SEA VIEW COTTAGE

ELLEN JOY

Created with Vellum

For Tina Durham-Bars. Thank you so much for all your help.

Click HERE or visit ellenjoyauthor.com for more information about all of Ellen's books.

Cliffside Point

Beach Home Beginnings
Sea View Cottage
Sugar Beach Sunsets
Home on the Harbor
Christmas at Cliffside
Lakeside Lighthouse
Seagrass Sunrise
Half Moon Harbor

Beach Rose Harbor

Beach Rose Secrets

Prairie Valley Sisters

Coming Home to the Valley
Daydreams in the Valley
Starting Over in the Valley
Second Chances in the Valley
New Hopes in the Valley
Feeling Blessed in the Valley

Camden Cove

The Inn by the Cove
The Farmhouse by the Cove
The Restaurant by the Cove
The Christmas Cottage by the Cove
The Bakery by the Cove

CHAPTER 1

Renee hurried across the front porch, waving, as the mailman pulled up the driveway. Marty stalled in the truck, rifling through the mail, which she took as a good sign, but the frown on his face as he stepped out of the mail truck said it all.

"Sorry, Mrs. Winthrop." He had gotten used to her rushing toward the vehicle.

"Nothing?" she asked.

He shook his head, handing over the stack of envelopes and fliers and magazines.

"Good grief," she said, taking hold of the mail. "How many magazines can three women have?"

The older man just raised his eyebrows. "That many."

She sighed. "Thanks."

"You bet." He waved and jumped back into his vehicle.

It had been weeks of nothing. Weeks of complete silence. Not even static on the other end.

Renee stood, watching Marty leave as she hugged the stack of mail against her chest, and she realized this was her life. Sitting around, waiting for a sign that wasn't coming. If he hadn't tried to communicate after all these weeks, would he ever?

She rubbed her swollen belly. Six months pregnant, or twenty-two weeks, she supposed. The websites and books went by weeks. She wished they went by days. What was tiny George doing inside there? According to the books, his little lungs were expanding and growing. He was learning to grab things like his ears and umbilical cord. Maybe even respond to light.

God, she thought. *I'm going to be a mother.*

Already, Renee had failed at this role. When she found out she was pregnant, she thought about what it meant to provide as a mother. She'd read about the benefits of a child being raised by both a mother and a father.

Since she couldn't keep a husband, she looked at other ways she could provide, like the basic necessities, such as food and shelter. She was currently failing in that area as well.

Renee could've provided had she stayed working at the restaurant back in Chicago. It wasn't like she hadn't been making money. As head chef at one of the hottest restaurants in the city, she'd made a dang good salary. She could've afforded at least a two-bedroom apartment, but she couldn't stay in the city. She couldn't stay working for Harry.

Renee could've kept her job. In fact, she was positive Harry would give it back to her if she returned, but why would she ever want to go back? He didn't want to be a father. He didn't want to be married. He didn't even want a relationship anymore. And she knew all of this going in. He had told her for goodness' sake! She knew better. She wasn't some naïve girl who didn't know the rules.

Secret kisses stolen in the back room. Hidden dates at each other's places. The stolen glances throughout work. She enjoyed the excitement of it all. The thrill of not getting caught. She never meant to fall in love with her boss, never expected to get married, and she certainly never meant to get pregnant.

Renee never imagined that at twenty-eight, she would live with her mother, Evelyn, and her mother's two retired friends—who she referred to as the Golden Girls—and wait for the mailman's daily delivery each morning as she devoured French pastries. But there she was, dropping the daily mail on the counter.

"Please stop making croissants," her mother said, stuffing a pain au chocolat in her mouth. She patted her hip with her free hand and mumbled, "I'll never lose these last ten pounds."

Renee walked to the steaming tea kettle and poured a cup of chamomile to go along with her own croissant.

"You look great," Renee said as she bit into her flaky treat. Her mother looked better than she had in twenty years. Every day, she and her friends walked the beach. If anything, Renee was the one carrying the extra pounds.

She wondered what the ladies would do once the weather on Martha's Vineyard started to change and head into winter. She had lived in Chicago almost a decade, so she knew winters, but she didn't know ocean winters, and from what she had heard from everyone around town, nor'easters were nothing to stick around for.

"Where do we go if there's a storm?" she asked her mother, returning to the topic they were talking about before Marty and the mail showed up.

"We can head to the mainland," she said back, unconcerned.

"But with a baby? On a ferry?" she asked.

"We wouldn't leave during the storm," she said.

"But sometimes storms just come out of nowhere, I heard." Renee suddenly noticed all the glass her mother put in around the house. French glass doors along the whole back end, large picture windows in every room. Even three extra dormers in her mother's master bedroom on the third floor. The lake effect was a real powerful force, but she imagined the Atlantic Ocean was a beast.

"Do you think it's safe to have a baby on the island?" Renee had doubts.

"This isn't *Gilligan's Island*. People have lived here for hundreds of years."

"Where's *Gilligan's Island*?"

Her mom stared at her. "You don't know *Gilligan's Island*?"

Renee hadn't ever heard of it. "Is it near here?"

Evelyn rolled her eyes. "Never mind."

Renee moved to another one of her many concerns. "Do you think the local hospital can handle a delivery? What if I need an emergency c-section? Remember Cousin Janey had one?"

"We can always head back to Minnesota if you'd rather have the baby there," Evelyn said.

Renee didn't want to go back there. She'd avoided it for five years. What was another five? She might not ever go back, and that would be fine too. She had too many memories of when life was perfect. She'd lived the childhood dream, with a backyard playhouse to prove it. She and her sister, Samantha, had had everything their hearts desired. She had been grateful, but like any kid with privileges, she hadn't appreciated it. She'd had no idea how truly lucky she'd been until everything changed the night her dad had died.

Renee had stepped out of her body the moment she'd heard. For the next two weeks, she'd gone through the motions and never once got emotional. Not when her mother had broken down, not when Samantha couldn't speak at the eulogy, not even when they had scattered his ashes in the St. Croix River. She'd never be able to explain it any other way, but something had taken over her mind so she wouldn't have to feel.

Then she'd met Harry.

And now she was in Martha's Vineyard, literally barefoot and pregnant and living off her mother's goodwill.

"You ready for tomorrow's writers' group?" her mother asked.

She almost came back with a smart remark. She wasn't a teenager anymore, but an actual professional chef that had run a forty-table restaurant. She'd overseen two assistant chefs, prep staff, and a pastry chef. And she had run a pretty darn good kitchen at that. She'd prepared her food with care, cooked with flare, and her plating had been perfect. But now she was cooking gluten-free finger foods.

"Yup." She sighed, thinking about the summer appetizers she'd rather make, but it wasn't her party, or her restaurant, or her house for that matter. It was her mother's.

She looked at Evelyn, standing at the island in her newly remodeled kitchen. Every window had a view of the ocean. The kitchen had turned out like a home interior magazine. It was stunning.

The best part of it all was that her mother looked happy, happier than she had been in years. The house made Evelyn happy, her friends made her happy, helping Renee and the baby made her happy, but what made Evelyn happy most of all was her new boyfriend, Charlie.

And Renee wanted her mother to be happy. She really did. But something deep down inside her broke a little seeing them together. Her mother had moved on, and Renee couldn't help but be sad about it all.

This new life her mother had found was wonderful, but Renee had never had to share her mother with anyone besides her sister. Who, at that very instant, as Renee checked social media, was living the dream life in Scotland with a hunky man wearing a kilt in the highlands.

"When is everyone coming?" Renee asked. She'd make the almond flour first. "I should start the tarts."

"Hank can't eat apples," her mother said.

"How many allergies do they have?" Renee couldn't keep up with all the different guidelines—gluten-free, dairy-free, soy-free, free of any taste. "He's going to have to pass on the meeting in September."

She would be using apples *and* gluten when she made her apple pies. She had read about the apple farms on the mainland in Vermont and New Hampshire. Hank was going to have to deal or not come.

"Any mail today?" Evelyn asked.

Renee loved her mother, and she had been impressed by the fact that Evelyn hadn't pressed her about Harry. She had been nothing but supportive and joyous about becoming a grandmother. But Renee's arrival, landing on the doorstep during her mother's rebirth, wasn't part of the plan. Just when all of Evelyn's hard work from writing had paid off, now her adult daughter moved into the guest room. It was like the comic relief plotline in her novels. The heroine's troubled pregnant daughter is getting in the way of her new relationship. When will the leachy daughter move out? When will the heroine finally have her happily empty nest?

Then there was her mother's boyfriend, Charlie. If her dad could pick anyone for her mom, Charlie would be the top pick, for sure. He was nothing like George. He was quiet, for one. He didn't talk much, except about books and writing. He also didn't like to cook or watch television or talk sports, but George would have loved the guy as much as her mother. He made her mom as happy as her dad had. Like her father, he gave small gifts, little gestures to show he cared. He'd pull out chairs, open doors, and look at Evelyn as though there wasn't another woman in the world.

She wanted her mother to enjoy this part of her life with someone who treated her like a queen. She deserved a second chance. It just hurt more than Renee had expected, seeing her mother with someone else.

It wasn't the new-daddy complex. It wasn't even her grief for her father. It was the fact that she couldn't find the space where she belonged now. And the more the weeks passed by, the more she felt like an outsider.

"Well, good morning, girls," Bitty said, walking into the kitchen. She wore a silk robe, her hair already spritzed and sprayed, and her make-up already applied. She grabbed a chocolate croissant, then mumbled, "You know, we're going to have to up the ante with our walk this morning."

Renee ignored their complaints, because the pastries would

be gone by lunchtime. All three women enjoyed the treats. She opened the fridge and pulled out the dough she had made the night before for her pastry puffs. She would fill them with a crab and herb cheese filling. She had picked up the crab at the fish market already that morning.

"Oh, goody!" Wanda said, heading straight for the croissants. She closed her eyes and moaned out in delight. "Mmm. They're better than men."

Bitty and Evelyn giggled at Wanda's comment, but Renee groaned silently in her head and wanted to gag. Her mother and her friends were all single, all over fifty, and treated Renee like their *Sex and the City* buddy, frequently throwing out comments and quips that were highly inappropriate, even if she was an adult and about to become a mother. She didn't want to think about these ladies getting it on with some old guy, especially her mother.

"Oh, sorry," Wanda said, wincing in her direction. Renee's face must have shown her discomfort.

She almost told Wanda to eat two croissants. The already petite woman looked frailer today than she had yesterday.

"I made those protein smoothies." Renee opened the fridge again and pulled out the one she'd made especially for Wanda. "I added extra ginger."

"That sounds good," Wanda said.

The ginger was good on Wanda's tummy. The chemotherapy had been causing her nausea, and she frequently didn't want to eat. They'd prescribed medicine to ease the queasiness, but she still didn't eat enough, in Renee's eyes. Evelyn had said the treatments for breast cancer were just the beginning of a long journey.

"Yup, counter the pastry with the protein." Evelyn slid the drink to Wanda.

"Hmm, this is delicious." Wanda sucked on the straw but stopped after a sip. She didn't take another bite of pastry, either.

"How about some fruit salad?" Renee asked.

"I'm afraid I'm not that hungry right now." Wanda picked up the protein shake in good effort but didn't drink from it. "Did the paper come?"

Evelyn passed the newspaper as Renee went back to her bowl of dough and dumped it on her mother's new Italian marble countertop. It was a splurge her mother had bought under her insistence. The whole kitchen had basically been designed by Renee, and it was beautiful if she did say so herself. Top of the line appliances throughout, white cabinets on the surrounding cabinets, but a dark navy set of built-ins under the Italian marble waterfall counters. Three modern gold pendants hung over the island, matching the rest of the hardware. White herringbone tiles made up the backsplash, and there was a deep farmer's sink and windows everywhere.

She sprinkled out flour on the marble's surface and unwrapped the cellophane from the dough. The women started their morning coffee klatch by discussing the grocery list for the week. Today was Thursday, and it was grocery day.

"Knock, knock," a man's voice said from outside the screen door. The kitchen sat at the front of the house but had a side door that led out to a screened-in porch. Mateo, her mother's contractor, stepped inside the house.

The three older women swooned as the handsome builder came into the room. All three smiled their goofy smiles as they greeted him a good morning. Renee could see why every time Mateo stepped onto the property the women couldn't control themselves. The builder was extremely attractive in his worn jeans and fitted T-shirt, his biceps tight in the sleeves, those big brown eyes, and his great smile. She didn't understand why a guy like that was still on the market.

"Want a croissant?" Renee pointed to the table where the plate sat with the women.

"Are those the ones with chocolate inside?" Mateo asked, reaching out for the plate. He stuffed one into his mouth before she answered. "This is delicious. You really know what you're doing."

She smiled at his compliment. She had heard it from others plenty of times, and she knew it was true, but lately she hadn't been feeling her talents; more like doubting them. If she was that great, wouldn't Harry have begged for her to come back? If he had loved her so much, wouldn't he have fought for their marriage?

"Hello?" Harper, Charlie's daughter and Evelyn's new assistant, came inside the front door of the house, her hair done up in two pigtail buns on the top of her head. Renee wondered what she would look like if she tried something like that. Most likely, it would look messy and unkempt, but Harper looked bohemian beautiful. She wore a flowing sundress down to her feet, which were covered in sandals, with ankle bracelets and fashionable foot tattoos.

"Good morning," Harper said as she fluttered through the kitchen.

"Want a croissant?" Renee asked.

Harper scrunched her face. "Does it have white flour?"

"Oh shoot, sorry," Renee said, forgetting Harper had started her cleanse a couple of days ago. "I'm making blueberry scones with almond flour."

"Thanks, but I'll pass." Harper bounced over to the coffee and turned her attention to Mateo. "Hey, Mateo."

Renee turned her attention back to the dough and slapped it, concentrating on the pastry puff, not the conversation she wasn't a part of, until she heard Mateo say, "Do you think we could talk for a minute?"

"Now's not a good time," Harper said to him. "Maybe later?"

Harper grabbed the French press and poured herself a cup of coffee as though she, too, lived in the house. As though she, too, were a daughter and a roommate. The only differentiation between her and Renee was that Harper got paid for what she did.

Renee wondered what her sister, Samantha, would think of Harper. She'd love her; that's what. Even Renee had to admit that Harper was hard not to like. She didn't seem to care what people thought of her, which made her more likable. She went by the beat of her own drum, which coming from the world of hospitality was refreshing. Harper was incredibly humble, even though she had every reason to brag. Renee should be glad this woman came into her mother's life as well as her own. By the looks of things with Harper's father and Renee's mother, they could end up being one big happy family. She should be glad.

So why wasn't she?

"Did you guys hear about Mateo?" Harper said, loud enough for everyone to hear.

"What's that?" Bitty asked.

"Last night, Mateo was inducted into our high school hall of fame," Harper said.

All the women started clapping and cheering. Bitty even did a little whoop-whoop.

"Wow!" Renee said a bit too enthusiastically, and she could feel her cheeks warm as he looked back at her. "That's awesome!"

"Thanks," he said.

"That's great," Bitty said. Her mother and Wanda nodded in agreement.

"How wonderful!" Evelyn patted him on the back.

Mateo just shrugged. "I played some football back in the day."

"And you happened to score the winning touchdown in the state tournament," Harper threw out.

"That's really cool." Renee hadn't known Mateo had played football. She thought his big build had been from his construction work. She imagined he looked pretty good in a uniform. She wondered what the women would say after hearing this.

The conversation moved on to what the day looked like in terms of her mother's renovation, that Mateo would oversee. The old Victorian beach house was one of the original properties to settle in The Vineyard Hills. Set back from Sugar Beach, the house overlooked the Vineyard Sound. To the right stood clay cliffs that glowed in the sun's reflection, and to the left, down the shoreline, was the harbor the locals called Eastport. Her mother had put an extension on the back end of the house, including the upstairs bedrooms and attic. The century-old house would be completely updated by the end of the project, but the original character of the house was built into the new construction. All the new rooflines aligned with the old, the woodworking and trim duplicated and design replicated.

Every room had a view of the water or of the seagrass hills and valleys. Every window had been decorated with a beveled glass border on top, casting rainbows throughout the space. Every room had built-in shelves and cabinets, and fireplaces in most. The house was going to be gorgeous when completed.

"My guys are going to be up on the roof today," Mateo warned them. "We're starting on the extension in the master bedroom and attic."

This meant Renee would be sleeping on the couch downstairs.

"We can't wait to get started," Evelyn said. She put her empty plate in the sink. "Can you show me what you were thinking for the bathroom?"

Mateo swiped another croissant and winked at Renee. "Thanks, Renee."

She gave him a salute, then from the corner of her eye, noticed his hand grace Harper's. A gesture so small and intimate that no one else in the room seemed to notice.

Renee slapped the ball of dough again, wondering about the two. They were both attractive people, both single, and they hung out together all the time. When she first came to the island, she'd suspected the two were a couple, until Harper had told her otherwise.

She looked down and saw her belly touching the counter. It didn't touch yesterday. Baby George was getting bigger, the size of a papaya according to her Google search.

Of course, a guy like Mateo would chase a girl like Harper—someone successful at twenty-eight. She had a novel being published within a few months by a big publishing house. She'd even landed Evelyn's agent, who brought huge deals and opportunities.

Renee let out a long sigh.

What was she going to do? Eventually, she'd have to return home to Chicago. She'd have to make decisions she wasn't ready to make. But when would she ever be ready?

"You okay?" her mom asked as she was about to follow Mateo out of the kitchen.

Renee picked up the dough and threw it down onto the counter, pushing her palms into it and kneading it hard. "I'm fine."

A line creased between Evelyn's eyebrows. A worry had hung on her face since Renee had confessed about her pregnancy.

"I'm fine," she said again, trying to reassure her mother.

Evelyn's forehead wrinkled, and in front of Bitty and Wanda, she said, "It's okay not to be fine." Evelyn looked to her friends. "We all have days like that."All three women stared at Renee, waiting for her response or reaction, waiting for her to fall apart.

"I'd be better if I could get these puffs made without the Spanish Inquisition." She could hear her tone, and she hated herself for it, but she just couldn't help it.

Evelyn gave a look to Bitty, then to Wanda. The three mother hens would be discussing her behavior on their walk, no doubt. Renee picked up the dough and slapped it again. *Like a baby's bottom*, she thought to herself.

Oh, dear Lord, she was going to be a mother.

The fact was, she *had* to be fine. She didn't have any other choice. The man she loved didn't love her back and wanted nothing to do with the baby or their marriage.

How could she explain that this pregnancy felt more like a loss than a blessing, like Evelyn had kept saying? How could she explain that losing everything that had defined her—her career, her independence, her community—felt like a death? How could she explain that she had hit rock bottom by moving back in with her mom and retired roommates when this was supposed to be the happiest moment of her life?

Renee had wanted children, just not yet. She didn't want to put off her own career, her own happiness, her own dreams to raise a child. Yes, her mother was a success, but Evelyn sacrificed everything before that success for Samantha and her. Her mother put everyone before herself, even now. Even in her golden years when she should be celebrating her success, she put Renee first. And the obvious truth glared at her. She wasn't an Evelyn.

No, she thought. She'd keep all her doubts about becoming a mother to herself.

CHAPTER 2

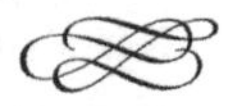

Mateo didn't know what had changed from last night to today, but Harper had. He was afraid of this. He tried going through the motions with Mrs. Rose, but also trying to read Harper as she stood with Evelyn, taking notes about what she needed to do to help.

"Do you think you could run to the hardware store and get me these supplies?" Evelyn passed a list to Harper.

"Yes, of course." Harper's eyes were on Evelyn, or Renee, or her phone, but not since their kiss last night had she looked at him.

He thought their kiss had been perfect. Their first kiss, and he was pretty sure she had liked it, too, by the way she had stood with her mouth open as he'd pulled away, her eyes still closed. She had even whispered, "Wow," as she let out an audible sweet, light hum.

Then she said good night.

He'd gone to sleep on cloud nine, then woke up and practically jumped out of bed, singing to the rising sun. He had been waiting for years for that kiss. He had been in love with Harper Moran since grammar school. And he'd finally done it. He'd finally kissed her.

They had always been friends. They were friends while she dated Bobby Cooper and James Cipriano and Matt Walsh. They were friends while she went from one bad relationship to another. They were friends while she came running to him and cried on his shoulder.

But last night was different. Last night, when he'd received his award, he'd felt like he could conquer anything, and with a double shot of whiskey to kill the nerves, he had finally taken the leap and kissed her.

But after he sent a text to say good morning, she sent back: **I think we should talk.**

His heart had dropped.

He hadn't texted back. Instead, he'd planned on catching up with her before meeting at Evelyn's, but that had been easier thought than done. She had seemed to stick around people all morning. With two failed attempts, he finally got her to step onto the porch alone with him.

"What's going on?" he asked as his stomach twisted. "I thought we had a nice time last night."

"It was nice." Harper's tone was upbeat, but her eyes said it all. The kiss hadn't meant the same thing to her as it had to him. "I just think we should stay, you know, friends… like we are."

She playfully punched him in the arm with her hand, then backed away as if afraid of giving him the wrong impression.

"So, what was last night?" He may be confused right now, but he hadn't been confused last night. She'd enjoyed kissing him just as much as he'd enjoyed kissing her. "You liked that kiss."

"It was nice."

"It was more than nice," he said, taking a step closer, but she backed away.

She took in a deep breath, then blew it out. "I can't live here forever."

She stepped back again, throwing her arms out at the water, and he realized this wasn't about being friends.

"No one said you had to live here forever."

"My family's history is literally buried on this island." She crossed her arms against her chest.

"What does that have to do with kissing me? I know you felt something between us."

She could come up with all the excuses she wanted, but he knew she'd felt it.

"It was nice, but..." She lowered her eyes away from him. "I don't think I feel the same way about you as you feel about me."

A jolt of pain flashed through his chest and straight into his heart, like a javelin slicing through his rib cage, stealing his breath on the way out.

She didn't feel the same way?

He opened his mouth to ask why she had been spending all that time with him all these months if she had no feelings, when he stopped himself.

"Yeah, fine." He stuffed his hands into his pockets, stiffening up.

"It's just that I want more than what this island has to offer." She went in for the final blow. "I'm planning on finding a place in the city, maybe Boston." She continued to tell him her newest plan. Just like all her other big plans that she never followed through with. "I haven't really thought it all out yet, but I'll be getting a percentage of all my book sales."

"So you're determined to leave the island?" He had heard these plans for over a decade now.

"Yes, as soon as I find an apartment."

This was her excuse?

"And you want more than someone like me?"

"That's not it at all." She bit her bottom lip. "Mateo, I don't want to lose my best friend."

Another excuse.

He stuffed his hands further into his pockets, and she rattled the car keys in her hand. "I should go and get Evelyn's errands done."

He nodded, not saying another word. Instead, he pulled out his phone and opened his reminders. When he looked back up, Harper had walked down the porch steps to her tiny car that could get stuck in a puddle.

He watched as she sped down the driveway and saw her face as she drove away. He knew her well enough to recognize the look of relief as she took off. As if she had just finished a dreaded task. *He* was the dreaded task.

When he walked back into the Rose house, Renee slid a cup of coffee to the edge of the counter as he walked by.

"There's cream and sugar already out." She motioned her head toward the table. There sat a small glass pitcher filled with cream and a fancy silver-plated sugar bowl.

His face flushed in embarrassment, recognizing that Renee probably heard the whole conversation of him being dumped.

"Blueberry scone?" she asked, holding out a plate of sweet, sugary smells.

He shook his head. "Nah, I'm good, but thanks."

He grabbed his leather portfolio, where he kept his calendar and all his notes and to-do lists. "I should go meet with your mother."

"Do you mind me asking you something?" Renee said.

He hoped this wasn't the inevitable "You're too good for her" speech that came whenever anyone was dumped.

"What's with all the candles in the cove?" she asked.

"Candles in the cove?"

"Yeah. Have you gone to the cove over there by the lighthouse on Gray Head?" Renee pointed over her shoulder in the direction of the water.

He shook his thoughts of Harper away and remembered what Renee was talking about. "Oh, you mean the prayer candles?"

She tilted her head. "They're prayers?"

"Way back, wives of fishermen started lighting them as a prayer for their husbands' safe return."

Renee's hand went to her chest. "That's beautiful."

"I forgot people did that," he said. When was the last time he had gone to the cove? "Locals used to call it Prayer Cove, but nowadays, I think teenagers hang out there."

He smiled back at her, relieved and grateful she hadn't brought up the scene with Harper. Putting his portfolio on the counter, he changed his mind and picked up a warm scone before taking a bite.

"Mmm," he mumbled. "This is really good."

He grabbed the cream and poured, then sipped the coffee. It made the crumbles even better going down. God, she could make a good cup of coffee, not to mention the scones.

"Great coffee," he said, holding up his mug. "Thank you."

She nodded and returned to rolling out her dough, pushing the long wooden rolling pin over a rectangle piece.

"What are you making now?" He couldn't imagine the four women in the house could eat all this food she made.

"A pastry puff for my mom's writers' group. They're having their meeting here tomorrow, and I'm prepping some appetizers for it." She sprinkled some flour on the dough, slapped it with her hands, then picked up the pin again.

He grabbed his portfolio and gave a nod. "I should get to work. Do you mind if I keep the mug for now?"

"Not at all." She stretched over the countertop, and that's when he noticed she held her hand against her belly so it wouldn't hit the counter. He knew Renee was pregnant, yet he hadn't noticed the actual baby bump until now.

He had seen pregnant women before. His older sisters and sister-in-law, who he'd felt were moody and ornery the whole time, had only complained about how swollen and uncomfortable they were. But Renee glowed in pregnancy. He never understood the reference to glowing before now.

He noticed the large diamond wedding ring on her finger. He wondered what kind of guy would leave a woman like her alone and pregnant.

"Do you always cook this much?" he asked, looking out at the dough.

She nodded. "Only when I'm stressed and have no job."

The bluntness pierced him.

"You should sell this stuff," he said, taking his last bite of scone. "I bet you'd make a killing at the farmer's market."

She stopped pushing the pin and stood up straight, looking at him. "How expensive do you think a spot is at the farmer's market?"

He shrugged, taking another sip of coffee. "I don't know. Maybe a hundred dollars?"

She picked up the dough, stretching it even more with her hands, then she flipped it over and slapped it. She stuffed her hand into the flour jar, sprinkled some on top of the dough, and went back to rolling.

"I haven't really thought about selling pastries," she said. "I usually just cook, not bake."

She stood on her tippy-toes, trying to push the pin to the farthest corner of the dough.

"Thanks for the scone," he said. He put the mug in the sink and began to leave the kitchen.

"She's a fool," she said to him before he left.

His heart dropped. Here came the speech. He could see the sympathy all over her face.

"Thanks, again," he said and left.

After meeting with Phil about the plumbing and showing Evelyn the next steps for the master bedroom, he left to go back to his office, which was really the spare bedroom of his house. He pulled into his seashell gravel drive and got out of his truck before grabbing his bag and other stuff from the back seat.

He looked out at the small cottage that had cost him a fortune. The house Harper encouraged him to buy with the cute back porch she could imagine a family sitting on one day. The same porch she'd sat on with him, night after night. The same porch he'd kissed her on last night.

What had spooked her? Or was he so clueless of the fact that she'd had no interest all this time? Had last night been a test? Had she kissed him to see if she did have feelings?

Renee was wrong about Harper. He was the fool.

CHAPTER 3

Evelyn could hardly keep it together with this whole pregnancy and failing marriage business. Her mantra *What Would George Do?* did not seem to help at all in this scenario. The problem with Renee was that she was so dang independent. She'd never once told her there were problems. Not once had Evelyn suspected Renee's marriage ending with a baby on the way.

How bad had it been?

But anytime Evelyn got close to prying, Renee had told her she was doing so.

"Maybe I should pry!" Evelyn complained to the women. "I'm her mother, after all. Besides, at twenty-eight, I didn't know what the heck I was doing."

But at twenty-eight, Evelyn had had a one-year-old Renee already.

"You're doing the right thing by supporting her," Bitty said, letting the waves wash up to her ankles. "She'll come to you when she's ready."

"That's the problem. We Roses don't like to talk about our feelings." Evelyn could write about anyone else's problems, but talk about her own? Never. She had just started to talk about

George's death with a therapist, and it had been five years. "Did he have an affair? Or commit a crime? Or is this whole thing a complete misunderstanding?"

"It seems unlikely she'd uproot herself because of a misunderstanding," Wanda pointed out.

Evelyn sighed. She was right. Renee wouldn't leave a dream career, her dream city, and her dream husband because of a misunderstanding.

"Then maybe I should reach out to him." Evelyn didn't know what else to do.

Bitty gave her a look. "That would be meddling."

Evelyn shook out her hands. "I thought now that my daughters are adults, things would get easier."

Bitty let out a loud laugh. "Don't I know it."

"I need to understand." Evelyn didn't see how Renee could walk away just like that. This was the fact she hadn't been able to wrap her head around. She'd thought Renee and her husband were happy together. But maybe they hadn't planned on having children. Or maybe he had freaked out.

"This must be the hardest part of parenting," Wanda said. "Knowing when to let go."

Evelyn groaned silently inside her head. Wanda had made a point she didn't want to admit to. "I know I should just be there when she needs me. I just want to understand why she thinks she needs to hide it. You know? Like, am I that bad of a mother that she can't confide in me?"

"Evelyn, you're a wonderful mother," Bitty said, stopping in the sand. Sea-foam wrapped around their ankles as the Atlantic waves came to shore. "She just needs some time."

"She doesn't have much time left." Evelyn didn't want to sound heartless, but losing George without being totally prepared had been hard on her as a mother.

"If she's divorcing her husband, she should hire an attorney on her behalf before the baby's born, for sure." Wanda stated the practical things Evelyn's mini-heart-attacks confirmed. "She needs to establish parental rights."

"If he thinks he can get out of his responsibility—ugh!" Evelyn couldn't understand what had happened. During the holidays, they'd visited, and everything had seemed fine. Samantha had never said she'd noticed anything. They had seemed like happy newlyweds; not a couple unwilling to talk to each other when they had a child on the way.

The women kept walking their usual route along the beach. First, they headed north, up Sugar Beach to Gray Head Cliffs, where they turned around, walked past the beach house, and down to the harbor where The Wharf Hotel sat at the end.

When they turned around to head home, Evelyn couldn't shake the feeling that she needed to get Renee to talk at least to someone. "Wanda, would you try to talk to her?"

Wanda looked surprised. "Me?"

"Yes, you just went through all of this. You could give her some advice." Evelyn realized she didn't know much of her son-in-law. She had met him a dozen or so times before they'd decided to get married at city hall out of the blue. What she did know was that Harry Winthrop owned more than a dozen restaurants in the Chicago metropolitan area. He owned the fancy apartment where they lived. He also owned the restaurant where Renee had worked as head chef.

"I'm just heartbroken for her," Evelyn confessed. "I want her to be as happy as I was when I became a mother. The only worry I had was naming her."

"She'll be a great mom," Wanda said. "She doesn't need a man, that one."

"No, she certainly doesn't," Evelyn agreed. This wasn't about having a man; it was about having a partner. Having George by her side through all their stages together had been a blessing. There were times she'd had to pass her children off and leave. He'd also had a totally different kind of relationship with the girls; something she could never replicate. She could help as much as possible, but she wasn't their father. "But she should know her rights as his wife."

Wanda and Bitty nodded in agreement. Both women had been through divorces. Both women had talked about the difficulties they'd had during them.

"The best thing she could do is hire an attorney," Bitty suggested.

Evelyn had already made a call to her own attorney she'd had since George and her had moved into their house. She would continue to encourage Renee to call him back.

When they made it back to the beach house, she followed the sound of Mateo's saw slicing through wood. He had set up a workshop in the detached garage with makeshift workbenches with all sorts of power tools, hand tools, and planks of wood.

"I'm starting the built-ins in the bedrooms." He opened his phone and showed a picture. "I started last night in my own garage."

He let her hold his phone as she checked out the photo of his hand-built maple cabinets. "They're beautiful."

The new cabinets would make the space fit the grandeur of the rest of the house. At some point, someone renovated the attic into a large room but did it on the cheap—bad drywalling job, inexpensive commercial carpet, no lighting, no bathroom, hardly any electrical outlets, and economical, but basic, windows.

The built-ins were just the beginning of the third floor, which at some point would be the master bedroom. She wanted maple flooring, electrical outlets, a working fireplace, a wet bar, and a soaking tub, all with a view of the Atlantic. But maybe it would be perfect for a nursery until Mateo and his brothers finished the garage.

The garage would transform into a cottage for Renee. That's if she wanted to stay. Evelyn didn't want to pressure her, but she'd love to have them stay with her on the island, either on the third floor or in a separate guest house. The idea of being close to her daughter and grandbaby would make Sea View perfect in her mind. Would little George call her Grammy like her daughters had called her own mother? Or Nana like George's? Or would he come up with a name that was special from him? Besides, Renee had no idea what motherhood was like at this point. Who would help her in Chicago if Harry wasn't in the picture?

The rest of the morning, she thought about talking to Renee about everything. Then she changed her mind. She'd have Renee come to her when she felt comfortable. But what if she needed her help and didn't even know it? If Renee couldn't find the courage to tell Evelyn, what kind of trouble was she hiding?

Had she had an affair?

Was the baby even Harry's? Maybe the baby had a different father.

She hadn't even thought Renee may have been the one who had made a mistake. Or was it a mistake?

"What would you do if you were in my situation?" she asked Charlie at the bookstore later that afternoon. She gave Stan a homemade dog treat.

"I'd probably talk to her," he said.

"But she just shuts the conversation down," she said quickly, feeling like she was making up excuses, but it was the truth.

He smiled patiently at her. They had been through this at least a dozen or so times since Renee had arrived, and he'd told her the same thing, with the same smile.

"She'll talk to you," he said. "Just give it time, and be ready when she does."

She plopped into a burgundy velour chair, which had become her favorite for her afternoon chats with Charlie.

"I should talk to her," she said, rubbing the armrest with her hand, making patterns in the fabric.

"I know you want to help, but she's not going to be receptive until she's ready," he said.

"But you told me to talk to her," she said, confused.

"Yes, but listen too," he countered.

"What?" She dropped her head into her palm.

"Just keep talking to her, let her know you're there, and at some point, she'll end up being the one coming to you." He said it as though it were that simple.

This whole situation was anything but simple.

"All I want is for her to be happy," Evelyn said.

"She's going to figure things out because she's got you," he said.

"I think you have way more faith in me than I deserve." Evelyn didn't have a relationship with her daughters like he had with Harper. The two of them were tight, in a healthy way, and she couldn't help but be a little jealous. Maybe she should've been more open about her own feelings all these years. She hadn't complained when life was hard, because she didn't believe in burdening her children with her problems, especially when George had died. They'd needed her to be strong, not dump her feelings on them. But maybe by keeping her feelings so tight, she'd taught her girls to close off the world.

Maybe Renee was closing off Harry?

"Talk to her, but… don't talk at her." He winced. "Are you okay?"

She nodded, but she wasn't sure. "I can't believe I'm becoming a grandmother."

Another moment in their lives George was missing.

"You look too young to be a grandmother," he said to her, leaning over the arm of the velour chair and sniffing her neck.

"You are being very unprofessional, Mr. Moran." Evelyn glanced around the bookstore to see if any customers were seeing him necking her in public.

Luckily, the place appeared to be empty.

"Is it usually this empty at this time?"

"Business starts to dwindle by late summer." But his look seemed more concerned.

"Is everything okay with the store?" she asked, paying closer attention to his reaction.

But he waved her worry away with his hand. "No, yeah, things are fine. Just the season. No tourists and stuff."

She supposed that was what being a local on Martha's Vineyard was all about. Roughing it during the months no one else wanted to stay.

"Renee's worried about having the baby on the island in the winter," she said.

"Tanya gave birth in LA next door to a woman who had suffered a gunshot wound. That was scary."

"Didn't they have a maternity ward?" she asked.

He chuckled. "Yes, the gunshot lady was also becoming a mother."

The one beacon of light through this whole situation: Baby George.

She stared out in disbelief. "I'm going to be a grandmother."

So much had changed in a couple months' time. She had to wonder what was in store for them next.

CHAPTER 4

Renee stood in the kitchen, watching Harper hum something as she walked along the back porch into the kitchen, with cloth grocery bags dangling from her arms.

"Did he leave?" Harper asked as she walked into the kitchen.

He, Renee was sure, meant Mateo. "Yes, he left with his brother, José."

Harper dropped the bags onto the counter, her multiple bracelets clinking against the countertops. Renee looked at her bare hands, short fingernails, no jewelry on her fingers or wrists. She had even taken off her wedding ring yesterday and hadn't bothered to put it back on. She wore earrings sometimes, but for the most part, Renee was simple, especially compared to other chefs in her profession, who wore tattoos as sleeves and hairstyles more colorful than the food. Harper had tattoos, but they worked on her. They were delicate and beautiful, and totally stylish, like everything else about Harper.

She could see why Mateo was head over heels for her. Harper oozed femininity. Her curly long brown hair always flowed down her back or was tied up in silk scarfs with tendrils and twists. Her big eyes stood out from her other soft, tiny features, like a doll's face. Her feet were probably a size five.

Renee wasn't going to ask, even though she was dying to know. What was it that Harper didn't see in Mateo?

He was very attractive—hot, even. She may be hormonal and pregnant, but the Golden Girls confirmed this every time he would enter a room. They'd swoon over the young contractor. He was also very successful, owning his own contracting business with his brothers and working on million-dollar homes like her mother's house with complete confidence. He ran a tight ship, too. His workers were there on time, worked long hours, and got the job done efficiently and without much difficulty. She had worked with contractors in the restaurant business many times, and projects always ran into snags, went over budget, and never went as planned. But Mateo and his brothers ran a very successful business.

It was no surprise he won the award as the hometown hero, because every person who came around Mateo enjoyed their time with him. He just made people feel good in his presence. People would stop by the house while he was working just to let him know what a great job he was doing and how impressed they were. His subcontractors always seemed to be happy to work with him. Her mom was overjoyed with the progress he had made and what he had already accomplished. The kitchen looked like something out of *Better Homes and Gardens*. So what was Harper's problem?

"It's none of my business, but—" Renee stopped herself. She could hear Evelyn tell her to stay out of Harper's business. "I'm sorry, it really isn't my business."

"You want to know why I'm not into Mateo, don't you?" Harper plopped her canvas bag onto the floor and fell onto a stool, dropping her head in between her hands. "I don't know what's wrong with me."

Renee wasn't expecting that.

"He's like the nicest guy in the world, right?" Harper's eyes moistened.

"Yeah, he's super nice," Renee said back, hoping Harper's

emotions cooled down. Renee didn't handle emotion very well, and being pregnant, she might start to cry herself. Instead of feeling her emotions, she usually cooked, or now with Baby G, she baked. She pushed a plate of crème puffs she had made with the leftover dough.

Harper held out her hand. "My cleanse."

"There are cucumber sandwiches in the fridge," she said before popping a puff into her mouth.

Harper shook her head. "I'm good."

"So, he's just too nice?" Renee was more curious than ever.

Harper blew out a long breath. "Yes, he's that nice. And he deserves a woman who wants the same things he does."

Renee popped another puff and asked, "What does he want?"

Harper traced a vein in the marble with her fingertip. "To get married and have a big family. He's already got the house just waiting for it to happen."

Renee could feel an ache in her heart. She would give anything for Harry to want to live the rest of his life with her and the baby.

"You don't want to get married now? Or like... ever?" she asked her.

"Ever." Harper said it fast and hard. "Have you met my parents?"

Renee didn't know much about Charlie besides the fact that his wife had left him and Harper when Harper was young.

"I don't really remember them together," Harper said. "My mom was basically MIA after that."

Renee couldn't imagine losing a parent like that. It was one thing to lose them by death; it was another when it was a choice. "You must be afraid of commitment?"

"Totally afraid." Harper looked at her. "Mateo deserves someone who is ready to be that wife and mother he's dreaming about. I'm just his sidekick."

"He seems to think you're more than a sidekick." Renee didn't know Mateo very well, but she knew he poured his all into his obligations. He was committed to doing a great job renovating her mom's house. He was committed to his family, working with both of his brothers. He was committed to his community, always hiring local workers. He had no red flags.

Unlike Harry Winthrop.

"I could see you two together," Renee said.

"Could you?" Harper wrinkled her forehead, and Renee thought about it for a moment.

Maybe a bit of an odd couple.

Harper slouched in the stool, resting her elbows on the counter and her head on her hand. "I'm just selfish, and I'm not ready to settle down."

Ugh, she was honest. Why couldn't Harry have just been honest? Would she be here if he had, or would they have worked things out? Renee rubbed her belly, wondering what life would be like in a few months. How being selfish wasn't even an option anymore.

"You're adorable, you know that?" Harper said, bouncing off the stool. "Can I touch?"

Before Renee could answer, Harper's hand went to her belly, and she palmed her with both hands.

"It's so hard," she said, feeling with her fingertips. She leaned over and got up close with her mouth. "Hello, baby George. You're a lucky little guy to have this lady as your momma."

Renee tried to smile, to pretend she enjoyed being talked to, but all she wanted was for Harper to get out of her space.

"He has no choice," she said and immediately felt rotten. Harper was being kind, like always. And Renee, negative Nelly again.

Harper didn't flinch. "You're going to be fabulous. Besides, you have all of us to help out."

Harper stood up straight and pulled out her phone, completely unaware of Renee's clenched smile. *Hold it together,* she silently prayed to herself. *You don't want to lose it in front of Jolly Miss Sunshine.*

"You're coming tomorrow, right?" Harper asked.

Renee would rather stick a cocktail wiener in her eye than go to their merry writers' group, but she made a face of regret.

"I'm going to have a night out with a friend," she said. If by "friend" she meant herself.

"Aw." Harper made a face, looking genuinely disappointed. "That's too bad. I was hoping we could hang out afterward."

Renee felt a tinge of guilt, but not enough to change her mind. "Next time."

Harper began texting and said, "I better get going. Your mom wants me to pick up Wanda's medication."

"Sure, see you later."

Harper was wonderful, positive, and kind. *Harper* would make an incredible mother.

Renee, on the other hand... The verdict was still out on her. She was moody, jealous, and dependent on everyone. She had no idea what she was doing, so she just baked, which had certainly caught up to her by thirty extra pounds. She didn't take after Evelyn's side of the family, where all the women were pixies. No, she'd inherited her father's big-boned family genes, where the women were farmers.

She put the lid on the puffs, grabbed her stack of books Charlie had given her, and sat on the back porch.

She looked out at the view. Sugar Beach sat about a hundred yards from the backyard of the house. Its creamy sand and sparkling deep-blue water dominated the view, but Renee gave her attention to the unending sky. Grassy rolling hills sat between the backyard and Sugar Beach, their stalks swaying as the wind blew off the water.

She opened the book with a pregnant woman rocking in a chair on the cover. After turning to the table of contents, she skimmed through the subjects until her eyes fell to one of the last chapters: Fathers are Expectant, too. She flipped to it and pressed down the binding to the big, bold black lettering. Wanda stepped outside.

Renee heard Wanda approaching from behind and flipped the page.

"Hello," Wanda said. "Mind if I join you?"

Renee shook her head, wishing she had an excuse to leave. She liked her mother's friends, and she truly respected them, but Wanda made her uncomfortable. She spoke openly about unpleasant topics, like her cancer treatments and symptoms, how her husband had left her, and how Evelyn had taken her in when she was all alone at her lowest.

Wanda had way too many feelings.

"Hey, Wanda," Renee said, flipping to a whole new chapter. "Not at all." She turned back to face her and pointed in the kitchen. "Did you see I made those puffs you like?"

Wanda nodded. "Yes, they look delicious."

"There's also a strawberry and spinach salad with couscous for lunch." Renee may not want to talk one-on-one with Wanda, but her personal challenge to keep Wanda well and healthy through food, including lots of treats, seemed to only be semi working. Wanda had lost a lot of weight from her already-frail body.

"How are you feeling?" Wanda asked.

"Good," Renee said, which luckily, she did. After all her reading, she realized pregnancy was no joke. Many health issues seemed to arise, even in the healthiest women. Deli meat could cause complications, and don't bring up unpasteurized cheese. "I'm not really sleeping anymore."

"That's common, right?" Wanda asked.

Renee knew Wanda didn't have children, and she'd never asked why. It certainly wasn't any of her business. Besides, Wanda would probably tell her in due time. The older woman had nailed the art of gabbing.

"I was never able to carry to term," Wanda said.

Was it confession day with Renee? Did her baby bump make people open up to her? It certainly wasn't her energy. She wanted nothing to do with talking about losing babies. It was a little reminder that she wasn't in the clear.

"Oh, I'm so sorry." How was she going to get this conversation to stop? "I can't wait to get to full term."

Wanda sat down on the lounge chair next to Renee. She held a home design magazine in her hand, but her focus was on the water. Her eyes looked sad, and it was obvious the topic brought up a lot of emotions.

Renee pretended to begin to read again, when a seagull dropped on one of the wooden lantern posts along the path to the beach. Ugh, she wished her mother hadn't told her about her father's spirit animal.

"Your father talks to me through birds, especially seagulls," her mother had confessed one day to her.

"Dad talks through seagulls?"

"Every day." Evelyn had seemed so convinced, so Renee kept quiet about it.

But now she saw the dang things everywhere, and they pooped a lot.

Renee had always had a good relationship with her mother, but she had been a daddy's girl. And her father's death had changed her and her mother's relationship; it separated them. Her father had been the glue that had kept them together.

Evelyn supported Renee's choices, but only to a point. After high school, Renee had wanted to jump into the workforce. She had been working in a small mom-and-pop diner and had enough experience to land a job instead of heading to culinary school.

"Get an education first," Evelyn had said. It hadn't been a suggestion.

"But I don't want to waste four years and the money to get an education when I could just work." It'd felt like a no-brainer, but Evelyn wouldn't have it.

"You need an education on how to run a business, how to manage a staff, and taxes and everything else involved." Her mother had been right, of course. Getting her education in culinary school, taking business classes, and even taking marketing and advertising classes had been the right choice, but not *her* choice.

After one of the many arguments between her and her mother, her father had come into her room and said, "Whatever you want to do, we'll support you. Your mother just knows you could go even further than you think you can."

Always the mediator, always the healer—her father had always made things better.

She stared at the seagull. Could her mother have chosen a less popular spirit animal for her father while living on the beach? What did he want her to do right now? It flapped its wings, bobbing its thick neck.

"You must've been devastated." Renee continued the conversation like her father would have encouraged her to do.

Wanda nodded, and just like Renee had dreaded, tears formed in Wanda's eyes.

What was with everyone today?

Renee could bring up an easy excuse to leave, her bladder would do the trick, but another seagull flew by and landed twenty feet away. "You've got to be kidding me."

"Excuse me?" Wanda asked.

Renee shifted in her seat and faced Wanda. "Did you have signs?"

"You mean about the pregnancies?"

Renee nodded. George would've let Wanda talk it out.

Wanda let out a breath. "I never had a normal pregnancy. At least, not what I see from what you're going through."

Her chest opened again, and she took a deep sigh of relief.

"It must be hard seeing me." Renee rubbed her belly. "Like a reminder of disappointment."

Wanda shushed her. "Goodness, no." She smiled. "I like being part of it all."

Renee had to admit, even though the woman was chatty, she

was kind and positive. Sitting with a deadly disease running through her, knowing her time might be shortened, Wanda didn't seem to harbor any resentments.

"Well, you're going to be like an extra auntie," Renee said, liking the idea of all the aunties George would have. "And if I turn out to be a horrible mother, at least he'll have the aunties."

The seagull took off.

Even under her visor, Renee could see Wanda's face change to pity. "You're going to be a wonderful mother. Look at what you do for all of us!"

"I can keep him fed, that's for sure." But did she have an emotional handicap? Would she be able to raise a confident and productive member of society? Would he end up in a shrink's office on the couch, talking about all the things she'd done to him?

"'She fed me nothing but pastries until I was eighteen,' he'll tell his therapist," Renee joked. At least she had successfully turned the conversation around. "Are you going to the writers' group?"

Wanda nodded. "Aren't you?"

She shook her head. Not that she had anything against the group or the meeting. She just didn't fit in.

"You should write cookbooks," Wanda said.

Renee had never really thought about writing. Usually, chefs who wrote out their recipes either had the name to sell the books or had years of experience and a couple Michelin stars. "Who's going to want to buy my book?"

A book written by a no-name twenty-something chef who had gotten pregnant. She should write a public service announcement about not falling for your boss or marrying the man who paid you.

Renee opened the book again, when Wanda glanced at the top of the page where the chapter's title was printed.

"If you don't mind me asking, have you heard from the father?"

Renee shook her head. "Nope."

Wanda hesitated, but Renee could feel her curiosity brewing. The chatty Cathy wasn't going to be able to hold back, especially when the others weren't there to fend her off. But Renee didn't stop her either. She almost kind of wanted someone to finally ask for the truth.

"Do you know your rights as a mother?" she asked. "Like the fact that he has to pay parental support whether he thinks he's responsible or not."

Renee nodded. "I want nothing from him."

"And he's okay with that?" she asked.

She thought about Marty and her pathetic daily routine, waiting for a letter that was never going to come. Each day, she waited for an apology, or a declaration of his love for her, or a statement that showed her she was more to him than just a mistake, but it never came.

"Yes, he's okay with that."

Baby George was worth two million—that's what he'd offered.

It was probably more than she would receive if she did go the legal way and receive child support payments.

Bile rose in her throat as she thought about their conversation.

"Renee," he had said while taking her hands in his, standing in his sleek office in his sky-rise downtown apartment that overlooked the Chicago River. For a second, she thought he was going to propose. "I've been thinking about you and the baby, and I want you both to live your best lives. I want you to be able to live out your dreams even though we stumbled along this bump in the road."

"Bump in the road?" She looked at his position on the couch. He wasn't getting on his knee, his pocket looked flat, and there weren't any flowers or special music or lighting.

She had dropped his hands from hers, and that's when he had pulled out a check from the front pocket of his Italian silk button-down that had been tailored to fit his slim physique. The color had been handpicked to match his azure eyes. His hair had been slicked back and perfectly placed. She had always thought him nothing but handsome, but right then, he'd looked like a pig in lipstick. He'd handed the check to her, folded in half, and she'd opened it up.

There, in a quick script as though he'd wanted to get it over with, were the words 'two million dollars' written out.

She folded it back up, put it back into his shirt pocket, and left.

She blocked his number, never returned to work, and had flown out to Martha's Vineyard with only a forwarding address.

"He wants nothing to do with us," she told Wanda, and that, she was sure of.

CHAPTER 5

Harry Winthrop was not only one of the most successful restaurateurs of Chicago but also one of the most eligible bachelors in the tri-state area. A self-made millionaire, Harry owned a total of sixteen restaurants throughout the Chicago metropolitan area and had expanded to Wisconsin and Indiana, with three more opening soon.

When Renee had landed an interview for a sous chef position at his Michelin star restaurant downtown on LaSalle, she'd thought life couldn't get any better, but that was when she'd gotten the call from her mother. Her father was dead. She had to return home to Minnesota.

"I wanted to call and thank you for the opportunity, but I will need to cancel my interview," she said on the phone with him. She didn't want to cancel her dream interview, but what choice did she have?

"You're missing a big opportunity," he said snidely.

"Yes, I apologize." She didn't offer an excuse. She could barely get out what she had already said. She didn't need to say the actual words.

My father is dead.

"Yes, well, sometimes you need to make sacrifices for your dreams." He threw her words back at her.

In her cover letter, she had explained that working for someone as innovative as him was one of her culinary dreams. That throughout culinary school, she had studied the new entrepreneur who believed in the same culinary style she did—fresh foods, farm-to-table partnerships, and creating a community-friendly atmosphere that united neighborhoods with fine food. Her letter had outlined why she would be the perfect candidate for his restaurant. And she would've been if her father hadn't died.

"I'm really sorry." She couldn't get the words out. She couldn't say it. *My father is dead.*

"Don't expect to work in this industry," he said under his breath as he was about to hang up.

And before she could help herself, she snapped back at him. "I hope someday when you're at your lowest"—she may have wasted his time, but she didn't need some big-shot speaking to her about sacrifices—"that someone makes you feel even worse, with no other reason than they're just a jerk and they can."

"Excuse me?" he shot back, but she didn't hear what he was about to say next because she hung up the phone.

She forgot about Harry Winthrop the week of her father's funeral. She forgot about her dreams falling apart, because her whole life broke into pieces. It wasn't until she returned from the funeral that she found a bouquet of flowers on the kitchen island with a card that read **You have the job if you want it. Harry.**

"When did these arrive?" she asked her roommate.

Ashley shrugged. "Maybe a couple days ago?"

He left his number and email. She kept the flowers but threw out the card. She didn't want to work for a jerk like that. There were plenty of restaurants in Chicago. There had to be a job out there for her, even if she had to work at Perkins.

It took some time, and a loan from her mom, but she finally found a gig in a semi-chain restaurant in Irving Park. It wasn't exactly what she wanted, but she worked as head chef, kept up with the seasoned cooks, and found her rhythm.

Then one evening shift, when she was running the line, Harry walked through the kitchen and right up to her. "I'm still looking for a chef de tournant for my kitchen downtown."

"Order up!" she shouted out, completely ignoring his presence as she slid a plate on the rack.

"I'm sorry," he said. "I didn't know your father had died."

"That doesn't change the fact that you're a jerk, and I don't work for jerks." She wasn't going to bow down to anyone, even if he was the most successful restauranteur she knew. There were better ways to run a kitchen without being arrogant.

He cocked his head at her. "You like working here?"

She shrugged and returned to the line, calling out orders. "I need two cows, one clucker, and a side of grass."

Her two assistants stared back at her and rolled their eyes. They weren't in a Michelin star restaurant, and her line cooks weren't chefs. They pulled out two steaks and a half-roasted chicken and threw them down on the flat stove.

"Can I help you, Mr. Winthrop?" she asked. He hadn't taken her hint and left. She may not own the restaurant, but it was her kitchen for the next four hours of service, and she didn't want this man in her way.

He crossed his arms, looking at her. "Come work for me."

"As you can see, I'm busy. So if you don't mind excusing yourself—"

"I'll pay you double whatever they're paying you here," he countered.

She laughed at the offer. Double? Was this man serious? "I don't think so."

She went back to poaching her steak in butter.

"Triple."

She stopped and looked at him.

"What?" her assistant Jed exclaimed. "Dude, I'm willing to leave this place."

She laughed again, but this time to hide her nerves. She may not like him, but Harry Winthrop had a presence unlike any other man she had been around. He commanded the room. He stood over six feet with a large, very muscular physique. He intimidated her, no doubt, but he intimidated everyone.

But wherever this sudden interest for her came from, it didn't change her mind. A jerk with a beautiful body and the deepest bluest eyes she'd ever laid eyes on was still a jerk. "You don't even know if I can cook."

She returned to poaching.

"What will it take?" he asked, moving closer to the station.

Harry Winthrop stood there towering over her.

"I don't want to be an assistant." She looked out at him, meeting his eyes and holding his stare. She had nothing to lose at this point. "I want to run the kitchen."

He laughed and she almost joined him. She had barely any experience, even if she was running the kitchen she stood in. It was semi frozen, premade meals. It was no Michelin star restaurant. He may have been a jerk and felt bad about it, but he wasn't an idiot.

"Start in my kitchen downtown," he said. "And if you work out, I may have an opening for a head chef at my restaurant I'm opening on the east side. I'm looking for an innovative chef. Someone who understands the trends of Chicagoans' culinary interests."

She was head chef after a year.

And in love with Harry Winthrop.

How could she have been so stupid?

That exact question rolled around in Renee's head into the next day.

"Who are you meeting tonight?" her mother asked. It was

after breakfast, and they sat on the front porch swing, waiting for Marty.

Harper must've talked to Evelyn. She didn't know why she had lied to Harper, because of course, now it looked bad. "I'm actually just going to get something to eat."

"Why did you tell Harper you're going to meet someone?" Evelyn appeared confused.

"I just came up with an excuse and that came out." She should've known better than to lie about having friends. Her only friends were seagulls and retirees and her mom.

"So, you're not meeting anyone?" Her mom made that sympathetic face she so frequently wore, as though she knew what Renee was going through. As though she knew how she felt being alone. But Evelyn didn't know anything about it. She'd had a doting husband throughout motherhood. She'd lost her husband and found another love of her life. She didn't have trouble finding friends. Or keeping her career afloat. Or being successful while also being the best mother.

"I'm sorry, I just..." She shouldn't have lied.

"Why are you afraid to come?"

"What's the big deal about this group?" Renee shot back. She could feel her moody teenager coming out. She tried to hold back, but annoyance pulsed through her body.

Evelyn raised her eyebrows. "You okay?"

"I'm fine," she said back.

Evelyn sighed, pushing the swing again. "What's the harm in meeting new people?"

"It's a writers' group, and I don't write." Why was her mother pushing it?

"Harper's reading her first chapter to the group tonight," Evelyn said. "It's a big deal for her."

"Good for Harper." At the end of her sentence, she tried to change her tone, as though she wasn't being a complete brat, but it was too late.

Evelyn gave her the stare. The one that spoke of her quiet

disappointment. The one that made Renee instantly feel guilty as a kid and the one she had seen plenty up until adulthood.

"Sorry, I just don't feel like being around a group of strangers," she said, which was partially true. She didn't want to sit pregnant and alone with a bunch of people, explaining for the hundredth time where her husband was without sounding like a complete loser.

"Do what you need to do," Evelyn said, "but don't lie to Harper."

This was supposed to wake her up, make her feel bad about lying, but she didn't. She didn't care, because Harper wasn't her friend; she was her mom's friend. Worse, she was her mom's boyfriend's daughter, who had more in common with her mother than she did.

She wasn't feeling sorry for herself; it was true. She had very little in common with her mother besides the fact that they both loved and missed her father. That was the only connection she had with Evelyn these days.

Evelyn had a whole new life of her own. And though Renee was happy for her mom, she couldn't help but notice how easily she could disappear. Would Evelyn even miss her?

Evelyn had sacrificed her retirement house for Renee and the baby, which she never complained about, but her mother also kept reminding her it was a "temporary solution." She had mentioned renovating the garage into a small cottage for guests, i.e., Renee and child, but then told Samantha she could use it, too.

"I'm going to start looking for an apartment. Probably in Boston." She spoke before she thought.

Evelyn stopped swinging; her eyes widened. "Really?"

She nodded. "I'll be able to find a job. There are plenty of daycares that have better hours than around here."

"You're going to pay through the roof in rent. Not to mention child care is really expensive in the city. And you have free rent and babysitting right here." Renee knew her mother meant well and wasn't trying to be patronizing. It was stupid to leave her mother's house. She should save up, take advantage of the care, but she'd have to continue with this song and dance, and she didn't want to anymore.

"I'm in the way," she said. "I don't like that feeling."

"No, you're not." She was sure Evelyn meant that, too. "We're all looking forward to being here for you, you know that."

She did. Bitty had walked her through every step of pregnancy and childbirth one night, just the two of them. Wanda hadn't stopped talking about the arrival of baby George, Renee's pregnancy, how she looked, and any stories she had heard about pregnancies. She knew her mother would continue to support her. She should be grateful.

But it didn't change her feelings. She couldn't shake her bitterness. She couldn't stand that her mother was moving on without her. Her mother may have seagulls to get over her father's death, but Renee had nothing.

Not even her last paycheck.

"Is this about what I said about Harper?" Evelyn asked. She was getting warmer.

"I'm not a child." Renee would get her there. "I don't need you to scold me about what I said to Harper. I don't have friends. You're right."

Evelyn gave the look again. "Harper likes you, and you're treating her rudely by lying to her."

Renee could feel the sting behind her eyes. She took in a deep breath, holding back what sat right on her tongue.

"I think I should go." She picked up her phone, opened the screen door into the kitchen, and walked inside the house. She picked up her purse as Mateo came down the back staircase.

"You headed out?" he asked, just as Evelyn came into the kitchen and said, "Renee."

She gave a half smile to Mateo. "Yeah, I'm going to head out to get away from my mother."

His mouth dropped, and he said nothing.

"Sorry, I don't want to lie." She shot a look back at Evelyn, who rolled her eyes at her. "I'll let you know my plans later."

She didn't break her stride as she walked down the back steps and straight to her car. She had perfected storming out; she was good at walking away.

Being stuck on an island, she had very few options. She drove around the island for an hour, then pulled back down the main strip near the harbor. The little part of town they called Eastport was her favorite section of the island. The strip had gray-shingled buildings, all with the traditional white trim and white flower window boxes. Each building had a homemade painted sign hanging above its door, each unique, yet each a similar charming characteristic of one another.

She didn't know why she pulled up to the shop. She had no interest in getting books. She didn't even enjoy reading all that much. It had been a chore for her. Yet there she was, parking in front of Martha's Mysteries Book Shoppe.

She sat in her car, looking in the large picture window with new releases and best sellers displayed. She opened the door and stepped out, looking at the front door. The small store sat right in the middle of a bunch of different gift shops and touristy businesses along the harbor. A prime real estate location, she imagined. She wondered how well a bookstore did with the tourists, who were probably the main source of business.

Did they buy books while on vacation? Did a local bookstore keep up with what the tourists were looking for?

There were always bookstores in airports, she supposed. People going on vacation liked to read. But this strip wasn't a place where vacationers were looking to relax with a book. They were looking for trinkets to take back home, not the next great mystery.

She walked up to the front door and opened it. A bell rang against its glass. She hadn't been inside the bookstore in a while, but enjoyed the comfortable, warm, welcoming atmosphere. Just like Charlie. She may not like the fact that her mother was moving on without her, but she did like Charlie.

"Well, if this isn't a nice surprise," Charlie said as soon as he saw her. He held out his arms to her.

Charlie was the kind of guy who hugged everyone—affectionate. He reminded Renee a lot of her dad. She went in for it, something she had a hard time doing with her own mother. They were getting on each other's nerves so badly. She noted that she should hug her mom more.

"I needed to escape the house," she said, this time completely honest with no passive aggressiveness. She had needed to escape.

"Come here," Charlie said, waving her to a table in the corner. It sat next to the picture window looking out at Harbor Lane. He pulled out a chair and sat her down. There was a book that looked like a journal opened on the table with a half-drank cup of tea.

"Would you like my homemade lemon ginger tea?" he asked.

She hadn't expected Charlie to drink tea, especially homemade.

"Harper's making me do this silly cleanse." He poured from a large mason jar into a mug, then set the yellow concoction down in front of her. Her eyes watered from the spicy scent.

"What's in that?" She picked up the mug and sniffed, her eyes watering again.

"Lemons, cayenne, turmeric, a pinch of sea salt." He sat down next to her.

She took a sip, wishing she had brought her own hot cocoa and treat. "I wonder if anyone's going to eat my food tonight."

"Oh, are you going?"

She clenched her hand around the mug. "Nope."

"Ah." He nodded. No more was said.

"This is a fantastic spot." She looked around the space. She could picture an eight-person booth set up instead of a reader's nook. A perfect place for a little restaurant—a bistro with a trendy menu. Right there next to the harbor, across the street from the hotel. "You must get a ton of traffic."

He shrugged. "Hardly any these days."

This surprised her. "Really?"

She looked around the space. The bookstore nailed the cozy atmosphere, but with a deeper look, the interior was a bit rundown, the rugs worn, the shelves stuffed with stale titles, and cheesy displays to market their stock that didn't move. He had lots of choices to read, but no trinkets or tchotchkes for the tourists. Not even a postcard rack. Not that he needed to cater to the crowd, but who was looking for a random mystery?

"You should sell some comfort foods to go along with a good book," she suggested, thinking about the fancy bookstores in Chicago. "You know, like the big stores do. Maybe some gourmet coffee instead of out of the carafes."

She nodded her head toward the coffee counter, which had way too many carafes, along with too many plastic creamers and types of sugar packets and straws. The station looked cluttered and messy.

"You know what would be good are those scones you made yesterday," he said, pointing at her.

She noticed there was no table stocked full of the island's own bestselling author, Evelyn Rose, whose number one series was trending on Netflix, The Vineyard. Her mother's hit series had been inspired by the quaint village of Eastport. She wondered if someone would want to eat a fruit tart while reading an Evelyn Rose romance.

"Maybe choices like biscotti and macaroons." Chocolatey, sugary, and sweet—all of Baby G's favorites. She rubbed her belly thinking about it.

"Oh, I almost forgot," he said.

Charlie got up from the table, leaving the journal open. She peeked at what looked like a map. She studied the drawing, recognizing some of the words written, like Sugar Beach, Red Brick Lighthouse, and Gray Head listed along points on the map.

She recognized the shoreline and its inlets and coves drawn along the edge.

"I thought about our last conversation." He handed her a book that had a red cover with a gold character and the word Connection written underneath. "It's the book your doctor recommended on yoga and meditation."

"Thanks," she said, flipping through the pages and noticing illustrations of poses. "Do you practice?"

He scrunched his nose and shook his hand. "Sort of. Most days I just try to do some stretching when I wake up and before I go to bed. I stand for a long time at the store and then sit doing other stuff."

She nodded but then wondered if she needed to lose some weight. Was this a way to get her active? "I should do more stretching."

She traced the gold letters, and the stinging crept back behind her eyes. Before she could pull them back, one dropped onto the cover, and she quickly wiped it away.

"It's not easy becoming a parent. I remember being filled with anxiety when I found out my wife was pregnant." He rested his arms on the table. Stan, his dog, sat underneath and scratched at his ear, then turned in a couple of circles to finally sit down next to her feet. "She had just left me when she found out she was pregnant. I convinced her to stay married."

She could feel the weight of his admission and his hesitation to tell it. He didn't look at her but pushed a napkin toward her. She picked it up, wiping her eyes and wishing she could hide under the table with Stan.

After a long pause, he continued. "But the years I forced our marriage to work made us both miserable, and Harper suffered the consequences. She was an anxious kid, cried all the time, didn't eat or sleep well. It got worse once Tanya left us, because I became obsessed with controlling every situation. I had to be the best father *and* the best mother. Then one day, daycare called and said Harper had to leave. She was too aggressive with the other children, and she couldn't stay. That's when I knew I had to change things."

"Harper was aggressive?" That she couldn't believe.

He nodded and laughed. "She was a habitual biter."

He nudged her with his elbow. "What I finally realized was that family came in all shapes and sizes. I felt ashamed moving back into my aunt's apartment, divorced and a single parent. Believe me, I know what it's like to live with the Golden Girls." He winked at her. "But when I allowed myself to receive help, the happier I became, and the happier Harper became."

A lump sat in her throat as she looked out the window. The point of the story hadn't been lost on her, but the reality hit her. "I know I have my mother and the women."

"And us," he interjected.

"And you." She hesitated and took in a long breath, holding it as long as she could. But it didn't matter. The truth clung to her ribs like a vise. "But what if I'm like your ex-wife? What then?"

Her eyes brimmed with tears, and he took her hands in his and shook them.

"You are not Tanya." He said it almost too matter-of-factly, as though he wouldn't even consider the possibility that Renee just might not be up to the job of parenting.

He squeezed them one last time and let go.

She scraped her thumb against the corner of the cover. "Thanks for the book."

"Renee, I'm positive you are going to be the greatest mother to this baby," he said. "I'm sure of it. Just don't forget to make yourself happy, too."

"By stretching," she said, holding up the book and pushing her emotions down. She pointed to his journal. "So, this is the infamous treasure map?"

"Oh, your mother has told you about it?" He slid the journal in front of her, letting her get a better look.

"This is drawn beautifully." She noticed the details were close to perfect. She sniffled and collected herself.

He took a sip of tea, and his mouth puckered. "My aunt drew out these maps in her journals. I'm piecing them together with the stories she used to tell us as kids about the treasure." He turned a page to another drawing. This one was of more detail of Gray Head and its mighty cliffs. The inlets were drawn out perfectly, matching the rock's natural creases and crevices that the tides had created over the years. "But I'm not sure if she made it all up, or if there's something actually out there."

"What kind of treasure?" It was hard to imagine pirates hiding chests of gold on the posh and swanky Martha's Vineyard.

He shrugged. "Not exactly sure. But from the time period and the supposed pirate looting back then, there should be a pot of pirate's gold." He pointed to a spot on the map where there was an actual drawn *X*.

"Blue Rock," she read aloud. "This isn't that far from the house."

He shook his head. "I've been looking for months, but no luck yet."

"Do you use a metal detector?"

He nodded. "Even old Stan does some digging."

She looked under the table as Stan shifted his position. They sat in silence for a few minutes. She knew he was trying to be helpful. She should take care of herself, but nothing comforted her anxiety. Not baking, not talking about it, and sure as the waves rolling to shore, not some silly yoga poses. She was alone and absolutely unprepared to become a parent. Downward dog wasn't going to fix that.

"Thanks for the book, Charlie," she said, leaving her full cup of tea.

"Anytime, Renee." He stood up, pulling out her chair for her. "Next time you make eclairs, you should make a few extra and sell them here."

She looked around, noting no new customers since she arrived. "Sure, why not?"

CHAPTER 6

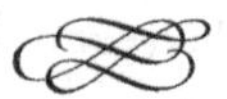

Mateo parked up against the garage that he was using as a makeshift wood shop. He had taken on all the carpentry work in the house. All the built-in bookcases, window seats, wooden surrounds and mantles. Evelyn Rose was spending a bundle to add these personal touches to each room, and he was going to do it right.

He went around to the back of his truck and pulled out knotty, honey-planed pieces of maple he would use for bookshelves, when he heard a car pulling into the drive. Hidden behind his truck, he could see Renee pull up to the house and get out of the car. From the back seat, she pulled out a couple of bags and a yoga mat.

He watched her as she juggled the bags and mat in her hands, balancing all of it on her stomach. He groaned silently to himself, then he ran out from the shadows.

"Let me help you with that," he said, jogging up to her.

She startled, the bags slipping from her hands. "I didn't see you there."

"I was inside the garage." He pointed to the open door hidden behind his truck.

"Thanks," she said, handing over some of the bags.

He peeked inside the first bag to see a couple of books and notebooks. In another were baskets, decorative plates, and silver platters, and craft paper and art supplies. "What's all this stuff?"

She looked at him and shrugged. "To be honest, I don't really know what I'm doing, but I think I'm going to try to sell some of my pastries... like you suggested."

She gave a half smile, and he could see her face was splotchy like she had been crying. He shook one of the bags in his hand. "That's a great idea!"

"Well, first, I'm going to start with selling a few things at the bookstore," she said. "Charlie has a table I can set up as a display next to the coffee counter."

"That's an awesome idea." He hadn't thought of the bookstore, but didn't big bookstores have food in them nowadays?

"I talked to someone at the Tinsbury Farmer's Market," she said. "I have to apply and get approved. I don't know how long that's going to take, so I think I'll try to sell at the store in the meantime."

He nodded, glad to hear she was doing something with her talent. "You're going to do really well. Your pastries are great."

She shrugged again. "We'll see."

"The mat?" he asked.

"I need to find my center," she said while rolling her eyes. There was a hint of sarcasm.

He let out a chuckle. "Maybe I could join you."

She gave him a look. "You always appear centered."

This made him actually laugh. "You heard the conversation with Harper yesterday, didn't you?"

She made a face, scrunching the bridge of her nose. "Sort of."

"Now, she wants me to go to the dang writers' club to listen to her read her book," he said.

Renee shook her head. "You don't have to go, you know."

He looked at her and wondered if it would be selfish to skip Harper's big night. "Sure, I do. She's my friend."

She looked at him for a moment, tilting her head as she stared. "You're really too nice."

The way Renee said it, it didn't seem like a compliment. Was he a fool for going?

He shook away the thought and followed Renee as she started walking toward the house and up the steps to the porch. He bounded ahead of her to grab the door.

"Thanks," she said when he opened the side door to the kitchen.

She dropped the items on the kitchen table.

"Are you coming tonight?" he asked, suddenly hoping to have another friendly face in the crowd.

"No." She took the bags from his hands and placed them next to the others.

"You should. Maybe even try out some of your food you're going to sell for the bookstore," he suggested.

She looked at him again, giving that melancholy stare of hers, which made her look like a modern-day Michelangelo. So beautiful, yet so sad.

"What are you doing instead?" he asked. Her bedroom on the third floor was under reconstruction. She'd have to get out of the house to avoid the group.

She shrugged. "Maybe go looking for some buried treasure?"

He pointed to the garage. "I just bought some boards for the bookshelves upstairs. I'll have extra. Enough to make a crib."

Her eyes widened. "You'd make a crib for me?"

"Sure." He didn't have enough wood like he'd said, but he could run out tomorrow and get some more. He didn't mind spending the money on it, either—as a gift. Didn't people have showers anyway? "Think of it as a baby present."

Her eyebrow raised as if she were suspicious. "You just want to make a crib?"

He stood, frozen, not sure what she meant by that.

"Stop being so dang nice," she said.

"Oh." Now he was completely confused. "I'm sorry."

"There you go again!" She dropped her hands on the table, shaking her head. "Ugh!"

Then out of nowhere, she began to cry. Really cry with tears and snot and hiccups. Unable to escape, he wished he had paid more attention to his sisters when they were pregnant. Had they acted this irrational? Maybe he was being condescending by offering to make a crib?

"I don't have to make a crib. I just thought… you might need one…" She wasn't stopping with the crying and Mateo couldn't tell if he was making things worse by talking. "I should go."

"Stop!" She held up her hand, hiccupping in between her words. "I'd love for you to make my baby a crib."

She reached across the table, grabbed a napkin, and blew her nose. She closed her eyes, dabbing another napkin in the corners and under her chin. Then, she exhaled a long, deep breath. Her body shuddered as she took in air, and she buried her face in another napkin. "I am so sorry. I didn't mean to lose it."

Her eyes began to tear up again and he shook his head, waving at her. "Nah, it's no big deal. I've been around my pregnant sisters enough to know to sit patiently through the storm."

She smiled, then immediately frowned, anxiety washing over her face. "Are there a lot of storms on the islands during hurricane season?"

She bounced from one emotion to the next, and he couldn't keep up. "They're usually very mild if they do make their way up the coast."

"Like when was the last time?" she asked, her anxiety increasing.

"You know, the last time Martha's Vineyard was hit with a bad hurricane was the day I was born," he said, thinking of the family legend of his birth. His father always told it the night of his birthday dinner as he gave grace. "My father delivered me in the back of their Chevy."

"That's my worst fear," she said, looking off into nowhere.

"You'll be fine," he reassured her. "Storms are really rare on the island. Plus, there's a good hospital that will be able to deliver your baby through any storm."

"I hope so," she mumbled.

He kept the fact that his parents couldn't get to the hospital because of downed trees and washed-up roads to himself. No need to worry her when the odds of a storm during her delivery were incredibly slim, especially with a winter baby.

"He's coming in November, right?"

She looked up at him. "You remember?"

He nodded. "You ladies talk about it every day."

"You do all the cabinetry work yourself?" She looked at the cabinets he had built especially for her mother's kitchen. He designed them with the Victorian style reminiscent of the millwork back when the house had been built.

"I like to work with my hands." After business started growing, he'd hired more subcontractors to take on a lot of the handwork of the job. He no longer did the tiling, or the floors, or the drywall. He told others when and where to do it. But with Evelyn's house, he hadn't hired a carpenter. Instead, he'd decided to do all the cabinetry work himself—at night in his free time—and he loved it.

She studied him. "You're an artist."

He slanted his head, not sure if he should take her statement as a compliment. "Thanks?"

"The work you do..." She spanned her arms out behind the counter. "It's gorgeous. Back in Chicago, I'd have killed to have someone who could create a space like this."

"Why don't you look up a design you like for a crib," he said, "and I can show you different styles of wood I have at my house."

"When?"

"What if we swing by after we hear Harper's chapter?" he suggested.

She smiled, and for the first time since he met Renee, she looked pleased.

"Fine, I'll go. But only for the reading part."

She started emptying out the bag, when he realized he had been staring at her. Renee was a beautiful woman. The kind of woman that was way out of his league. He didn't know much of her story other than what he had picked up here and there from Harper, but he did notice that the ring that had been on her finger was now gone.

He walked back to the door, ready to go back to the garage and get working on the shelves, and said, "Find me a picture of a crib, and I can start tonight."

She smiled at him again, and an electric shock went straight through his body.

Whoa, he thought to himself as he walked down the porch steps. *What was that all about?*

CHAPTER 7

Renee baked even more foods, mostly pastries, all day long. Bitty and Wanda became her taste testers.

"I think this is a great idea selling pastries at the bookstore," Bitty said, biting into the crispy éclair's outer layer and releasing the vanilla pastry crème from inside. "Hmm. This is to die for."

Wanda dipped her biscotti into her coffee. "What about a logo? A name for your business?"

She hadn't thought about it. "I don't know."

"I worked for years at my father's business," Wanda said. "It's all about branding that elicits an emotion. What do you want your customers to feel?"

"Comfort," she replied.

Wanda pulled out her phone. "You want to choose colors that complement each other and think about packaging."

Wanda continued to rattle off things to think about, which had been helpful. Harry had taken care of all things business when it came to the restaurants, where Renee focused her attention on the quality of dining.

Renee pulled out the notebook Charlie had given her at the bookstore and started writing things to do. She needed a name, a logo, business cards, labels, and branding. A menu simple enough that tourists can quickly pop in and out. She wasn't going to make up fancy signature dishes but give them classics that were memorable.

"You should claim your name and create an LLC before you do anything." Wanda kept telling her more and more information. "You'll need a professional website that looks sharp and clean."

"Wanda," she interrupted.

"Yes?"

"I'm only selling baggies of treats at a bookstore," Renee said. She loved the support, but she didn't want to get ahead of herself.

"Someone wise once said that a dream written down becomes a goal, and a goal broken down becomes a plan, and a plan put forth becomes reality." Wanda tapped the notebook. "You should create a vision board."

Vision board? "I don't even really know what my dream is."

"Close your eyes," Wanda said.

"What?" Renee wasn't going to start this mumbo-jumbo stuff.

"What do you imagine doing, if you could do anything with your talents?" Wanda asked. "Come on, close those eyes."

Renee hesitated, but when Wanda didn't stop staring at her, she lowered her lids.

In her mind, she saw Harry and the restaurant. Everything appeared dark, in shadows and empty. She could see herself stressed, rattling out orders, but no food anywhere. Her heart started beating faster at the images. She opened her eyes and looked to find the ocean. Then squeezed her eyes shut, pushing the dark images away with the sparkling of the beach. She imagined the bookstore and its bright light coming in from the front windows.

"I see a bakery, but more like a kitchen," she said. "Like a place to sit and relax and recharge. Comfortable."

Renee could picture people reading while eating, relaxing with friends after shopping, and families coming in from the beach.

Her image suddenly popped when she thought of the costs. "How do I get from selling treats in a bookstore to owning my own bakery?"

"This is just one step in your journey." Wanda patted Renee's back. "Now, let's think about what you need to do next."

After Wanda ran out of the best Tony Robbins quotes, Renee went to her suitcase and looked at what she had to wear for the writers' group thingy.

Nothing.

She looked at her standard outfit since arriving on Martha's Vineyard—yoga pants, a loose-fitting T-shirt, and a zippered hoodie in case she got cold. She walked into her mom's room and opened her closet. Her mother always had something nice, but just as she found the perfect top, she realized she wouldn't be able to fit into anything.

She was too big.

She rubbed her belly and combed through more of her mother's shirts, when she finally found a blue button-up that she could put over a plain white tee. She would wear it with a pair of leggings that hopefully still fit.

She'd need to go shopping soon.

"You're back," Evelyn said, walking into her room. "Help yourself."

Renee made a face. "I decided to come to the reading after all."

She wouldn't mention that it was Mateo's idea or that he was the person who had convinced her to go.

"Good, I'm glad," Evelyn said.

"I wasn't trying to be a jerk," Renee said.

"I know." Evelyn sighed. Her mom came up to her, wrapping her arm around Renee's waist. "I didn't mean to be so harsh. I know you're going through a lot, and I'm trying to be supportive, but I feel like sometimes you're leaving me out on what's going on."

Evelyn was right. Renee hadn't told her mother anything.

"I don't know what there is to say." That was an actual lie.

She had so much to say, but she didn't know how she could. Everything she had to say would so deeply disappoint her mother that her feelings would immediately and forever change.

"I hired a lawyer for you," Evelyn said. "I won't pressure you to tell me what's really going on with Harry, but you should know your rights as a parent."

Renee froze. Her mother was only trying to help, she had obviously talked to Wanda. Evelyn wasn't trying to butt into her life, but Renee didn't want to leech off her mother more. "I don't need a lawyer. I want nothing from Harry."

"What if he wants something?" Evelyn said. "You should know what your rights are."

"I'm fine, really." Renee wished she could bet on Harry's noninvolvement, because she'd be rich.

"Look, Renee, you should know your options." Evelyn was smart enough to know her daughter couldn't afford it on her own.

"I don't want his money." Renee shouldn't have brought it up. "I don't want anything from him."

She didn't need her mommy to hire her a lawyer. No, she was an adult, whether she appeared to be or not.

Evelyn looked out the window as two cars pulled into the driveway. "Renee, tell me what's going on, please."

"Looks like you have guests arriving." She couldn't tell her mother, because the minute Renee spoke the words, they'd come to life and become her reality. Right now, she could pretend none of what happened in Chicago had been real.

Evelyn sighed but left the bedroom.

Renee took her position behind the kitchen counter as more people began to arrive.

She texted her sister. **I can't believe you still haven't come out here. I need you.**

Dots flashed at the bottom of the messages, then they disappeared. Apparently, Samantha was still mad. Renee put her phone down and went to the fridge, where she pulled out a tray as more guests arrived.

"Renee, you've outdone yourself," Charlie said, trying her mini beef tartar bites.

Then he handed her a piece of paper. She opened it up as others came in the front door. She could hear her mother greeting them with a boisterous hello. Inside was an address in Boston.

"Your mom said you're headed to Boston tomorrow," he said.

She had agreed to go to Wanda's treatment.

He pointed to the paper. "It's a small bakery that I know you'll just love to see."

"Bottega Del Pane." Renee held up the paper. It was a map of an address in the North End of Boston. "Thanks."

Evelyn whisked through the kitchen in a flowing sundress, her hair tied up in a French twist, and she wore strappy sandals on her feet. Renee's mom was adorable. She was so happy as she floated through the house, introducing everyone to Renee as the chef and showing off the renovations. Each one told Renee how much they "loved" her mother.

"This is my talented daughter, Renee," she said to a woman who looked to be in her sixties.

"She's beautiful, too," the woman named Margery said. "When are you due?"

"November," Renee answered. November twenty-third. It sounded so official and felt so far away six months ago.

"Ah, you must be dying in this humidity," Margery said to her.

Renee looked down at her feet, swollen in her flip-flops. "I am."

She patted Renee's arm and popped a puff into her mouth. "Mmm!"

Renee met a man named Hank, an older woman named Anita, and the plumber, Phil, and his partner, Dan.

"Nice to see you again," Renee said.

Phil removed his hat as he shook her hand. "Your mother thinks the world of you."

She smiled and realized what a jerk she had been. She had almost skipped her mother's party because she was jealous, when all her mother seemed to do was gush about her and Samantha. She was the worst daughter in history.

Just when she thought of how glad she was that Mateo had pushed her to go tonight, he walked through the side door with two bouquets of flowers.

"Wow, those are beautiful," she said, admiring the purple hydrangeas mixed along with black-eyed Susans, and big white Gerber daisies.

"For you and your mom." He handed over the first bouquet. "They're from my garden."

"You garden?"

"My mom planted a bunch of stuff." He held the extra bouquet in his hands. "I wouldn't say I garden."

"Thank you so much," she said, pulling down a glass vase from one of the cupboards. She filled it with water and placed the flowers inside.

From across the counter, she could smell the cologne Mateo wore. He had shaven and cleaned up. "You look nice," she told him.

"Thanks. You do, too," he said, then quickly added, "Happy."

"Thank you." Ugh, he must think she's a complete nut job after her crying fit that afternoon. "I clean up occasionally."

"You're glowing."

She stopped arranging the flowers and looked at him. "I'm glowing?"

"You keep rubbing your belly and smiling." He grinned at her. "It's nice to see you happy."

She hadn't noticed, but when she looked down, her hand rested on her belly. She smiled back at him.

He sat down at the island, watching the commotion from afar.

"Don't want to go in?" she asked, also watching the crowd

interact. Their voices gained momentum and bass as new arrivals came through the front door.

That's when she noticed who he was looking at. Harper stood in the foyer, greeting the room. Renee could hear Harper's laughter from the kitchen, the soft and soothing melody that eased those around her. With a silk scarf as a headband, Harper wore her hair down, and it flowed down her tan and slender shoulders. She wore a sleeveless linen dress that was perfect for a cocktail hour, but then Renee noticed the butterfly tights.

Harper was so cool.

"I want a pair of unicorn tights," Renee murmured to herself.

"What?" he asked, snapping out of his trance.

"Nothing." She pushed a plate of chunky chocolate blondies in front of him. "Try these with this."

Next, she pushed forward a tumbler of high-quality bourbon. She had asked Charlie what Mateo liked to drink earlier.

"How did you know?" he asked, taking the cookie and the drink.

"I always find out what people like to eat and drink." She shrugged. "I'm basically just nosy."

He smiled as he bit into the blondie. "That's delicious."

He turned his attention back to the crowd as Harper made her way through it.

"Everyone!" Evelyn called out. "Let's all gather on the porch, and we'll eat after Harper's reading."

He sighed. "Remind me why I'm here torturing myself."

"I don't know," she said honestly, leaning her elbows on the counter.

He nodded. "Yeah, maybe I should've skipped this."

She almost suggested he leave after his bourbon, but then she felt a kick. "Oh!"

He sipped the bourbon as he looked at her. "You okay?"

She put her hand on her belly. "I think George just kicked."

"That's just weird." He made a face as if she had an alien in her stomach.

She moved around the counter and grabbed his hand, then put it right on George's little kicks.

"Do you feel that?" she asked. "Isn't it incredible to think there's a tiny, little person inside there?"

"Holy moly!" His eyes widened as George kicked again as if on cue. "That's really incredible."

He shook his hands out as if he got an electric shock. He went to put his hands back on her belly but stopped just as he was about to place them. "Can I feel again?"

She laughed. "Sure."

She took them in hers and placed them where George had kicked before, but now nothing was happening. She waited, then jabbed at the spot. "Come on, George."

"Are you hurting him?" he asked, concerned.

She laughed again. "I hope not. I'm pretty sure he's just bouncing around in there."

Then just as she was about to give up, he kicked again.

"Oh, I felt that." He shook out his hands again and laughed with her. "That's so weird."

"Tell me about it." She rubbed her belly with both hands. "So, you going to go out there and listen like you said?"

"Yeah," he said. He picked up the bourbon and shot it back before clenching his jaw from the sting. Then he bit into the cookie. "That's a great cookie."

She walked up to him and placed her hand on his back. "Let's go listen."

He nodded. "Cool."

She led him to the porch, where the group sat around in folding chairs that Charlie had brought over. The dozen or so people sat around with copies of Harper's chapter in their laps.

"I got these from my proofers," Harper explained to someone sitting next to her.

Evelyn sat next to Charlie, leaning close to him as he whispered something in her ear. Renee had to admit they looked good together. She noticed most of them were eating something. She wished she could interrupt them before they started and have them take notes on which foods they preferred.

Charlie stood up once everyone found a seat. "Thank you all for coming tonight."

He looked to Harper. "If someone told me the hardest thing about parenthood was letting your child dream big, I would've thought you were making things up." He paused. "Harper got the bug of storytelling before she'd learned to write. Drawing stories in notebooks, on menus, in books, on walls..." The group laughed. "She had the gift of story, and I knew what kind of heartbreak writing could create."

A murmur echoed from the group as everyone nodded in agreement, mumbling something to one another. Harper beamed.

"I cannot tell you how proud I am that she's more stubborn than I am and chased her dreams anyway." He looked to Evelyn, who stood up and pulled out a cooler. "I brought Harper's favorite Riesling, and I'd like to make a toast."

Renee and Mateo got up and helped Evelyn pass out the plastic cups to the group of people as Charlie poured everyone a glass.

Charlie filled his cup last and held it up. "May we all continue to chase our dreams. To Harper!"

"To Harper!" Everyone touched cups around the circle, and Harper squealed in delight.

Renee watched Mateo look on like a puppy dog as Harper began to read. She started shaky and nervous, stopping every once in a while to get a drink of water, but soon she gained a rhythm and her voice flowed. Renee's thoughts quickly disappeared, and she entered a thriller she hadn't expected from happy-go-lucky Harper.

When Harper finished the chapter, everyone clapped, including Renee. "That was excellent," she said aloud as the others followed the unspoken rules of their group.

"We wait our turn," Anita said to her.

"Thanks, Renee," Harper said, and she looked relieved by the comment. "I'm so glad it's over."

People took their turns, just like Anita had said, telling Harper everything they loved about the chapter.

"It's wonderful," Evelyn said. "I'm so proud of your hard work."

Harper and Evelyn hugged, and that's when she felt the bubble that had grown all afternoon burst. She watched as Evelyn squeezed Harper's arm when they broke from their hug. Then her mother kept telling her something that made Harper tear up. They hugged again.

"Hey," Mateo whispered. "I'm going to grab myself a water. You want something to drink?"

He held up his empty glass. Renee put on a smile. "I'm good. I actually need to run to the ladies' room."

She could feel her emotions growing, and the heat from the night made her sweat. She got up before Mateo could say anything else, rushed inside, and ran into the bathroom. She studied her reflection in the mirror. What was it that bothered her about Harper and her mother's relationship? It wasn't like Evelyn was blowing her off. Her mother had been nothing but supportive through all of this, even when Renee hadn't deserved it.

She didn't know.

"I'm such a brat," she said back to herself, turning on the water and splashing her face with it.

When she opened the door, Mateo stood in her way.

"You okay?" He looked worried.

"Yes, I'm fine," she said.

"You looked like you were going to be sick," he said. "Are you sure you're okay?"

She didn't know what Harper was thinking about Mateo. He was a catch, for sure. "I'm good, really."

She looked out to the crowd of people, everyone still huddled around Harper and Evelyn. They wouldn't even notice if Renee was there or not. She just broke the rules anyway.

"Are you still willing to let me look at those samples of wood?" she asked.

Getting out of the house, away from the lovefest that made her morph into an angsty Twilight character, sounded like the best idea she'd had in a long time.

He smiled. "Can I have another chocolate chip cookie first?"

She drove after convincing him to have another glass of bourbon with the cookie.

"It's so chocolatey," he mumbled.

"I made homemade milk chocolate," she said, as if that were no major undertaking for just a chocolate chip cookie.

He stared at her.

"What?" she asked.

"So you don't like Harper, huh?" He rested his arm on the door, half out the window. His dark curls blew around, and she noticed his defined bicep.

"I do," she said with a grimace. She hoped her secret wasn't out. "Why, do I act like I don't?"

His head tilted sideways. "You looked upset when she and your mom hugged."

"Oh." She looked out at the road.

"Turn left up here," he said, pointing to the street ahead. "None of this is my business, of course."

She didn't say anything for a while, and neither did he.

"I do like her," she finally said. She contemplated how she could explain her feelings without sounding even more of a wackadoo. "I'm jealous of how free she is."

He stayed silent but raised his eyebrow.

"I want to show up to a party where everyone's proud of me, and I'm wearing butterfly tights." She smacked the steering wheel with her palm.

"You mean unicorn?"

"Yes, exactly!" She threw her head back on the headrest. "I just hate being the pregnant daughter in the background, living off her mother's good fortune."

"Your mom is wicked proud of you," he said, his Vineyard accent coming out.

"She loves me, but she's not proud of her twenty-eight-year-old pregnant daughter who lost her husband." Her poor mother had done everything right. "I'm a mess, and she keeps having to clean up after me."

She didn't even want to think about what he thought of a leech like her.

"Harper is the daughter I wish I could be."

There was her truth.

He eyed her. "Do people ever tell you how dramatic you are?"

"All the time." She winced at how awful he must think she is.

He chuckled and put his phone on the console. It displayed a navigation system. "Turn left up here."

She cautiously threw on her blinker for good measure and turned on the street, waiting for him to jump out of the car and tell her to buzz off, but when he fiddled with her radio, she figured he'd forgotten the whole conversation.

"This is the cutest neighborhood." She leaned as far into the steering wheel as her tummy would let her, trying to get a better look. The neighborhood they drove through reminded her of a movie set, everything perfectly manicured and landscaped.

"That's my place over there," he said as they drove up to a two-story cape. "The one with the window boxes."

"I love it." Renee pulled into the driveway next to the garage.

"Let me just open up the garage, and I'll show you the pieces," he said before they got out of the car. Her eyes caught his muscular arm as it shut the door behind him. He pulled open the garage door from the ground and let the light shine into the dark space. Inside was no ordinary garage, but a woodworking dream shop

She got out of her mother's station wagon and walked up to the shop. "Mateo, do you have every tool there is?"

All along the walls were tools positioned like art on a wall. Numerous drills, saws of all different sizes, clamps, sanders—some looked brand new while others looked antiqued. Large workbenches took up the center of the room, along with large machines and mechanical saws. She walked up to a cabinet and knew exactly where it would be placed once finished.

"Is this for the bedroom upstairs on the third floor?" Renee asked.

He nodded. "The kitchenette."

It looked like a piece of furniture with large corner posts, decorative molding, a top with handcrafted edging underneath, and hardware that fit perfectly with the rest of the house.

"Is your house like this?" She could only imagine what he could accomplish when it was his to do whatever he wanted.

"Um, well, I wasn't really expecting anyone," he said, walking deeper into the garage. "Besides, don't you want to see the different wood?"

She stepped into the garage and up to the door that led inside. "Come on, I don't care."

He hesitated, but only for a minute. "Alright, but no peeking in my closet."

"Is it a walk-in?" she asked.

"Yes."

"Then I can't make any promises." She turned the doorknob without another word and walked straight into the kitchen.

Mateo watched her reaction. Her mouth dropped, then she covered it with her hands.

"Oh my god, Mateo, this is gorgeous." She trailed her hand along the butcher block counters he had picked up in Providence. Her finger ran along the grout lines of the subway tiles of the backsplash.

"Where did you get this Viking gas range?" She had never fallen in love at first sight, but she was in love with that stove.

"I actually got that from a client who didn't like it." He rubbed his hand on the back of his neck as Renee continued through her self-guided tour. "Want a glass of water?"

"What are you doing here?" She pointed out the kitchen window to the newest project he'd started. The whole front yard was a mess. All the landscaping had been dug up against the house. Four concrete footings, and all the leftover rocks and boulders he had dug up to put in the footings, and the siding he had to replace sat under a huge blue tarp.

"I'm putting a farmer's porch on the front."

She looked back at him. "That's going to look amazing."

He walked up behind her and leaned over the sink, just close enough that she could smell his musky scent mixed with bourbon. He pointed out the window. "You can see just a little of Gray Head through the trees."

She stood on her tippy-toes and looked out. She could see the water sparkling through the branches. She glanced over at his face, pride shining as bright as the sunset's reflection.

"This is a really great house." She meant it too.

He nodded. "It works."

She rubbed her hands against her belly.

"The baby kicking again?" he asked.

She moved her hands in circles. "Not now, but I'll let you know if he does."

He stepped back and walked through a doorway. "Come on in and see the rest of the place."

Renee had never been the kind of person who dreamt of interiors like her sister and mother. She was practical and wanted an organized space and a clean house, but when she'd walked inside Mateo's fisherman's cape, she'd fallen in love.

"Oh my."

Her jaw dropped as she stepped into the living room. Her attention immediately went to the ceiling. Large wooden beams ran along the width of the room, with wood crown molding around the perimeter. He had two camel-colored leather chairs set up in front of a wood stove inside a wooden surround. Bookshelves flanked either side, and a rug and a chunky ottoman sat in between the chairs. Books were everywhere.

"You must like to read," she said, picking one up and reading its title. "*The Grapes of Wrath*."

"Harper gives me books to read, and…" He didn't finish.

She put down the untouched book and noticed titles on the shelves, their bindings broken in multiple spots. Biographies and memoirs of Churchill, Eisenhower, and Lincoln. Books on Afghanistan, Japan, Scotland, and more. Novels about Little Bighorn, The Revolutionary War, and a complete set of Louis L'Amour.

"You're a history buff?"

"I like non-fiction, mostly."

"And Westerns." She plucked a tattered paperback off the shelf. "My dad loved *Lonesome Dove*."

A memory crossed her mind: her dad sitting at the kitchen table, drinking his coffee, watching the sunrise and his birds, and reading his books.

Keep it together, she thought to herself.

Just as the image faded, she looked to see a copy of The National Audubon Society's familiar green cover. "Do you go bird-watching?"

"Not yet, but I'm hoping to go soon." He wrinkled his brow. "Do you?"

She shook her head, still holding *Lonesome Dove* in her hands. "My dad loved bird-watching."

"Where does your dad live?" he asked.

"He lived in Minnesota with my mom." She'd said it quickly, putting the book back on the shelf.

"I'm sorry to hear that." he said, understanding the use of past tense. "I lost my father about five years ago."

Usually, when she told of her father, she was met with sympathy, but Mateo gave a knowing look of pain and sadness, and nothing needed to be said, and it was refreshing.

"Would he have liked living at the beach house?" he asked.

She thought of all the different kinds of birds, sanderlings, sparrows, ducks, hawks, eagles, and seagulls around the beach. So many birds.

"Yes, he'd love it." She walked along the shelves, peeking at all the titles. "But what he loved more than birds was a project. He'd love your garage. He'd be following you around the whole time trying to be your assistant."

Her dad would've loved following around Mateo.

"I've had clients like that. Retirees who have nothing better to do." He started to laugh. "It's kind of nice having someone to talk to while working. A lot of times, I'm alone."

"Wow, more books." Renee looked into the bathroom, which was modern and clean but had a stack of books. She moved through to the back porch, her hands resting on her belly. She peeked out the windows to the screened-in room and backyard.

"Oh, how cute." The tiny postage-stamp backyard had more than just a few plants. "This looks like an English garden."

She went to the sliding glass door and opened it. "Do you mind?"

He shook his head and gestured his hand toward the garden. "Go for it."

She couldn't believe her eyes. Beach roses made a natural border around the backyard. A small pond with a running waterfall sat in one corner, and on the other end were manicured beach plums, rhododendrons, lilacs, and even a gorgeous apple tree. In the middle of the square yard was a stone patio under a cedar pergola, with grape vines growing up the four wooden posts.

"Mateo." She twirled around to see it all again. "This place is beautiful."

"Thank you." He looked around, and she could see pride across his face.

She pointed to the area near the sliding glass door. "You should build yourself an outdoor kitchen over there."

He pointed to a small spigot on the side of the house. "That's a tap to a gas line for that exact purpose."

Harper was out of her mind.

Mateo stuffed his hands into his pockets. "Can I get you something to drink?"

Five years ago, she'd have asked for a beer and then flirted with him. Five years ago, she'd have no trouble capturing his attention. But truthfully, five years ago, she wouldn't have bothered flirting with a contractor, no matter how hot or handy. She'd had her sights set on the first love of her life.

Cooking.

"I'd love a water," she said.

He lifted a finger into the air. "I'll be back. Make yourself comfortable."

She wanted to walk around the perimeter, check out some of the flowers she recognized from her own mother's garden, but her feet were swollen, and she needed to sit down. His garden was full of coneheads and brown-eyed Susans, tall pink and purple and white phlox, and purple flowered cat mint.

Mateo came right back with a glass of ice water and a bowl of cut lemons.

"Are you Martha Stewart's grandson?" she asked.

He laughed. "I'll assume that means you think I'm hospitable."

"What's that growing on the side of the house?"

"Honeysuckle."

"I love the smell of honeysuckle." She took a sip of water, and when silence entered the space, the need to fill the void made her blurt out, "You should set up a picnic back here with Harper."

Mateo shook his head, taking a sip of his own water. "She just wants to be friends."

"This place is so romantic." She waved both arms toward his flower garden. "String up some fairy lights, light some candles, and she'll be melting in your arms."

"She told me to back off." He gave a hard nod but didn't look at her. "And so that's what I'm going to do."

They stood there for a second longer in silence, and she moved toward a chair. She pointed to the one across from her. "Do you mind if I put my feet up on the chair?"

"No, of course not." Mateo hurried over and pushed it closer to her, sitting down in another chair.

She didn't know what it was, but *something* swept through her —a need to have Harper see what she saw in Mateo.

"You should host a tasting for your pastries," he said. "Your mother's place is a gorgeous spot. Invite some of the community, have people taste your food. If you're going to sell stuff, you should get opinions about what works and what doesn't."

"A tasting?" Renee gave him a look. "I don't know. I'm not opening anything. I'm just selling baked goods."

And her heart sunk as she realized why she was jealous of Harper. Renee wished more than anything she'd have a guy as nice as Mateo. "I should probably head back to my mom's place. Thanks for letting me see your house and garden."

"You didn't pick your wood," he said, looking disappointed.

She swallowed the lump digging at the bottom of her throat. "I trust you."

CHAPTER 8

Evelyn sat next to Renee and Wanda on the ferry to Falmouth. They were on their way to Wanda's second chemotherapy treatment, which luckily was now every three weeks versus her radiation appointments that were every day of the week. She thought back to a few months ago, when she'd first met Wanda. Crazy how much things had changed. She laughed aloud thinking of how she'd planned on ditching Wanda the second she could, and now Evelyn wouldn't leave her side.

"Do you need to use the restroom?" she asked her friend, seeing the shore coming into view.

"Does your mother still make you go before leaving the house?" Wanda asked Renee, who nodded and rolled her eyes at the same time.

"You'd think it was because I'm pregnant, but it's been going on for the past twenty-eight years." Renee browsed the news on her phone, which strangely irritated Evelyn, even though she had been doing the same thing.

"You do read more than just your browser for news, right?" she asked.

One of the things Evelyn gladly passed off to her virtual assistant was anything to do with social media and relevant pop culture. When having a social media feed meant "talking" with her readers, she became on board, but then people wanted personal effects from her life, like pictures of her pets, her house, and her family. Strangers came out of the woodwork and comments became less about "talking" and something else entirely.

Then George had died, and she had no use to be social. But her readers wouldn't have known it. She still enjoyed knitting, baking cookies at Christmas, and watching her Netflix series with friends. Photos of feet with knitted stockings worked for all three. Evelyn wasn't in any of them.

Her readers didn't even notice.

"Now I do have to go," Wanda said, dropping her purse in Evelyn's lap. "Do you mind holding that?"

"Not at all," Evelyn said, jabbing her elbow into Renee's ribs. "You should go, too, before we get on the road."

"Seriously?" Renee scrunched her eyebrows together but then handed her purse to Evelyn. "Here."

Evelyn smiled, thinking about when the girls and her would go shopping at a mall. When was the last time it was just her and her girls? She'd sit outside the dressing room, holding their coats or bags or purses, and wait for them to come out in whatever they were trying on.

She'd complain to George about how many different outfits there would be. How many times she was sent back for a different size or color. She'd give anything to get those days back.

George always had a meal ready to go when they came back. The girls would kiss him on the cheek as they walked past him in the kitchen and up to their bedrooms with too much stuff.

When the pair came out of the bathroom, Evelyn realized how happy she was that Renee agreed to go along with her and Wanda. She really hadn't been sure if Renee would follow through. Renee hadn't fully picked up the Wanda bug; instead, Wanda just bugged her. But moments like today—traveling, going to the hospital, showing this type of vulnerability of life and death—showed Wanda at her best.

"How long does the infusion take?" Renee asked as they walked back from the bathroom.

"A little more than thirty minutes," Wanda said, as though having poison running through your body was a normal, no-big-deal thing.

"Where will we shop?" Renee asked as they all headed down to the car. "I'd love to eat at Quincey Market or somewhere in the North End." She pulled out the paper Charlie had given her. "We told Charlie we'd check out this bakery."

"We'll take Wanda to her appointment, which will take about an hour, then we can go anywhere you want. Do you have an idea what you need for the baby? Do you want to focus on furniture or clothes?"

Renee shrugged. "I haven't really thought about it, but I already have the bassinette from Charlie, and Mateo said he'd build me a crib."

Evelyn couldn't believe it. "What a nice gesture."

Renee nodded. "Yeah, I don't understand what Harper doesn't see in him. He's the nicest guy."

Evelyn frowned. "Harper doesn't like Mateo?"

Renee shook her head. "She likes him as a friend, if you know what I mean."

Wanda clucked her tongue. "I could tell something was happening between the two of them."

"They're such a handsome couple," Evelyn said.

"I think they're really good friends, and she doesn't want to ruin it," Renee said. "But, don't you think she'd be really happy with him?"

"I guess that's up to Harper," Evelyn said, but she completely agreed with Renee. She could see them very happy together. As they reached the station wagon, she thought about how cute their babies would be.

"He's got a great place," Renee said. "You should see what he's done to the interior. Talk about a kitchen."

Evelyn jerked back. "You were at his house?"

Renee nodded. "Mm-hmm. I went last night."

Evelyn thought about the night. She had thought Renee went out by herself.

What was she doing with Mateo at his house?

"I thought you were out on your own last night?" Evelyn hadn't noticed her leaving with Mateo. He had been there for the reading, then she'd seen him with a drink. Had he left after that, when Renee had left?

"I was planning on it, but then I stayed to listen to Harper read, and he offered to build a crib, and we ended up going to his house." She said it all like it was no big deal, but for some reason, it was a very big deal to Evelyn.

"You went to Mateo's at night?"

Renee's face immediately turned defensive. "What's that supposed to mean?"

Evelyn tried to hold back. She could feel herself losing her cool, and it wasn't the appropriate time. She looked through the garage of the ferry for a seagull—something to help her do the right thing—but she didn't see anything, and her tongue wasn't listening.

"Should you be going to a guy's house while pregnant and still married?"

Renee's face dropped, and Evelyn could see Wanda wince.

"I'm twenty-eight," Renee reminded her as though that made a difference. "I can go to whoever's house I want to."

"This isn't about going to anyone's house. It's about the fact that you don't tell me anything." Evelyn was fighting her on this because she was right. Renee hadn't told her anything. Not about why she'd left Chicago, about her marriage suddenly ending, about the pregnancy and Harry's absence.

"What's the big deal?" Renee made a face that said Evelyn was being ridiculous. "You were busy with Harper's reading. You didn't even notice."

Evelyn could feel the passive blow. She couldn't really figure out what was happening with Renee and Harper, but something was simmering in Renee.

Wanda stood frozen next to the car.

"Never mind. I'm sorry I even said anything." Evelyn used her remote to unlock the station wagon. A beep echoed off the other cars. She thought of Charlie. If she had continued, she certainly wasn't allowing Renee to open up to her on her own. All she would be doing was starting a fight. But didn't Evelyn deserve a little decency of knowing about her daughter's life? She will always open her home to her daughter, but what was so bad about telling her the truth?

Renee took the seat behind Evelyn, and the whole ride up to Boston, Wanda did the talking while Evelyn and Renee hardly said two words to each other. But Evelyn could feel her nerves ramping up, and she needed to get herself together. This trip was to help Renee feel comfortable to talk, not push her away. But when would she ever tell Evelyn the truth about anything?

"Wanda, do you still feel up for lunch after your treatment?" Renee asked. "Because we don't have to go shopping, if you're not."

"No, that sounds fun." Wanda smiled behind her at Renee. "I've never really explored Boston besides the hospital."

Evelyn had a feeling Wanda was accommodating Renee's request. That was Wanda, Evelyn had learned—always trying to please. "Quincy Market is a great little stop. There's plenty to eat and shop."

"I can't fit into anything anymore," Renee said.

Evelyn looked in the rearview mirror. Her daughter looked out the window, her face melancholy like usual. Evelyn's own heart broke. The preparation of motherhood had only brought her joy and excited apprehension. She and George would stay up (when she could) and talk and talk about their child. What would he or she look like? What would they act like? Would they be smart and good at sports? Would they be a bookworm? What traits would they take on?

"Maybe we should do some shopping for the nursery." Evelyn suggested.

"That sounds fun," Wanda said. "They have such cute boy stuff nowadays."

Evelyn looked through the mirror at Renee's reaction. Her attention was still out the window.

"Renee?"

She didn't respond.

"Renee," Evelyn called out. "Do you want to go shopping at one of those maternity and baby stores?"

Renee looked up. "I'd rather see some bakeries." Her eyes went right back out the window.

Evelyn sighed. She would try Charlie's advice: stick with it for the trip. God hoped she could, but she was already losing patience.

The problem was that George would've been able to talk to Renee. George would have known exactly what was going on and how to solve it. Renee would've never kept this from George. Evelyn would've only found out because George would've been the one to tell her. Because the real problem Evelyn didn't want to admit was that she and Renee had never had a good relationship. Not a real one, at least. Even before George had died.

She loved Renee and she was sure Renee loved her, but there was nothing more to their relationship other than mother and daughter. Nothing like Harper and Charlie, or even Samantha and Evelyn. When Samantha called, she was full of conversation, telling Evelyn all about her adventures. Renee obviously didn't share anything or tell the truth of any kind. Or had Evelyn missed it in her own grief? Here she was blaming Renee when maybe it was really Evelyn who had been the one ruining the relationship.

This made her miss George more. He would have known what to do.

They finally arrived and walked into the oncology office, with its sterile look and neutral furniture décor. Over the past couple of months, Evelyn had become familiar with the routine of treatment centers. Familiar with its magazines that were outdated, familiar with its fake homemade signs of positivity and inspirational quotes.

"Ugh," Renee said, rubbing her belly. "He's moody today."

Wanda sat down in between Evelyn and Renee. Evelyn couldn't help but notice her smiling more than usual.

"Is this your family?" a nurse behind the check-in counter asked when she called Wanda up.

Wanda looked back at them and then to the receptionist. "Whether they like it or not."

Evelyn smirked, but then she shot a look at Renee as she opened her mouth to correct her.

"We'll call you in when we're ready for you," the receptionist said.

Wanda twisted her hands as she waited.

"You nervous?" Evelyn asked.

"I haven't started losing my hair yet." Her smile faded as Evelyn's heart dropped. "They say it takes two to four weeks."

"Maybe you won't lose it," Evelyn said optimistically. "I read that only about seventy percent lose their hair."

"I think I should shave it before it falls out." Wanda's hand went to her hair. "I've always been known for my red curls. What if it doesn't ever grow back?"

"My mom has the most fabulous silk scarves from Paris you could wear," Renee said. "You'll look like Audrey Hepburn."

"What if it's misshapen?" Wanda asked.

"You could buy really fun wigs." Renee twisted in her seat. "Like blonde or pink or even a sultry brunette."

Wanda's smile grew as she swatted her hand at Renee's suggestions. "You know, I always wanted to see what I'd look like as a blonde."

"Wanda?" a nurse asked from the doorway.

Wanda passed her purse to Evelyn.

"We'll be here," Evelyn said, putting the purse in her lap.

Wanda gave a look to Renee, then said to Evelyn, "You haven't left me before."

Evelyn turned to Renee as soon as Wanda left. "Am I babying her?"

"Yes." Renee didn't even hesitate.

"Really?" Evelyn hadn't even noticed this bothering Wanda until this morning.

"You tell her to use the bathroom all the time," Renee answered as though it was over the top.

"You should see how much she goes to the bathroom." Evelyn had met her in the bathroom after all. "Speaking of which, her treatment doesn't take that long, and they have a nice restroom here."

"Seriously?" Renee rubbed her belly again.

"Is he kicking?" Evelyn hadn't expected the movement of her grandson to be so remarkable, but the idea of a little, tiny George inside of her own baby…

"Are you crying?" Renee asked.

Evelyn started to laugh when she felt a tear fall before she could catch it. "I guess I am."

Renee scanned around the room. "How do you come here all the time?"

Evelyn noticed a few familiar faces. "It's actually therapeutic." She hadn't expected to confess that. She didn't want to burden Renee with more, but if she was going to get somewhere with her closed-off daughter, she would at least have to try what Charlie had suggested. She would talk to Renee. "With losing your father so suddenly, death was this sudden and scary thing."

Renee nodded as she rubbed her belly. "And this place makes you feel better?"

"Sort of." Evelyn exhaled as she spoke. "When he died, death became so frightening, because it happened out of nowhere. But here, death is just another day. The men and women who walk through these doors day after day, treatment after treatment, face it. And if you look around, they're not afraid. It's just part of their journey."

"When did you become Dr. Phil?" Renee asked. Sarcasm hung in the air.

"I'm sorry you were alone through all that," Evelyn said. "I should've been there for you and your sister more, and I'm really sorry."

Renee looked down at her hands, picking at her nails. "I should've stayed longer. I left right after the funeral. You were all alone, and we just left."

Evelyn got up and moved seats next to Renee, then patted her hand. "You aren't supposed to take care of your mother. Besides, you had your own life."

Renee's husband had come into the picture right after George's death. Evelyn could swing the conversation so easily to Harry and her marriage, what with Wanda in the infusion room —no harm, no foul.

But she didn't.

Instead, she pulled out her phone. "I wasn't going to show you this until I knew exactly what your plans were, but..." She pulled open the email and clicked the attachment from Schneider and Smith Design Group.

"What's this?" Renee asked, pulling the phone into her view.

"This is the guest cottage Mateo is going to build the garage into," Evelyn said with pride. It would be a beautiful space for her and the baby. Two bedrooms, two baths, a galley kitchen, and a wall of windows facing the water. "I'm even thinking about adding a wood fireplace. Do you love it?"

Renee pushed the phone back in Evelyn's lap. "This is too much."

"What?" Evelyn looked at the plans. It was hardly a thousand square feet. "I think you'll be fine living there."

"I mean, it's too much for you to do. We don't need it." Renee shifted in her seat, away from Evelyn.

Evelyn slowly put the phone away. Then a fear crept in. "Are you going back to Chicago?"

Renee shook her head.

"Okay, then let me renovate the cottage."

"Ugh," Renee said. "I don't need you to do that."

"Look, Renee, I don't know what to say or do with you lately." Evelyn spoke before she could stop herself. "All I'm trying to do is help."

Renee's lips pierced together. "I'm sorry I'm so difficult."

Evelyn squeezed the arms of the chair. "I'm not saying you're being difficult. I'm trying to be cool, I really am, but everything I seem to do is wrong with you. I don't know what's wrong."

The look on Renee's face said it all. She thought Evelyn was the stupidest person on earth. "Isn't it obvious my life is falling apart? How did the fact I'm here, alone and pregnant, not give you enough clues?"

Renee's eyes immediately welled with tears.

"I don't mean to upset you. I just care about you and the baby and want to help."

Renee's chin trembled. "Well, don't worry," she said, wiping her cheeks with her sleeve. "I won't keep your guest room for long. I'll start looking for a place today."

She held up her own phone and opened the screen, showing a website with rental properties.

"Renee, I don't want you to go. That's not what I'm trying to say at all." Evelyn could see others looking at them. "Please, I want to be here for you and the baby. I want to help."

Renee sniffled up a breath, covering her eyes with her hands. Evelyn pulled out a tissue from her purse and handed it over to her.

Well, that conversation hadn't gone as planned.

"If you want to help, then please don't ask me to tell you about Harry. Not yet," she said.

Evelyn's jaw set hard, as though she had been punched. "If that's what you want."

CHAPTER 9

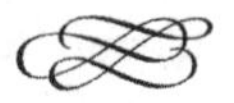

Renee couldn't tell her mother. If she did, there was no coming back from the truth. Harry didn't want his son. Harry didn't want his wife for that matter. Harry Winthrop didn't want his best chef. The worst part? She had seen it from the beginning. He was thoughtless, arrogant, and selfish.

She had thought he'd change.

And now, she didn't want her mother to know. Not yet. Not until the baby was born. Not until Harry got to see his son. Maybe then he'd change his mind, regret ever thinking of ending the pregnancy, and beg her back.

But even though she skipped Marty's delivery that morning, she knew in her gut she was only fooling herself. He wasn't going to change his mind and come back. Harry Winthrop wouldn't change. He'd been the same person all along and would continue to be.

They sat in silence until Wanda came out of her infusion.

She made a face when she saw the two of them. "Did someone pass gas?"

"No," Evelyn said.

Renee smiled knowing full well Evelyn didn't talk about passing gas, or heaven forbid, a fart.

"Well, why do you look like you've smelled something rotten?" She put her hands on her hips.

"She tried telling me to use the restroom," Renee mumbled, glancing sideways to see her mother's reaction. But Evelyn's attention was on Wanda.

"Are you feeling okay?" she said, concern on her face.

The petite-framed woman suddenly looked tired; more tired than when she had first walked into the room. Renee had almost forgotten Wanda had just undergone chemotherapy treatment.

"We don't have to shop," Renee said. "We can just go home."

"No," Wanda said. "You wanted to check out those bakeries in the North End, didn't you?"

"They'll be there next time," Renee said.

Wanda shook her head. "I want to try a real cannoli."

She winked at Renee, and in that moment, Renee had never been more grateful for her mother's friend. Maybe having another person in the mix worked out. Her mother wasn't going to press her in front of Wanda or Bitty.

Instead, Evelyn pressed Wanda with her questions, and just like that, the conversation was dropped.

Renee let out a sigh of relief as they headed out of the office.

Even though Boston would be considered a young city in Europe—where Samantha was—for Renee's midwestern roots, Beantown felt ancient, with its modern skyscrapers mingled among the red brick buildings of the colonial era. The roads were designed with no design in mind, and every street seemed to be one-way. The summer heat did not deter tourists, who seemed to be everywhere, sitting on green duck buses, walking the Freedom Trail, and taking selfies everywhere.

Evelyn navigated through the city with no trouble at all. She drove like an expert without needing to use the GPS once.

"Wow, I'm impressed, Mom," Renee said as Evelyn drove through the Back Bay to the North End.

"That's Quincy Market over there," Evelyn pointed out. "And Faneuil Hall."

"I forgot you used to live here," Renee said, looking out the window at the golden dome. "What's that church?"

"That's the old state house," Evelyn said as they passed down Congress toward Hanover.

"Charlie said everyone goes to Mike's Pastry, but he told me to check out another bakery." Renee held the paper with the name and address.

"Charlie told you about this place?" Evelyn smiled. "That's awfully nice."

It had been, but even still, Renee felt the tear in her chest. She liked Charlie, a lot. He was a nice guy. Plus, her mom was an adult, who had every right to make her own decisions for herself. Renee certainly didn't like it when her mother got into her business, so Renee understood why she needed to get over herself. So why couldn't she just do it?

She rubbed her belly.

Would it have broken her dad's heart if another man ended up with her mom? Would George, the husband, be sad to see Evelyn move on? Would he feel possessive of his daughters and grandson with this new man? Would he want Charlie fitting into the role of grandfather?

She wondered how he would've reacted about her being pregnant and missing a husband. How he would have reacted to learning he was becoming a grandfather. Or would he be a Poppy?

Renee wished her mother would slow down or drive around more. "Boston's such a great city."

"Expensive," Evelyn said as she turned right. "That's the house of Paul Revere."

When they finally parked, Renee looked out at a brick storefront with the name Bottega Del Pane written in black paint on the window. The second Renee stepped out of the car, she could smell the aroma of bread floating out from the shop.

She was home.

"That smells divine," Wanda said, stepping out of the car.

"Why don't you two take a seat, and I'll grab some treats for us," Renee said.

Wanda put her visor on. "I'm not that hungry. Maybe a café latte if they have them."

"Water as well?"

Wanda nodded. "Yes, that's perfect."

Renee could see the toll the therapy was taking on her body. Her mom may not be overreacting after all. "We don't have to stay. We can go home."

"No, please, this is adorable. I love going places and sightseeing." Wanda patted Renee.

Evelyn opened the door, and a rush of air-conditioning came out as they all stepped inside. The space was small, probably smaller than Evelyn's new kitchen at the beach house, but it was the most gorgeous bakery Renee had ever stepped into. She felt as though she were truly in an Italian bread shop.

The floors were a dark stained wood but looked original to the centuries-old building. The tall brick walls warmed the space, and refrigerated glass cases were filled with sweet and bright pastries. Ricotta cakes with candied peels, chocolate chip and pistachio cannolis. Chocolate-drizzled sfogliatella, airy and light panbriacone, and maritozzi sweet buns filled with whipped cream.

George started to kick. "Let's take it all."

"Do you have a sampler selection?" Evelyn asked the girl behind the counter.

The girl smiled and nodded. "I can put something together for you ladies."

Renee walked around the small space as the girl packed a dozen Italian pastries.

"Could we take a couple of those loaves of bread, and a café latte?"

The young girl nodded and got to work. Renee grabbed a chocolate milk from the refrigerator.

“Go out with Wanda and get a table,” Renee said, nodding to the empty round table on the sidewalk out front.

“Okay, text if you need help.” Evelyn ushered Wanda out the door to the table.

“Mind if I take some photos?” Renee held up her phone to the other women behind the counter.

The older woman shook her head. “Not at all.”

She began taking pictures of things she liked that they did in the bakery. For one, the style and décor was spot on. The inside had soft neutral colors. The back wall had chalkboards with all the different items they sold. Wooden crates held different types of loaves and types of bread.

“Can I get you anything else?” the younger woman asked, handing her the filled pastry box.

Something inside of Renee wanted to cling to the space and never leave. The smells, the sounds, the sights—everything. Charlie had been right. She loved it.

“Is everything made here in the bakery?” Renee asked.

The younger woman nodded. “My mom bakes everything you see.”

The woman from behind the counter looked up. Her hair was pulled up in a messy bun, and Renee noticed her pastry hands—working hands. Her apron was dusted in flour, the company’s name stitched on the front. “Hope you enjoy your treats.”

Renee stood there dumbfounded. She didn’t look much older than forty. “You run this all by yourself?”

The woman smiled. “I have help, but yes, this is my bakery.”

“I’m a chef,” Renee blurted out, suddenly wanting this stranger to feel the immediate connection she’d had with her. But when the young woman behind the counter’s eyebrows lifted at her outburst, she felt a bit silly by her reaction. “Well, I was in Chicago.”

The woman smiled. “Ah, a fellow culinary friend.”

“Is most of your business storefront?” she asked, noticing the cakes in the tall refrigerator. "Or is most of your business catering weddings?"

"We have a large volume of tourists who come to the shop, but a lot of my pastry goods are bought from local restaurants and hotels. I also do a lot of weddings."

Renee thought about all the hotels and restaurants on Martha's Vineyard. Were they large enough to have a full kitchen staff or did they already hire out for desserts? Would they be willing to buy pastries and desserts from a local chef?

"You've got a great place here," Renee said, noticing Gia smiling at her mom.

"Thanks." The chef held out her hand. "Lisa."

"Renee." She shook her hand while balancing the box on her belly.

"When are you due?" Lisa asked.

"November twenty-third." Renee held the box again.

"Gia, help Renee with the bread, and I'll help with the drinks." Lisa picked up the three cups, and they all walked outside to Evelyn and Wanda.

Gia set bags of bread on a chair, standing up.

"Enjoy your pastries, ladies," Lisa said to the women.

The two went back inside as Renee sat.

She looked to Wanda, who sat quietly. The usually chatty Cathy was low on energy, and Renee felt guilty making her go on this adventure in the city. Was this too much? On top of the ferry ride back to the island. "We don't have to stay, Wanda. We can go home."

"No, no. I like people watching." Wanda looked out at the busy street with all sorts of people walking and rushing around, cars passing by. "Besides, I think this place will give you inspiration for your own bakery."

"It's definitely inspiring." Renee wondered if Charlie knew the pastry chef would be a woman. A woman with a daughter.

"I bet people would love a little place like this on the island," Wanda said.

Evelyn's face perked up. "Or someone to do catering for events and parties."

Renee thought about the island. It was a magnificent place no doubt. The water, the beaches, the quaint villages and harbors. But would she be happy stuck on an island? Would she be able to run a bakery and handle the business side of things as a mother? It was gorgeous but isolating. She couldn't just leave whenever she wanted. She had to plan, count on fair weather, and go by someone else's schedule for the ferry.

She looked behind her into the bakery's window. The volume of the inventory, dealing with staffing and payroll, and all the other things in between. She wouldn't be able to do it on her own. Or afford a place like that on the island. "Who's going to watch George?"

"Renee!" Evelyn shook her head in dismay. "We've been telling you all along. We will."

Wanda nodded.

"I can't ask you to do that for me." Renee scowled. "You should be retired, not child-rearing. Bitty isn't planning on staying forever, and—"

She stopped herself and looked to Wanda. She was in no shape to take care of a baby.

"I want nothing more than to be a grandma," Evelyn said back. "I can't wait to have Baby G around."

"And I'm looking forward to becoming a great auntie." Wanda rubbed Renee's knee with her hand, which felt cold.

Evelyn leaned in, making Renee look her in the eyes. "We want to help you become a success."

Renee looked down, immediately embarrassed and scared and grateful at the same time. The pastries in front of her started to blur from her emotions rattling inside.

If she took the offer, took their help, she could do it. She felt it deep in her bones. She could open something up, a bakery, a small boutique eatery, or maybe a Euro-hip coffee and pastry shop. If her mother and Bitty and Wanda did help, for just a few hours a day, she could possibly do it. Possibly. At least save up some money by living with them.

How could she ever repay her mother and her friends for this? She blew out. "Okay, maybe I'll stay on the island while I figure out what I'm going to do next."

Renee inhaled a breath, noticing a look exchanged between Evelyn and Wanda. They both smiled. Renee didn't want to admit it, but a wave of relief rushed through her. She'd stay at least the first few months after George was born. She could use that time to really plan out her next step. Did she really want to run a bakery? Or would she be just as happy working in a kitchen, any kitchen, if she was baking?

Bottega Del Pane's pastries tasted better than they looked. Even Wanda finished a cannoli topped with pistachios.

"Did you enjoy your treats?" Lisa asked as Renee returned their cups and plates.

"Everything was delicious," Renee said, looking around the space one last time before they headed out. Wanda and Evelyn had hit the restroom, of course.

Wanda returned and said to Lisa behind the counter, "Our Renee is planning on opening her own bakery."

Renee's face instantly heated, and she could feel sweat forming on her chest.

"Is that so?" Lisa grinned and glanced at Renee. "Well, good. We need more women in this business. Come and see my oven."

Lisa waved her to the back room, and all three women followed her and Gia behind the swinging door. Instantly, Renee felt at home stepping into the heart of the bakery—the kitchen. Lisa kept it impeccable. Shining stainless steel appliances, gleaming stovetops, and smudge-free refrigerators. The kitchen sink, though full of dirty cookie sheets and trays, had clean counters and a drying system with a commercial grade dishwasher running quietly next to it.

"You have a Baxter standing oven?" Renee had dreamt of having an oven like that back in Chicago, but Harry hadn't seen it as a necessary purchase. Most baked goods were done in mass production with large commercial machines.

"I lucked out and got it used from a bakery in New York that had shut down because of a divorce." Lisa poked Gia in her ribs with her elbow. "Remember when we drove down there to get it?"

"I'll never forget." Gia lifted her eyes to the sky. "Mom made me drive a U-Haul."

"You drove it through a parking lot," Lisa said.

"It was still huge!" Gia argued back to her mother.

Renee watched the mother-daughter dynamic. In a matter of months, she would no longer only relate as the daughter in that kind of scenario, but also the mother.

As Evelyn and Wanda asked more questions, Renee picked up that Lisa wasn't married. For one, she didn't wear a ring, not that it meant she wasn't married, but for two, she never mentioned a husband or Gia's father. She talked about her business partners and investors, but not a man. Renee wished she could ask how she did it on her own, *if* she did. She had read somewhere that one in every five bakeries fail. It must've taken Lisa a lot of hard work to make it in the food service industry, which was dominated by men. Even getting a loan from a bank to help finance could not have been easy.

"Thank you for showing us around," Renee said as they began to leave.

"You call me if you have any questions." Lisa handed her a card with the bakery's name and information.

"You might be sorry you gave this to me," Renee said back to her.

Lisa went back behind the counter. "It's all about using your resources."

Renee tucked Lisa's card into her wallet and waved goodbye. She would call Lisa and return to Bottega Del Pane. Charlie had been absolutely spot-on.

"Thank you so much for coming with me," Renee said to Wanda and her mom as they got back into the car.

"Of course," Evelyn said, turning on the engine and adjusting the rear view mirror.

As Evelyn drove out of the city, toward the ferry in Falmouth, an energy grew in Renee's chest as she stared at Lisa's card, and the more she looked, the more the energy grew.

I'm going to do it, Baby G. I'm going to open a bakery.

CHAPTER 10

With one hand, Mateo dragged the sandpaper over the wooden slats that made the side of the crib. He followed a pattern that was considered one of the safest designs to regulations today. Hopefully, Renee would be able to reach inside and pick up the baby from the mattress. He couldn't remember her exact height, but he recalled her being up to about his chin. He was about six foot two, which made her, if he had to guess, around five foot six, maybe?

He finished his sandwich just as he heard a car pull up the driveway to the Roses' beach house, Sea View. Harper slid her Mini Cooper to a stop in front of Mrs. Rose's house. With the top down and her sunglasses on, she looked like a Hollywood movie star in her silk headscarf and sundress. No doubt about it, Harper was gorgeous.

"Hey," she said, waving at him as she pulled out bags of groceries.

"How's it going?" He dropped the paper and walked out of the garage. "Can I help you bring anything in?"

"Yes," Harper said, dropping the bags she had in her hands into his.

"Anything else I can take?" He looked inside the small car.

She reached in the back and took out the remaining bags. "I've got it."

He let her lead the way to the house and helped grab the door.

"Thanks," she said, dropping the bags onto the counter. Something that looked like a root fell out of the bag, and he picked it up.

"What's this?" he asked, examining it.

"Ginger," Harper said. "It's for Wanda. It helps with the nausea."

"Is that because of the chemo?" he asked. He didn't know much about Wanda's condition, other than that she had breast cancer, but she frequently rested throughout the day on the back porch under blankets.

"Yeah," Harper said.

"I feel so bad for her." Mateo thought about his own mother, who was sixty-five. He'd die if she were to ever get sick.

"It's so nice of Evelyn to let her stay here," Harper said, emptying the bags to the counter. "I think it's really remarkable they all moved in together to take care of her."

He nodded and gathered up the bags, and the conversation stilted. Things had changed between the two of them. Would it take time to get over the kiss and his broken heart, or would this be the way it was?

"Nice job last night on the reading." He had listened to the story, but his thoughts had been spinning about everything. About how good she looked while reading. How proud he had been of her. How being friends just didn't seem like a good idea anymore.

"You didn't stick around." Harper held a bag of loose lettuce in her hands as she waited for him to respond.

Did he tell her the truth? That he had needed to split before he did something stupid like try to kiss her again. Or did he just confess everything? That all this time, all these years, he'd been head over heels for her. He'd only freak her out even more. The crux of the situation was that, looking back on everything, he should've seen the red flags with their relationship. They were some of the only people left on the island who were single and their age. She was stuck and hated her job. They both had obligations to their families. They both loved to read. It made sense she would be friends with a guy who visited the bookstore where she worked. It wasn't her fault he felt the way he did.

The worst part of it all: he would hold her back if they became serious. She'd always wonder what would have become of her if she had left the island. She'd end up resenting him. It was better this way, to avoid all that.

Then why did it hurt so much?

"I should go back to the garage." Mateo gestured his thumb behind him toward the garage. "I'm working on the built-ins for the third floor."

Harper's left eyebrow perked up. "Looks like you're building a baby crib."

He shrugged. "I have some extra lumber."

"That's really nice of you." Harper stood there as though she were waiting for him to spark up another conversation like he would've before the kiss, but he didn't. He couldn't. Things were different.

He lifted his hand as he walked out of the house and left.

Would he go back and change things so everything could return to normal? No. He didn't believe in going back. He may have ruined their friendship by kissing her and letting her know how he felt, but he wasn't going back.

By the time he decided to stop for the night, he almost finished the basic frame for the crib. He locked up the garage and left for the day. Usually, he'd go inside, see what Harper was doing before heading home, but he left without even saying goodbye.

José had called a meeting at the local bar in town, which was code name for getting out of the house.

"The mother-in-law is here for two weeks," José complained the second Mateo sat down at the table.

Mateo raised his hand at Allison, the regular bartender. "I'll have what he's having."

"Sure thing," she said to him, grabbing a glass and pulling the tap on a dark ale.

"What are you drinking?' Mateo asked as his brother chugged his glass empty while also holding his hand up to Allison.

"Two boilermakers!"

Mateo shook out his hands at Allison. "I'll just take a beer."

"Guess I'll need a ride home anyway," José said as Allison set his boilermaker down in front of him. He took the shot of whiskey, dropped it into his pint glass, and in one go, drank down the beer.

Mateo handed over a napkin for José's chin. "That looks like it hurts."

"She's driving me crazy," José said. "She's always saying things to Julia, like I'm a different subset of human because I didn't come from money."

Mateo had to admit, his brother's mother-in-law took the prize for being a nightmare. "You think getting drunk with me is going to make things better?"

"I can't sit in *my* house listening to her complain about *my* house."

"Why don't you offer to put her up at The Wharf?" Mateo suggested. He knew a couple weeks at The Wharf wouldn't break José's bank account.

"She says she's there to see the kids." He moaned. "I think she's there to torture me."

Mateo patted José on the back. "It'll go by fast, and she'll head back to Florida."

"God, I hope so," he mumbled.

"You already started without me?" the youngest Perez said as he came into the pub.

José lifted three fingers to Allison. "Let's do three this time."

"Just two." Mateo pushed his own beer aside. He'd be the sober driver tonight. When he gave his younger brother, Elias, a hug as he sat down, that's when he saw her out of the corner of his eye.

Outside on the patio of the pub was a couple sitting close to each other. At first, he wouldn't have noticed them under the shade of the trees beside the building, but he noticed her patchwork purse draped on the back of the chair.

That's when he saw the man sitting across from her reach out his hand to her cheek, lean over the table between them, and kiss her.

"I take that back," Mateo said. "Make that three."

He pretended not to notice Harper for the rest of the night, as she dangled over the man across from her. He also pretended to not see her when she left with him, or when she noticed Mateo and pretended not to see him. He also pretended not to care in front of his brothers, as if his heart didn't feel like it was being ripped out of his rib cage. That he didn't feel like a complete fool.

Harper was seeing someone?

When José's curfew came and went, Mateo got his brothers out of the pub and into his truck. He drove Elias with him to José and Julia's house, expecting not only an annoying mother-in-law but a very annoyed sister-in-law.

"Hey, Baby," José said as he stumbled out of the truck. Julia stood at the front door with her arms crossed as Mateo and Elias helped him out.

"I can smell you from here," Julia said.

"We had a business meeting." José slurred his words as he walked up to Julia. He kissed her on the lips and wrapped his arms around her. "I love you so much."

"You better now?" she asked him.

He kissed her again and nodded. "I promise to take the kids all day tomorrow."

"And you're doing dinner and bath time," she said.

"I promise." He held her against him in a big bear hug. "Thank you for letting me escape."

She rolled her eyes as he held her.

"You good?" Mateo asked his sister-in-law.

"Yes. Thanks, Uncle Teo," she said as she led her intoxicated husband into the house. "Thank you for being the responsible one tonight."

"No problem." He waited to make sure she got José inside the house with no trouble. He smiled as his brother continued to kiss his wife as she dragged him through the house.

"Is that Mateo?" he heard Julia's mother say from inside.

He rushed toward the truck when she called out, "Mateo, that is you!"

He swung around to see his brother's mother-in-law standing on the doorstep.

"Hello, Sandy," he said. "Good to see you."

"Always a pleasure," she said, holding out her hand as she waited for him to walk back up the stoop to greet her.

He reached out as he came close enough and shook it, but he was almost certain she would've accepted him kissing her like a queen.

"How was your business meeting?" she asked, but sarcasm oozed in her voice.

"Productive," he said. "We're working on multiple projects this summer and can hardly find time to meet."

She cocked her head. "Julia showed me the beach house you're working on."

"It's a beauty, isn't it?" Mateo said. He knew Sandy would admire the work they were doing with that project.

"Julia said it's Evelyn Rose, the writer." She sounded impressed.

"Yes," Mateo said. "She's completely renovating the Victorian."

"It's stunning from the outside." Sandy's forehead lifted. "You wouldn't happen to be able to introduce me to her, would you?"

He groaned inside. Was she really asking him that?

"I'll see what I can do," he said, but he wasn't planning on asking Evelyn about it.

"It's a shame my daughter doesn't have a house to entertain

in," Sandy said out loud. "It's really too small to invite more than a few couples."

Mateo looked behind her at the three thousand square foot house his brother had built for his new bride. José had put his heart and soul into the house that sat in the same hills as Evelyn Rose's beach house.

"I hope you enjoy your stay with your grandchildren." He waved as she continued to complain about how raucous her three grandchildren were.

"That is one miserable woman," Elias muttered under his breath as Mateo got into the truck.

"No kidding." There was no way Mateo would introduce her to Evelyn.

But as it turned out, he didn't have a choice. The next day, as he worked on the moldings around the dining room, he heard Sandy's voice coming from the back porch.

"Yoo-hoo!"

His stomach dropped as he looked out the window and saw Sandy barreling down the wooden planks toward the beach house.

"Who is that?" Renee asked as she walked out from the kitchen, watching the crazy woman trespass.

"I am so sorry." He immediately started climbing down from his ladder. "That's José's insane mother-in-law. She made a comment about wanting to meet your mother. I swear I didn't think she'd go as far as trespassing on her property. You should hide and I'll take care of her."

He expected Renee to get upset, but instead, she laughed. "I've never heard you speak so negatively about anyone before. I've got to meet this woman."

He groaned. "She's seriously the worst."

"Yoo-hoo!" Sandy called out again as she continued walking closer to the house.

He walked out of the French doors and onto the back porch.

Elias had been working along the side of the house and was the first to get inundated by Sandy.

"There you are, Elias." She waved.

Elias, who had earbuds in, continued working, not noticing the situation unfolding in front of him.

"Hello?" Renee said as she walked out with him.

"Oh, hello." Sandy waved once more. "I'm José's mother-in-law, Sandy."

"Can I help you?" Renee asked.

"I wanted to come by and introduce myself," Sandy said kindly.

Renee gave him a look as though he had been wrong. "That's nice."

To Renee, Sandy must've looked like one of the many grandmothers scattered on the beach with the large sun hats musing over her grandchildren. To Mateo, Sandy reminded him of how evil can come in all different forms.

"My daughter said you're the author of that Netflix show," Sandy said.

Renee shook her head. "Oh, you have me mistaken for my mother."

Sandy laughed, holding on to the brim of her hat as though it might fly away. "Oh, goodness. Sorry. Is your mother home, then?"

Mateo smirked at Renee. He wished he could say *I told you so*, but he wouldn't have to. Sandy was already starting to show her true colors.

"She's out, but I can tell her you stopped by." Renee stayed cordial, but he could tell she was picking up Sandy's vibes.

Sandy sighed as though that wasn't going to be good enough. "I'd love to see the house since I came all this way."

Mateo let out a groan only loud enough for Renee to hear. Elias conveniently continued to work on the side, just far enough out of view to not give attention to what was going on, but Mateo was certain he saw what was happening.

"Sandy, I didn't know you were stopping by," Mateo said, walking out of the house and toward her. He didn't want to make his brother's life more difficult, but this was a huge job. He didn't want Renee to think he encouraged this kind of behavior.

Just as he reached her to pull her back down toward the beach, Renee said, "Come and see inside. You will be so impressed with what your son-in-law has done to this house."

She held out her arm toward the house, and Mateo had never been more grateful. He mouthed the words, "Thank you," to her as she motioned Sandy inside.

"Let's start in my favorite room, the kitchen," Renee said to Sandy and ushered her through the dining room.

After forty-five minutes, Renee, Elias, Sandy, and Mateo all stood on the back porch.

"Thank you so much for the tour," Sandy exclaimed, clapping her hands together. "It's just gorgeous. Although, I think your mother made a mistake by not adding a master bedroom downstairs. People want that in a luxury house."

"You're welcome." Renee handed her a plastic container of cannolis. "Have these with your coffee tonight."

Sandy took the package and left without saying goodbye to Mateo or Elias.

"She's interesting," Renee said once she was out of earshot.

"You could say that," Mateo said back to her. "Thank you for dealing with her and saying all those nice things."

"I meant it," she said. "The work you guys have done is incredible."

"Thanks." Mateo meant it too. She had done him a solid. It could've easily gone the other way. "I won't let her come by again to bother your mom."

"Don't worry about it." Renee brushed her hand against his arm, and out of nowhere, his heart skipped a beat.

Whoa.

He checked to see if she had noticed something, but her hand went to her belly, rubbing in a circular motion.

What was that?

He froze awkwardly, hoping she didn't notice his mood suddenly changing.

"You okay?" she asked, her forehead wrinkled.

He froze. *Did she notice?*

He opened his mouth to answer, when from the front of the house, he heard the doorbell ring.

"Did she somehow get lost?" Renee asked, chuckling as she walked inside the house.

Mateo breathed a sigh of relief when she went to answer the door. He walked inside the dining room and glanced in the front hall. A man in a dark suit handed Renee a package. He held out a clipboard, having her sign. When he left, she just stood there, looking at the package.

"Everything okay?" he asked after a few moments of her not moving.

"My husband just served me divorce papers."

He noticed her hands shaking, and he immediately cupped her elbow with his palm, leading the six-month pregnant woman to a chair. How could a husband serve papers to his wife while she was pregnant?

"Let me get you a glass of ice water," he said, not really knowing what to say or do.

"That's okay," she said, getting up off the chair. "I'm going to need something a bit more than ice water."

She walked toward the kitchen to the tray of cannolis she had just baked and stuffed one into her mouth.

"He's such a jerk!" she muttered as she took a second bite. "He wants to divorce me because I want to have our child. Divorce me!"

She took another, bigger bite, practically polishing off the whole pastry in three bites.

She picked up the package and ripped open the cover. Inside sat a large packet of papers with the words "Petition for Divorce" in bold black print.

"I'm sorry," he said.

She took another cannoli, then pushed the tray in front of him, motioning with her head to take one. He wasn't sure what to expect next from her. How would one react to being served divorce papers? Was she going to break down? Would she break something?

He didn't expect her to... laugh?

At first it was a giggle, but suddenly, Renee's shoulders shook up and down, and her face turned a dark pink. She couldn't catch her breath, she was laughing so hard.

"And you thought Sandy was crazy." She shook her head.

"He's insane to divorce you," he said back.

She stopped laughing and met his eyes, holding them there, and in that moment, he saw something so beautiful and broken that he had to hold back his hand to not reach out to her.

"Do you have someone to help you through this?" he asked. He had never been divorced or even in a serious enough relationship, but he imagined it'd be hard on her own with a baby on the way.

She nodded, but her laughter had ended. "I'm fine."

She picked up the papers and stuffed them back into the package they came inside, then left the kitchen. He watched her go up the stairs. If there was something he could do, he'd offer, but he had a feeling she didn't want him or anyone else in her business.

And he didn't blame her.

Renee didn't come downstairs all afternoon, and Mateo decided to leave without bothering her further. When he got home, he couldn't help but do a quick search on social media for a man with the name Harry Winthrop in the Chicago area.

Right away, links to a website popped up for a restauranteur from Chicago. He looked older than Mateo had expected—in his mid forties, if he had to guess. He read over Harry Winthrop's bio, CEO of Dine Company, the parent company that owned all thirteen of his restaurants. He had to agree with Renee. Harry looked like an arrogant jerk in every picture. None of the articles of his famous culinary skills and great business talent talked about how he left his wife pregnant and alone. It was lucky Harry Winthrop didn't live on the island, because Mateo would enjoy letting the world know what a jerk he was.

He may not know exactly what had happened, but the way she had stared at the papers, shaking as she'd held them in her hands, he wanted to do whatever he could to help her out. It didn't take a genius to see she was in trouble.

CHAPTER 11

Evelyn woke up as a faint light hit the earth. Even though the bats floated around the sky in the front yard, birds began to sing their songs, waking the earth below. She didn't move from bed, glad she forgot her phone downstairs, and just stared out at the horizon, waiting for the real show to begin when the sun rose above the ocean.

Every day she counted her blessings as she watched the world come alive before her. She waited until she saw the usual flock of seagulls and began to pray.

"Morning, George," she started. "If you could tell Samantha to return my phone messages, that would be helpful." She adjusted her position, moving the pillows as a backrest, sat up, and grabbed her journal sitting on the nightstand. She usually wrote an inspirational quote, a goal she wanted to reach that day, a wish, or a short prayer, but today she wanted to talk to George. "Something happened yesterday with Renee while I was out with Charlie, but like always, Renee isn't talking. She just holed herself up in the guest room and didn't come out, like she would do as a teenager. Remember when she got braces?"

She laughed to herself.

She could just call Harry. It would be a quick call. Would it really be snooping to call her son-in-law?

She blew out and pulled the covers back, when she noticed Renee walking across the backyard to the walkway toward the beach. She wore a hoodie over her head and carried a bag with her. Evelyn almost ran to the balcony to get her attention, tell her to stop and wait up so she could join her, but she hesitated. Renee was leaving the house literally at the crack of dawn. She didn't want anyone joining her.

Evelyn would respect her privacy. She wouldn't call out or ring her on her phone. She'd listen to Charlie and stay the course since Renee was staying on the island until at least the baby came. She wouldn't push things for now, but she was going to ask Samantha about what was going on. She may be enjoying traveling the world one hostel at a time, but it was time Samantha be part of the family again, whether she wanted to or not.

Her sister needed her. Evelyn was sure of it.

Evelyn showered and went downstairs to make coffee. Renee had left a post-it with a note: *There are fruit tarts in the fridge, granola in the pantry, and freshly squeezed orange juice.* After opening the fridge, Evelyn pulled out a fruit tart with kiwi, strawberries sliced paper thin, and plump blackberries placed perfectly in rows. Renee had such a gift.

With a quick knock, Mateo came inside. Right on time. "Good morning, Mrs. Rose."

"Please, call me Evelyn," she said for the hundredth time.

"Elias and some of the crew should be putting in the floors on the third floor today," he said, going over the schedule on his phone. "Hopefully, I'll be able to finish the shelves after that."

"That's great, Mateo. I can't tell you how happy I am with how everything is running right on schedule," she said. "Do you think the room will be finished before November?"

"Definitely." Mateo seemed sure. "Phil's coming in to finish the plumbing, and then I'll have my tile guy out here."

She couldn't believe how smoothly the whole process had been. "You've done a really wonderful job, Mateo."

"Thank you." He stuffed his phone into his pocket. "I was hoping to catch Renee. Is she around?"

Evelyn shook her head. "No, I'm sorry. She went out for a walk this morning. She was headed up the beach."

He nodded. "Will you tell her to come find me if she gets back this morning?"

"I will." Evelyn's curiosity peaked as Mateo left. What did Mateo have to tell Renee?

She called Charlie. "She's been gone for hours. Now Mateo is asking to talk to her, and I know something happened yesterday."

"Evelyn, she's an adult who's figuring things out on her own right now. She'll come back, I promise you," he assured her. But she wasn't convinced when it turned noontime and Renee still wasn't around.

"I'm calling her to make sure she's okay," Evelyn said, picking up her phone as she sat with Wanda on the porch.

"Evelyn, hold on." Wanda pointed out toward the beach as Renee walked up the path back to the house.

"Where have you been?" Evelyn said as Renee walked across the lawn to the back porch. "I was worried sick."

Renee's face looked red and burnt, her eyes swollen and puffy.

"Are you okay?" Evelyn asked. "You don't have to tell me what's going on in your life, but will you just let me know if you're okay?"

Her heart started pounding harder the longer Renee stayed quiet. She expected Renee to walk past her as she came up to the porch, but she didn't. Renee went straight into Evelyn's arms and began to cry hard sobs into her chest. Evelyn swooped her arms around her daughter, just like she had when Renee'd gotten her braces and when she'd lost her father, and held her.

"Harry served me divorce papers yesterday," she cried. "He didn't even fight for me." Her sobs tore through her chest and vibrated through Evelyn's body. "He didn't even love me."

Evelyn held her daughter in her arms as tight as she could. She would not let go until Renee broke away, but Renee didn't break away. She continued to cry, and Evelyn said only one thing over and over. "Let it out. Let it all out."

It was Renee who ended up sitting down first. Bitty brought her water.

"You were served papers here?" Wanda asked.

"Yes." Renee hiccupped. "Yesterday, a man came and handed them to me. There's all this stuff from his lawyer. I don't want anything from him."

The second Renee calmed down; Evelyn was going to call her attorney. Plans of taking Harry Winthrop down filled her head. He wasn't going to get away with treating his wife and the mother of his child this way.

"Now is the time you need to know your rights as his wife," Wanda said.

Evelyn intertwined her fingers and squeezed them hard together. She was sick thinking Renee had gone through a whole day alone with this. "Don't worry about a thing, Renee. We'll make sure you're taken care of."

"That's the thing. I don't want anyone to take care of me," Renee said, tears still streaming down her face. "I just want to be a family. I just want to live as a unit, together, like you and Dad had. I want my son to grow up playing baseball with his dad and have brothers and sisters."

Renee's breath heaved in and out.

"You are going to give that baby the best life ever," Evelyn said. "Sure, it would've been nice to have Harry on board, but that doesn't mean this is the end. This is your new beginning." She reached out for Renee's hands.

Renee began to cry again and wrapped her arms around her mother. It could very well have been a coincidence that the flock of seagulls on Sugar Beach floated above them, calling out, and she was being ridiculous, and it wasn't George. But she liked to think it was him flying above them, watching over them, because at that moment she knew he was telling her that everything was going to be alright.

CHAPTER 12

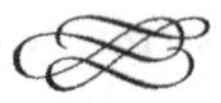

Renee stood in the law office with her mother. She felt like a child, even though she could no longer see her ankles with her protruding belly. She had removed her wedding ring, but the indentation sat heavy on her finger.

At first, she had thought she was gaining weight. It hadn't occurred to her that she was pregnant. Things had been extra tense between her and Harry. He had been opening another restaurant while ignoring the glaring issues with the one she ran, the one she swore he'd put no effort into.

The restaurant she had run was named Bliss. It was in a perfect location, right in the center of the Chicago Loop downtown in the financial district. High-powered money brokers came for a good meal over business. Her reviews had been stellar. She had won awards. Her kitchen had run like a well-oiled machine. Yet, the better business got for her, the more Harry had detached himself from the restaurant.

To say they had been having problems was an understatement. He'd started a habit of staying at the office late into the night. He had rarely made it into her restaurant, even though it had been the most successful. Things they used to do together as a couple had suddenly stopped in the name of busyness.

With the demands of running a restaurant and Harry's bad moods, she hadn't noticed she had completely missed her period until she'd missed her next. All the signs had seemed clearly obvious. Her breasts were bigger and had deep purple veins running through them. Her sudden disdain for coffee and her aversion to the smell of vinegar had become glaring. Her exhaustion had felt heavier than she'd ever felt before.

She had been on birth control but had taken antibiotics. As she sat on the bathroom floor staring at two bright pink lines, she knew her marriage was over.

When Renee told Harry, he didn't even hesitate when he said, "It's not too late to terminate it."

He'd said it as if she were removing a mole, not their child growing inside her. She'd almost thrown up.

But she had expected this reaction. She had wished—no, prayed—he'd somehow change his feelings about children from hearing the news of becoming a father. She'd drawn in a breath, taking his hands into hers, and had said, "I'm keeping the baby."

He had dropped them. "I told you I don't want children."

He had explained that before they were married. She had known going in that he didn't want them. She clasped her hands together, squeezing them. "I expect nothing from you, but I'm keeping *our* baby."

He'd stood, almost as if he had to get away from her, then looked down, shaking his head like a father disappointed by his daughter's actions, not a husband whose wife was pregnant.

"That's your choice, and I will do what I have to do to support you, but don't expect me to be involved."

He walked away after that, swiping his keys off the counter, and left.

That night, she had packed her bags, left a note with her mother's address, and headed for Martha's Vineyard.

Now he was divorcing her.

"It looks like he wants to set up a trust fund for your son, along with child support payments." The female attorney was all business. "You're very lucky your ex-husband is being so amicable."

She faded out every time the attorney congratulated her on her fortune of having such a willing participant of divorce.

"He's offering to pay you monthly support payments until the child is eighteen," the attorney continued. "While also voluntarily giving up his parental rights."

In other words, he gave up his son, Renee thought in her head.

"I'll need time to think through everything," Renee said.

"This is one of the most generous divorce settlements I've seen. You'll be lucky to have the courts grant you a fourth of what he's willing to payout." The attorney passed the papers across the table from where they sat. "The hardest part in a divorce is removing the emotion. You want to do what's best for your son."

Renee took the thin sheets in her hands. They felt like the weight of the world. How had she gotten herself here? Twenty-eight, pregnant, and on her way to being divorced?

"Thank you for your time," Renee said, leaving the office that was closing in on her every second she sat in there.

Evelyn followed her out to the car, and when they got in, her mom turned in the passenger's seat to face Renee and said, "I will support you no matter what you decide to do."

Renee held the steering wheel, her eyes looking out the window, but her focus was back on the past. "I just didn't think he'd let go so easily."

Her hands turned white from her grip. How could he just pay her off? And how could she just accept it?

"Do I take what he's offering and that's that?" She flung her body back against the seat, her hands on her stomach. "How can I not feel my emotions when making this decision? I still love him."

She was ashamed of her truth. How could she still love someone who had thrown her away like trash?

"I don't know." Her mom spoke quietly. "I don't know how you've held up all this time."

That was a joke, she thought. She had been hiding this whole time at her mom's, waiting for this imaginary Prince Charming who had been under an evil spell to come back to his senses and sweep her back to his kingdom.

But fairy tales only belonged in books.

"How could he just leave us?" Renee didn't understand how he couldn't pivot. She'd never meant for this to happen, but life didn't always go as planned. What's worse, how could she still love a man so willing to let her go?

The two women drove back home in silence until they reached their street.

"You should go to Chicago and collect the rest of your stuff," Evelyn said as she parked the car. "I'll go with you."

"I don't think I'm ever going back there." Renee didn't care what she had left behind. It didn't matter at this point. It was just stuff. It had been Harry's apartment. She had been the one who had moved into his space after they'd gotten married. His furniture, his books, his stuff—none of it was really hers.

"It must be hard having advice being thrown at you," Evelyn said. "But the baby's coming faster than you know it. You should get everything in order so you don't have things hanging over you when he arrives."

Renee sat looking out at her mother's house. Her big, beautiful, expensive beach house. Her mother got here on her own. Evelyn never gave up, even when the cards were falling around her. Even when they were pulled out from underneath her. Evelyn kept going. This house proved more than anything that Evelyn was right. She had to figure things out.

She could take the money and never worry. She could open a bakery, buy a house, and live wherever she wanted. She could take her mother's offer and stay at the cottage on the island. What would it prove by not taking Harry's offer? That he didn't have any consequences for breaking his vows to her.

"I'm going to sign the divorce papers," Renee said, "but I can't take his guilt money. You sure it's okay that I stay here with you for now?"

Evelyn extended her arms out, leaned over the console, and wrapped Renee into her arms. "This will always be your home."

Renee wished her mother's hug would make her pain disappear like it had when she was a girl. Whenever Renee or Samantha got sick or hurt or scared, they'd run into Evelyn's arms, and everything would magically feel better. But she didn't feel better when her mother let go, or when they went inside the house, or when she called the attorney to let her know her decision.

So, she decided to bake.

First, she called Charlie.

"Are you sure you don't mind me selling my pastries at the store?" she asked again.

"I think it's a great idea," Charlie said back. "I can set up a table next to the coffee station."

"I'm thinking almond croissants, macarons, scones, maybe even some crème-filled donuts," Renee said over the phone.

Charlie hummed while she listed off the different baked goods. "That all sounds delicious. Tomorrow… I'm closed, but the following day, you could open with us at eight. You could come by tomorrow and get it ready however you want it."

With a little stretch, Renee could feel her heart expanding. She'd never thought she'd be glad her mother had a new man in her life, but she was glad that since there was a new one, it was Charlie.

"That sounds great." She could feel George kick, and she instinctively rubbed her belly. "I'll be there by eight."

She decided to start a plan. She put everything in order of what she had to do first to be ready to sell anything. She needed market research. Harry would pay for this kind of research, but she knew exactly who'd love to find out this information and would be just as good as any marketing company.

"Wanda," Renee said as Wanda sat on the porch with her visor. "What do you know about bookstores and cafés?"

Wanda's downward frown instantly lit up. "Most of the big

book chains have them inside as a part of the store. Even the big retail stores are putting in cafés or coffee shops."

She pulled out her big tablet and started opening up tabs.

"I'm thinking of doing a small menu. Stuff that people would be looking for if they were to go to the store. You know, what's already being sold at the big retailers."

Wanda understood immediately. The biggest retailer with a physical store name was on top of her page.

"Almond croissants," Wanda said immediately. "They're at the large retailers, but also at the large coffee shops."

Renee had made plenty of croissants, but she'd have to perfect the pastry so that visitors would come back to Charlie's bookstore for more.

"What do you think about branding? Will I look just like the rest?" she asked as Wanda found more chain stores and menus. "How will I stand out?"

How could she compete with the other retailers that were already established?

"You will show them that you have familiar items, but you use only the freshest and purest ingredients," Wanda said. "Familiar and fresh."

Renee would have to nail everything.

As Wanda scoured the internet of every bakery in the area, Renee got baking. First, her almond croissant. She combined the water and the yeast and had it sit on the kitchen table in the sun as she made the almond paste. When the paste was sticky and perfectly mixed, she moved onto the croissant dough. After grabbing her yeast, she combined all her ingredients into her standing mixer bowl and started it up. Within a few minutes, the dough began to take shape, and soon it was smooth and flexible. She greased a large glass bowl and put the ball of dough inside it before covering it with plastic wrap. She'd let it sit in the refrigerator for a couple hours while she worked on something else.

Just as she closed the door to the refrigerator, Harper came walking into the kitchen. "My dad just told me about you selling your pastries at the store."

"Yes," Renee said. She checked Harper's reaction. Would Harper think it was silly? But like always, Harper looked perky and cheerful.

"What are you going to bake?" Harper asked.

"Almond croissants," Renee said, covering the almond paste.

"Oh, I love those." Harper lingered and stood next to the counter. "Are you baking them today?"

Renee shook her head. "I'm just making sure they come out okay."

"Everyone's going to love your baking," Harper said. Although Harper rarely ate any of Renee's stuff, citing its gluten as the issue.

"I don't know if I'll sell anything," Renee said. Truthfully, she worried if she'd hit the mark. What if the island tourists also wanted sugar-free, gluten-free baked goods?

"You're going to do fantastic," Harper said, trying to be reassuring, which was nice. Harper was nothing but nice.

Renee opened her notebook to her notes and reviewed her checklist. After a few moments, she noticed Harper hanging around, tapping her fingernails against the counter.

"I know it's none of my business," Harper said suddenly. "But I'm sorry to hear about your divorce..."

Renee gave a half smile while silently praying this wouldn't become an advice session from a woman who was carefree and had the whole world at her feet. She cringed as Harper opened her mouth.

"Sometimes divorce is the best thing for everyone," Harper said.

Renee almost laughed. Was she serious right now? What did she know about divorce? But then Renee saw a sadness in Harper's eyes she hadn't before.

"Sometimes people aren't supposed to be parents. And my mom, well, she wasn't supposed to be a mom." She played with her nails, which were painted with designs. "When I see you and Evelyn together, I think, 'Wow, she's so lucky to have a mom like her.'"

Like a curtain being opened, Renee saw Harper in a whole new light. There stood a woman who, as a child, knew more what Renee's child would be going through than Renee. The pain and hurt in her eyes could be felt. How could Renee have judged Harper's circumstances without learning about her circumstances? Yes, she knew Harper's mom wasn't around, but she had been a brat about everything. The vibe she had been throwing toward Harper all this time was negative, and she could suddenly feel it. She felt ashamed.

"I'm sorry," Renee said.

Harper crinkled her forehead. "For what?"

"I haven't been very welcoming and I'm sorry."

"Oh." Harper's face blushed. "Did your mom say something?"

The comment confirmed it, Renee had been judgmental and harsh. Here Harper was, so welcoming, thoughtful, and helpful, and Renee pushed her away. And for what reason? Because she was jealous?

"I'm such a jerk." Tears brimmed the edges of Renee's eyes. Never had she felt so many emotions all at once. She was grateful for her to keep coming back, being kind, offering advice.

"No, don't cry." Harper pushed herself off the counter. "I didn't mean to make you cry."

"You didn't." Renee grabbed a dish towel and covered her face. "I just cry all the time now with this baby inside me."

Harper passed a tissue to her. "Do you like being pregnant?"

"Sometimes." Renee instinctively rubbed her belly. "Most of the time, I love it."

"What does it feel like when he kicks?" Harper asked.

"Right now, it feels like gas, and most of the time it is." She giggled to herself, then before she could squeeze her muscles, she broke wind. Her face immediately heated. "But my body is no longer my own."

Both women laughed hard, and Renee had to run to the bathroom before she had an accident.

When she came back into the kitchen, Harper had a teakettle ticking on the stove. "Want some tea?"

A day ago, this scene would have driven her batty, Harper just doing what she wanted in the house, but today, she had never been more grateful for Harper. "I'd love some."

The two women ended up chatting all afternoon, and Renee learned they had a lot in common. They were both twenty-eight, both played clarinet in band, loved all John Hughes' movies, and wanted to travel to the south of France.

"I've heard it's gorgeous," Harper said.

"My sister's been all over, but I've never really gone anywhere," Renee said. Would she ever? Or would she take George on adventures and give him the travel bug young? If things had worked out with Harry, what would life have been like? Harry had longer work weeks than her, and she had worked at least sixty to eighty hours depending on the week. He had always been too busy before everything fell apart. What made her think a baby would make Harry Winthrop do a one-eighty and suddenly become a family man who came home to spend time with his wife and kids?

"I always wished as a kid to travel to Paris," Renee confessed.

"Have you ever thought about going abroad? I mean, you're an amazing chef. Why not go for your dream location?" Harper's voice was filled with optimism.

"I think I want to open a bakery here," she said. It came out before she could take it back. Harper's eyes opened as if she understood the magnitude of what Renee had said.

She patted her knees with her hands. "You planted your seed of intention."

Renee didn't know if she had planted it or said it or what, but by midafternoon, Bitty, Wanda, and Harper all believed Renee's hopes and dreams would come true by "releasing it to the universe."

"Let me just get through labor first, and I can start thinking about opening a bakery," Renee said. But secretly, she hoped for the seed to find the soil and grow its roots.

"Are you planning on taking Lamaze soon?" Bitty asked.

Renee had dreaded this. The stereotypical class where husbands sat with their pregnant wives between their legs for eight hours, learning how to take care of them.

"Don't you think I could just watch something on YouTube?" Renee said.

"A lot of classes are taught by ob-gyn nurses or midwives," Bitty said. "You can ask questions that pertain to you and your situation. You should really take an in-person class."

"You're right," Renee said, groaning inside. "I just don't want to go alone."

"I'll go with you," Harper said. "We can make a date of it."

Renee was just about to say no, when out of nowhere, a seagull swooped down from the sky and flew above them, floating in the wind. The bird continued to glide in the wind above them, screeching even, as if to make sure she knew it was there.

"Okay, that sounds great," Renee said, secretly cursing the hovering bird.

Later that night, when the three women had their Jeopardy on television in the living room, Renee snuck out of the house with a candle and a flashlight and followed the path to the beach. A sliver of pink sat on the horizon as waves gently rolled up the shore. Darkness settled around her, yet the sand radiated a soft glow from the moonlight above. Her feet sunk into the sand as she walked toward Gray Head, still warm from the late summer sun. Soon, autumn would arrive, and so would baby George.

As she reached the inlet, she turned off her flashlight, pulled out a small lighter, and lit her own votive candle she'd found at a stop near Charlie's bookstore. She walked around the rock cliff and saw a candle already lit inside, but no one else was around. She set her bag on a large boulder, then one by one, she lit the abandoned candles once lit with a prayer. The candles' flames illuminated the inlet, flickering movement against the amber clay cliffs and casting shadows.

She didn't have a plan besides making one wish, but the weight of it made her sit and hold off. She wanted to think it through. There was so much she wished for, and she needed to focus. She sat down in the sand, resting against the boulder, groaning into a position. She set the candle in front of her.

Should she pray? Or should she call it out into the night?

"I want to find peace with becoming a mother," she whispered to the candle.

She sat, listening to the waves, waiting for a sign. She gazed out at the black horizon that blended into the night sky. Stars twinkled in the sky and water. Shadows danced as a breeze blew through the inlet.

She grabbed her bag, pulled out her notebook, and opened to a new page.

The first step to becoming a strong mother was to provide for her son. On top of the page, in big bold lettering, she wrote, "The Bakery." Then, with bullet points, she created a list: make a sample platter, create survey cards, type up fliers, buy a chalkboard, collect cutlery, design a logo, come up with a name.

She looked up at the stars, thinking back to when she was a child dreaming of her own bakery. She had made a Barbie bakery where everyone, including Skipper and Ken, liked to hang out. She'd named it The Sweet Spot. Not exactly the vibe she was going for nowadays, but the idea of a community gathering spot was what she wanted. She wanted something sophisticated for the kinds of tourists that came to Martha's Vineyard yet comfortable and welcoming for even locals to relax and enjoy a good cup of coffee and a delicious pastry. She wanted a local bakery where families could order something special like a wedding cake but also grab a treat to have on a Sunday morning. She wanted to sell finger treats to eat while strolling through town but also delicacies that one had to sit down to enjoy. She wanted her bakery open like a kitchen, but with equipment and designed for productivity.

On another page, she wrote ideas for names. The Gathering Place? Savory and Sweet? Bread and Chocolate Café?

"Renee?" a voice said.

She jumped in her spot, dropping her notebook in the sand. She looked up and standing in the inlet was Mateo.

"Mateo? What are you doing here?" She rocked back and forth trying to get up, her heart still racing in her chest.

"Please, don't get up," he said as a smile widened across his face. He walked toward where she sat. "Mind if I join you?"

She shifted her back end and waved her hands out before her. "Not at all."

Cradling her belly in her hands, she hoped and prayed that Mateo didn't overhear her wish.

"You had mentioned this place the other day, and I thought I'd come and see if people still came here to light candles." He sat down in the sand.

"Apparently, just me." She felt foolish suddenly, knowing he had been the one who told her about the wishes. "I had to come and see what it looked like at night."

"It's really something." He glanced around, resting his arms around his legs. "Did you bring all these candles?"

She shook her head. "No, only this one." She pointed to the candle in front of her.

"Did you make a wish?" he asked.

She laughed and then confessed, "Just before you came."

His right side of his mouth perked up. "I hope I didn't disturb you."

She shook her head. "Nah, just getting out of the house, really."

But it had been more than that. An energy grew inside her. Something had shifted, and she could feel it. "You come to make a wish?"

He shrugged. "Just the usual health and happiness."

She studied his expression as he focused on the candle. His thoughts were somewhere else completely. Did he wish things had worked out between him and Harper?

She thought about how she didn't wish for her marriage or Harry to change his mind. If the past few months living with the women had taught her anything, it was how futile it was wishing for someone else to make her happy. She was in control of her thoughts, her goals, her dreams, and her own destiny.

"I hope your wish comes true," he said.

She focused on the flame and smiled. "I'm going to make sure it does."

CHAPTER 13

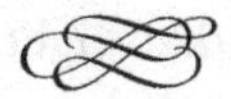

Mateo hadn't talked to or texted Harper in a few days. It was the longest they had gone without talking for the past few years. Usually, she'd send him a silly meme or GIF, then he'd ask what her plans were for the day. When she started working for Evelyn, they'd frequently talk and have lunch or dinner. Now, as he pulled up to the Roses' house, he dreaded seeing her.

Luckily, she had been doing a good job avoiding him too.

He wondered how long she had been dating other people. She had never mentioned anyone. She must not have considered him a friend if she kept secrets from him. The realization of that alone made him want to avoid her, no matter how ridiculous he may appear. He'd stayed in the garage when she pulled up to the house. When she stuck around, he'd leave for his other sites. But today, she walked into the garage, trapping him inside. "I know you saw me the other night."

He froze, unable to think of what to say. "I did."

"I wish I had told you about Gerard, but after the kiss, things were weird." She stood in the threshold of the garage door and the outside.

"Gerard?" Never once had she mentioned a friend or an acquaintance named Gerard, and they had talked every day.

"He's an artist," she said.

His heart sank.

"I want to be friends." Harper's worry lines between her eyes deepened.

"Why did you kiss me that night?" He wanted to know. He wanted to get any lingering questions answered.

She looked away. "I wanted to make sure I didn't have feelings."

"I take it that you don't." He felt used. Like a favorite book read over and over yet tossed to the side when a new one came along.

"I'm sorry, Mateo."

Her words stung, then burned since the little voice inside his head had been right all along. His brothers had been saying it as well. Harper had been using him as a placeholder until the right one came along. And apparently, the right one was an artist named Gerard.

"I'm glad you've figured things out for yourself," he said, hoping she'd step out of the threshold and back inside the house.

"I'm really sorry I've hurt your feelings," she said, tears welling in her eyes.

He thought about his wish from the night before in Prayer Cove. He hadn't really planned on wishing for anything, but then as he walked there, thinking of the past few weeks, he'd wished for the ability to let go of everything that had happened between him and Harper and move on. He didn't want to hold animosity or anger toward her, but he couldn't drop the feelings.

She rubbed her thumb in her palm, hard. "I think I was getting confused because I do love you, Mateo. It's just that I'm not..." She paused, looked him in the eyes, and said, "In love with you."

He swallowed the lump in his throat, along with his pride. "Sure, great."

"I'm sorry."

"Please stop apologizing," he said, holding his hands up. "It only makes things more awkward."

"Oh." She stepped back again, and out of the garage entirely. "I want to be friends. Always."

He nodded, trying to take in a deep breath, but he said nothing.

He hadn't ended up using his wish that night. Instead, he had wished for Renee's good health and fortune in the next few months. A woman in her situation deserved his wish. He was just a fool, and there was no wish to help with that.

"I'm helping Evelyn and the women plan a baby shower for Renee," Harper said, gesturing toward the crib. "Do you think you'll be done with the crib in a couple of weeks?"

He had been working on the crib at his place at night. "Sure."

"The room upstairs looks great," she added.

"Thanks." Apparently, there wasn't enough artistry in carpentry.

"Would you like to come to the shower?" she asked.

"I thought those things were for women," he said.

She made a letter *b* in the drive with her flip-flop. "It's for her friends. My dad's coming, and Hank."

He had been working on the house for a few months now and knew the three women well enough to hold a light conversation, but hanging out with them for a party? And a baby shower?

"How about I just finish the crib by then?" he suggested.

She looked thoughtfully at him. "I hope you'll reconsider hanging out again."

"I don't think that would be a good idea," he said honestly.

She immediately frowned. "Okay."

He was hit with the urge to take back his words, like not letting go of a rope swing. It'd be easy to hold on and swing back to shore, but he let his fingers loose. He didn't want to hurt her, but he spent years being her friend, only to get his heart crushed. No, he couldn't be friends.

"I'll finish building the crib tonight," he said. "Then I'll have to stain it."

He had ordered a mattress, but maybe he should also pick up some sheets for it.

"Does she have a registry?" he asked.

She shook her head. "Not yet, but I'll let you know when she does."

Mateo didn't say anything more.

Harper made her fake grin as she gave a limp wave. "I'll let you know when the shower will be."

He turned away from her, reaching for his toolbelt. He didn't want to be rude, but if he hadn't turned as she left, he might've said something he'd regret later. Like the fact that she hadn't been his friend. That friends didn't hold secrets from each other or confess until after they got caught. Friends didn't kiss just for giggles or for curiosity's sake.

No, he couldn't be friends with her, because they never had been.

By quitting time, Anthony, his tiler, met him with Evelyn in the master bath. His stomach growled as smells from downstairs wafted all the way to the third floor.

"It's gorgeous," Evelyn said, touching the tilework in the shower.

"I told you you'd be happy," Mateo said. He knew Anthony would do a fantastic job. "Now, I can get the tub in."

An antique iron clawfoot soaking tub would be placed neatly inside the newly expanded dormer window with a stunning view of the Atlantic Ocean. Evelyn Rose spared nothing. Hand tile work, the two-sided fireplace, the floor-to-ceiling windows with a panoramic view, and that was just the bathroom. The whole floor could be considered an in-law suite or a master suite.

Hanging from one of the exposed beams was an antique light fixture she had found at a farmer's market. Its illumination showed off the space in a gorgeous light.

"When can we move furniture in?" she asked.

"Probably in a couple days."

This made Evelyn clap her hands together. "Well, that's fantastic. Because I'd like to start on the garage and turn it into a guest cottage next."

"Sure," he said. He'd figure out a plan. "What are you thinking?"

"Well, for now, I'd like to convert it into a two-bedroom, one-and-a-half-bath cottage. Something where someone could stay for a visit but also be comfortable staying for long periods of time if they wanted to."

He didn't know Ms. Rose other than through all the renovations, but if he had to guess, he was certain the guest house was for Renee and the baby. Evelyn Rose was one the most generous people he had met with that kind of money. He had worked on the island for years with some of the wealthiest people in the country, and never had he seen someone think about the people around them like she did.

When she had started the project with him, she wanted the spaces for her friend, Wanda, finished first. Then the kitchen for her daughter. The upstairs for the baby and Renee. Now the cottage.

"Tell me when a good time will be to talk about what you envision, and I can get things started right away if you want." He could rearrange some things Elias was doing.

"How about you stay for dinner tonight?" Evelyn said. "I have the architect's plans, and we can talk about everything then."

He almost asked if Harper would be staying, since he noticed she had been hanging around Renee and the women more lately, but he didn't.

"Let me clean up and I'll bring dessert," he said.

"We have plenty of desserts," Evelyn said. "Renee's been baking all day. Bring yourself at seven."

A scent of baked goods came from downstairs as Evelyn said it. "Sounds great."

Evelyn smiled. "Alright. See you at seven."

As Mateo drove home to clean up, he couldn't help but wonder what his father would think of him hanging out in the big houses on the water. The son of an immigrant living among the grassy valleys of Cliffside Point—never in a million years would his father believe it.

"Mateo," he'd begun to say when they had driven through the wealthy neighborhoods. "We might be the help today, but someday, we Perezes will own this island."

José, Sr. would be floored if he saw his three sons now.

It was the reason why Mateo included his brothers in the business. His father would've wanted it that way.

When his older brother, José, had gone straight into a trade, Mateo's mother figured he'd be next. They couldn't afford a four-year college. And what was wrong with a trade anyway? Weren't they successful? Hadn't they fed all six of their children? But Mateo had wanted more. He had wanted the island.

That was when he'd made the best choice of his life. He had joined the football team. Throughout his childhood, he had passed the football with his brothers here and there, and having two brothers made Mateo tougher, but his talent was his speed and precision. He could predict the players' moves before they tried anything and send the ball spiraling through the air and into the players arms before anyone knew where the ball was headed. He had worked harder than any other player on the team, put in more time in the weight room, watched more tapes, and did extra drills. It had all paid off with a full scholarship to play for UMASS, and he'd earned a degree in civil engineering. He was the first Perez to earn a degree. His father had died a month after.

Mateo had taken his death as a sign. He'd just been young enough with the skills to start and stupid enough to think he could do it. He'd started Perez Brothers Building. At first, he'd done decks, roofs, painting, anything really. He'd made sure to finish jobs fast and had barely paid himself. Word had spread fast since a lot of his customers had hired his father for help around their gardens and lawns. Job after job, Mateo had worked hard, focused on details, made sure he followed through with the customers' expectations, and then wowed them. José had joined first, then Elias after he'd gone to college as well—paid for by Mateo.

After ten years, Perez Brothers Building had a strong reputation of quality work, and that was what made Mateo most proud. People like Evelyn trusted him to build their dream home, and he took that very seriously.

After a quick shower and a new bouquet from the garden, he drove back to the house and didn't see Harper's car in the driveway. A sigh escaped him as he shut off the engine.

"Come on in," he heard a voice say from the screen door. Renee waved as he climbed the porch steps.

"This is even prettier than the last," she exclaimed, sniffing the flowers right away as she leaned against the door, propping it open.

He had mixed in purple hydrangeas, bright pink zinnias, and a small sunflower with deep green variegated hosta leaves as its border.

"Here," he said, handing her a book.

"*The Sweet Life in Paris.*" She held it up, and without warning, hugged him. "Thank you."

"You're welcome." He looked at the ground, stiff and suddenly feeling uncomfortable.

"Dinner should be ready in a few minutes." She led him inside as she walked behind the counter, and an aroma symphony floated throughout the kitchen.

"It smells delicious in here." It reminded him of his grandmother's house as a kid. "Thanks for letting me join you for dinner." He watched as Renee stirred a wooden spoon in a large pot. "What are you making?"

"I made a pasta alle vongole with the little neck clams my mom and Charlie picked up this morning," she said. "Along with homemade garlic bread and an arugula salad."

"You would've liked my grandmother. She cooked almost as much as you." Then he pointed at her. "Aren't you not supposed to eat shellfish while pregnant?"

"I made some pasta just for me." She pointed to a large bowl filled with creamy pasta.

"That's just for you?" It was enough to feed a family of four.

"Hey, I've got a linebacker inside me." Renee laughed.

He couldn't tear his eyes away from the way she crinkled her eyes. The easiness he felt sitting at the counter with her in the kitchen made him feel strangely at home.

"Here." Renee slid him another drink, premade like the last time he came for socializing. "What's this one?"

"A Manhattan," Renee said.

"Do you want to get me drunk?" Mateo sniffed it. "Is that a rye whiskey?"

"Yes, I do." She winked. Renee seemed to be in a much better mood than she was the other day. "I miss having a cocktail. Plus, Charlie likes whiskey." She giggled as he made a sour face.

He studied the drink up close. "I don't usually drink much, but my dad liked whiskey."

She tilted her head and gave a nod, her eyes acknowledging their common experience.

"My dad liked to drink gin," she said.

He took a very tiny sip of the drink. He pulled out the stool at the counter and sat, setting the tumbler down on a napkin.

"Everyone's on the porch out back." She nodded her head at the back of the house.

He looked out through the dining room to the porch. Evelyn and her friends sat together with Charlie. He didn't see Harper, but he didn't move. "I'm good for now."

She smiled back at him and leaned on her elbow. "Tell me what your grandmother made."

"My grandmother?" He had missed the connection.

"You said I reminded you of your grandmother," she said.

"Oh, right."

He noticed how Renee had worn her hair down tonight and how it made her look like an angel with her blonde silky curls around her glowing face.

"My grandmother was from Costa Rica," he said, remembering her tiny kitchen in the city of Liberia. "She was known for her casado."

"What was her protein for her casado?" Renee asked, and he did a double take. She knew about casados?

"Pork usually, but fish too." Fish had been the cheapest where she had lived by the beaches.

Renee took the pot and dumped the creamy pasta with clams into a large bowl.

"Can I help with anything?" Evelyn said, walking in with an empty bottle of wine. "Mateo, you came."

"Charlie, Mateo's here." Evelyn went in straight for the hug, just like her daughter had. He immediately felt welcomed in her home, as a guest this time.

"Ah," Charlie said, walking in behind her. "Just the man we were talking about."

He looked to Renee, who shrugged while slicing bread on a large wooden cutting board.

"The third floor looks amazing," Charlie said, patting Mateo on the back and going in for his own hug. Both Charlie and Evelyn smiled at him.

"Thank you." He appreciated the feedback, but he wasn't surprised. He and his brothers had been doing this long enough to know their talents. Their ten thousand hours had come and gone, and he was confident in their work. He'd had no doubt the cottage would turn out just as beautiful.

"It's gorgeous," Renee said. "I feel lucky being able to stay in such a beautiful space."

Renee's compliment made his heart skip a beat. He felt proud that someone as talented in her own craft appreciated his work. She thought what he had built was beautiful.

"What's your favorite dessert?" Renee asked, handing him

another bowl filled with salad.

"Empanadas de chiverre," he said.

She squinted her eyes, looking up as if she was going through her mental notes of Costa Rican cuisine.

"They're a pastry," he said to her, figuring she didn't know what they were. The Costa Rican dessert was hard to come by on this side of the earth.

She nodded. "It's a gourd type fruit, right?"

His mouth dropped. "You know about chiverre?"

His brothers didn't even know about the fruit their maternal grandmother would boil for hours to make into a syrup.

"You make honey from it," she said.

"Yes." He couldn't hide his surprise. "Do you know everything about food?"

Renee laughed. "I worked alongside a lot of Latin Americans who were happy to share their culture with me."

Mateo was about to tell Renee about his own family, but Evelyn ushered them out to the back porch. He wanted to tell the story of his mother coming to this country with nothing but hopes and dreams and that she worked in the food service industry. She hadn't been a fancy chef like Renee, but she had sacrificed everything working in the back of restaurants. As he looked at his family's work around Evelyn's house, he wished his grandparents from the old country could see that they had achieved what they set out for.

He lived the American Dream. His business was thriving. He had more houses slotted for work than he had ever imagined, and he wasn't slowing down. He wanted to start getting into new, bigger builds.

But first, he wanted to show Evelyn his idea for the guest cottage.

He pulled out his sketchpad from his bag and handed it to Evelyn as she sat down in a chair on the back porch. He had printed out a photograph of a carriage house from another Victorian on the island.

"I know you had plans drawn up with the architect, but I thought I'd show you some ideas I had for the cottage." Mateo hoped he wasn't overstepping.

He'd never done this with other clients, but something about Evelyn made him feel like she'd listen to what he had to say. He opened the sketchpad to his own designs—interior walls with built-ins, the fireplace along with kitchen cabinets. Space used smartly, everywhere.

"This is from a property on the other side of the island." The architecture mirrored Sea View's design, yet it clearly had been renovated. "Have you heard of the 'Build better, not bigger' motto."

"Like Sarah Susanka?"

"Yes." He smiled at the reference of the acclaimed architect who had changed his way of thinking about space.

In the design, he placed cabinets for storage under the stairs, built a window seat for the dining room table, and created a composition of continuity from the main house to the cottage. He wanted to create different ceiling heights to define each space. He also made sure every inch of the cottage was properly used.

"It's perfect." Evelyn traced the outline of the floorplans with her finger.

"The first floor should be open to the kitchen and living space with a half bath." He turned the page. "If we vary the heights, it will define the separate spaces, but without the walls." He pointed to the bedroom. "A balcony here and a widow's peak on top big enough for two to sit."

Her eyes brightened at the idea. "A widow's peak is a great idea."

He'd had a feeling Evelyn would like it, but when he saw her eyes mist, he couldn't help but smile.

As they talked plans, Charlie and the other women all made their way into the room and congregated around Mateo's plans.

Evelyn went through his whole spiel to each one, flipping through his drawings.

"That's going to be beautiful," Bitty said from her seat across the table.

"I love the idea of keeping the appearance of an actual Victorian carriage house," Charlie said.

Wanda nodded in agreement.

"It's beautiful," Renee said. She looked up from his design and caught his eyes. Something in his stomach did a flip, and he immediately looked away.

What was that?

"Let's eat," Renee said, getting up from her chair. He wondered if she had noticed.

Evelyn led them to the table set up on the porch. He counted six table settings, and his stomach stopped flipping and dropped.

"You made it!" Charlie said as Harper came around from the front.

Harper looked away from him as she said, "I can't stay long. I'm meeting someone later."

He sat into the chair on the other side of the table and silently prayed for the dinner to end as quickly as possible.

CHAPTER 14

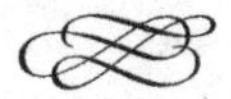

Renee could feel the tension boiling between Harper and Mateo. Something had gone on, and she had a feeling this was beyond the situation the other day. Before, he looked like a sad puppy. Now, he looked like an angry bull. He wouldn't make eye contact, and he barely spoke. By the time dinner was over, he had said nothing.

Harper didn't stick around for dessert. Instead, she said quick goodbyes and left without giving too much attention to anyone, but she and Mateo hadn't engaged the whole time.

If the others had noticed, they made no bother of it. After dessert, they sat around with coffee talking about what Renee had planned to sell at the bookstore.

"I want to sell foods they can hold with a book." Renee had visions of tourists walking around the harbor square eating pastries.

"There really aren't any bakeries around this area," Mateo said, which was something Renee also noticed. If someone wanted a Martha's Vineyard T-shirt or magnet, there were plenty to come by, but nowhere to just get a quick treat and coffee and a place to sit down.

When the sun had set and the air cooled, everyone returned

indoors. Bitty pulled out a box of dominoes. "We're playing a game if you want to join in."

Renee cringed as she waited for Mateo's reaction. Would this handsome single man want to hang out with the silver hairs?

"Sure, sounds fun," he said, pulling out a chair next to Wanda.

Wanda immediately glowed. She fluffed her hair with her hand when he wasn't looking, and Renee couldn't help but giggle to herself.

Laughter could be heard the whole time they played. It turned out that Mateo and Charlie had a comfortable enough friendship to tease each other, which made Renee almost pee her pants on two separate occasions. Bitty entertained them with wild stories of being a nurse, and Wanda told them about the quirkiest neighbors in her retirement community.

When the game had finished—Charlie had won—Mateo got up from his chair. "Thank you so much for inviting me." Mateo looked at the clock. "Wow, I didn't realize it was already that late."

"It's nine," Renee said, but she too couldn't hold back her yawn. She had prepped all day so she could bake in the early morning and bring it all to the bookstore.

"Tomorrow. I'll see you?" Charlie said it like a check-in as she got up.

"Yup." She nodded. She still had so much more she wanted to do, but she had to start somewhere, and now was as good a time as any.

When Mateo left, Renee headed to the bathroom to wash up, her mind racing about the day ahead. She would get up by three. Bake the six dozen different items she had prepped. She had bags tagged with her name. She wanted to be set up at the store by eight, get the coffee brewed, and sell her pastries.

But when she came out of the bathroom, her mom had already pulled out the sofa and was in the middle of making the bed.

“You don’t have to make my bed, you know.” Renee wondered if she’d always feel like a kid with her mother.

“I like to.” Evelyn put down the pillow and patted it with her hand. “Are you sure you don’t want to sleep with me?”

Renee shook her head. “I’m mostly tossing and turning these days.”

“Wait until menopause,” her mom said back.

Renee made a face. “Really? It’s late summer and I’m six months pregnant.”

“At least we’re not in Oklahoma,” Evelyn said as if that made any difference to her swollen ankles.

“Thanks, Mom,” Renee said.

Evelyn took a blanket and flung it up into the air before settling it down to cover the bed. “No problem.”

“No, I mean for everything.” Renee may be just selling cookies and treats, but tomorrow was the first step towards her new life. And she knew she wouldn’t be starting anything without her mother’s help. “I really appreciate you always taking care of me.”

“I appreciate the kind words,” Evelyn said, “but you’re going to find this is what motherhood is all about.” Evelyn pulled Renee into her arms, holding her like she did when Renee was little. She kissed Renee on the head. “Good night.”

“Night, mom.” Renee may have stumbled on hard times, but she had a solid foundation to get through it all.

Like she had said, Renee tossed and turned all night. By three, she had the ovens turned on. Everything was baked and packaged and ready to go by six, and then she sat around waiting for the rest of the time to pass until she could set up at the bookstore.

When it was time to leave, all three women gave her a hug, but she refused to have them come with her like they wanted.

“I can’t bring my mom to work with me,” Renee said to Evelyn. “I’m just selling pastries.”

Charlie met her inside the bookstore. She noticed the sign right away—a large chalkboard like the one she had been looking for, with a list of all the items she had baked.

"How'd you know?" she asked Charlie.

"Harper made it," he said.

A smile broke across her face. Harper remembered what she had made for today.

Renee got to work. First, she threw the French linen tablecloth she'd found at an antique shop in Edgartown over the table. Next, she placed her mother's glass vase filled with Mateo's flowers on top. Under a glass cake stand, she displayed her six baked goods—an almond croissant, a chocolate-crème-filled donut, a huge sugary cinnamon roll, a trio of biscotti tied together, a large chocolate chip cookie with homemade chocolate chunks, and a double fudge brownie. All the bagged items sat organized in baskets with clear signs and their prices labeled.

When she opened her own bakery, she'd have more than just finger sweets. She'd also bake breads and pies and cakes. She'd include special items like fruit tarts and crème puffs. She'd have crusty baguettes and hard dinner rolls. Maybe even offer soups and salads. Could she do all that with a child?

Lisa from Bottega Del Pane did.

She looked down at her pathetic display and shook her head. *Don't get too ahead of yourself*, she thought. She didn't want to pop the little bit of hope she had. She needed to focus on the here and now, one day at a time. Today, she would focus on selling all the pastries.

"Ready?" Charlie asked as he flipped the sign from closed to open.

She nodded. "As ready as I can be."

He unlocked the door and she waited. For the first twenty minutes, she stood behind the table, waiting for the stream of tourists to pile into the store. But when the tourists kept walking past, skipping it altogether, she had a feeling she might not meet her goal.

After an hour of no customers, she made a cup of tea. After two hours, she walked around the table to the window and watched the groups of people strolling along the harbor's sidewalk. Most of the shops had displays or signage to get their attention. Not Charlie. Except for Harper's chalkboard, there was nothing to tell the visitors that this was a bookstore that might be interesting.

"Do you put any type of window display outside?" she asked, looking at Harper's chalkboard. "Besides the sign?"

"I stopped dragging things outside because it didn't seem to make a difference," he said.

Renee didn't doubt he believed it, but as someone who had worked in the restaurant industry and had to reinvent herself every season, she knew how to catch customers' eyes.

"Do you mind if I make one for today?" she asked, pointing to a table filled with old titles and pictures of the staff.

Charlie placed his hands on his waist. "Anything you think will help."

She went outside and grabbed the chalkboard. "Do you know if she kept the chalk here?"

He pointed to a drawer in a desk. "She keeps all that stuff in there."

She took out white, pink, and yellow. On the board, she wrote, "Find your next beach read with a sweet treat." Then she drew a beach ball and a pail in the background. She searched the store for the perfect titles—romance, mystery, thrillers—and that's when she noticed something.

"Do you not carry my mom's books?" Renee asked Charlie. She had already noticed they weren't on display, but surely he had a few copies on the shelves.

He let out a long breath and shook his head. "No."

"Really? Why not?" Besides the fact Evelyn Rose was a best-selling author, she was his girlfriend. Why wouldn't he carry her books?

He shrugged. "I don't have a real good reason. It's just that I used to think I was the villain in all her books."

She hadn't read all her mother's books, and she wasn't sure if they even had a so-called villain. In fact, she had only read two from beginning to end. But she strangely could understand exactly what Charlie felt like. "I started reading one of her books, and it had a protagonist with two daughters. I stopped reading right away."

He let out a chuckle. "Yes, well, you do have to be careful around writers."

"Will you help bring out the table for me?" Renee asked Charlie.

With a lot of maneuvering, Charlie shimmied the table out of the store and onto the sidewalk. Renee followed behind with an armful of books.

She looked up and saw three women in sun visors and sunglasses peeking from the other side of the street. "Speak of the devil."

She waved at her mother.

"She's really proud of you, that's all," Charlie said, watching as Evelyn and Bitty and Wanda all sheepishly waved back.

Renee huffed out a laugh. "Proud of her pregnant divorced daughter who's living off her?"

Charlie made a face. "No, proud of her daughter who keeps getting up and brushing herself off."

Her mouth dropped, and she could feel the blood drain from her face. Her dad had said that exact saying throughout her childhood. He said it when she missed the ball in left field during the championship, and after the play when Kenny Baker threw up on her shoes, and when she didn't get into her dream culinary school in Paris.

She could hear him saying it in her mind, a vision of him with his hands on her shoulders. *Just pick yourself up and brush yourself off.*

"Is that Debbie Macomber's newest?" a woman asked, pointing to the book in Renee's hand.

Renee bounced out of her thoughts. "Yes, it is."

"Mmm," another woman said, standing next to her as she

smelled an almond croissant through its packaging. "Do we pay inside?"

Renee nodded and pointed inside. "There's also more inside."

The women opened the door.

"This place is adorable," the first one said.

Charlie patted her on the shoulder. "Here we go."

Renee realized four things while working at the store with Charlie that morning.

One, the bookstore was adorable. Inside the store, there was a clear view of the harbor. From almost every angle, one could see boats floating in the water, and the quaint gray clapboard shops. But it was also a tidy pigsty. Charlie clearly cleaned—the floors were vacuumed, the shelves dusted—but the space was full of books. They were crammed, and stuffed, and piled everywhere there was space.

The second thing: Charlie must not have a lot of business on Tuesday, or maybe any day, because he kept making comments.

"I haven't seen this many people inside the bookstore in years," he'd said that morning when a group had come in.

"Wow, they're still coming," he'd said after lunch. "Do you think they're coming because of the table?"

Third, Charlie had a way with customers. He made them feel as though they were neighbors, not just some random strangers in his store.

"At about seven o'clock, you should drive down to the lighthouse, and take some binoculars," he'd said to a customer who was looking for a restroom but ended up buying a dozen cookies and two Nora Roberts books. "When the sun sets, it looks like the whole world is on fire."

The fourth and most important thing she realized was how much she liked Charlie. Not just because he was nice to her mom or because he was helping her out, but she liked him for who he was. He had encouraged her to stay the day with him at the store. As the books on the display had been taken and bought, he'd allowed her to replenish with her choices. He'd taken notes about the sales throughout the morning.

"I can't believe how many books and pastries people bought this morning," Charlie said, watching Renee clean up the empty baskets. His face showed a surprised respect, as though he hadn't expected the idea to pan out like it had, and boy had it ever. It was just after noon, and she'd sold out of everything."

"I know," Renee said. "I can't believe it."

She cleaned up the display area, putting the old bins of coffee cups and sugar alternative choices back. She put everything into the empty baskets, including the flowers, when she looked up to see Mateo standing in the doorway.

"Mateo," she said, instantly smiling.

"How's it going today?" he asked, looking around for her setup.

"I sold out," she said, her arms gesturing to the empty table.

"You're kidding." Mateo grinned, but unlike Charlie's surprised smile, Mateo's was a told-you-so smirk. "That's great."

Just as she was about to say something smart back, in came her mother, Bitty, and Wanda. She laughed as they pulled off their disguises. They just could not help themselves.

"Charlie said you sold out," Evelyn said as she came straight up to Renee and embraced her in her arms.

"Mateo, it's good to see you," Wanda said, immediately bouncing her hair.

"Good to see you ladies as well." Mateo looked to Renee. "I should get going. Congratulations, Renee."

"We brought lunch for everyone." Bitty held up a wicker picnic basket. "Enough for you too, Mateo."

"Well..." Mateo rubbed his hands together. "I did come to grab a pastry, but since Renee sold out, a salad would be nice."

Charlie ushered the group to the table at the front of the shop with the picture window that overlooked the street.

"Women are your customers," Charlie said to Renee, sitting next to Evelyn.

When Mateo sat next to Charlie, from the corner of her eye, she saw Bitty and Wanda switch to different seats, leaving the only open chair for Renee next to the handsome contractor.

Oh dear, she thought to herself. What were they up to?

When she sat down, the three women instantly shot glances to one another. Charlie kept talking.

"Husbands will eat whatever their wives buy them, but it's women who are doing the buying." Charlie went through more of his findings. "The crème-filled donuts went first, which surprised me because I thought they'd be messier."

"Maybe because they look so dang delicious," Bitty said.

Renee thought about this. "I didn't display popular men's titles."

"Put some historical fiction up and anything Robert Patterson," Evelyn said.

"What about chairs outside?" Renee said. "Like Adirondacks where someone could sit with a coffee and read, watch their wife go shopping."

Charlie thought about it for a moment. "You know, this place needs something new to jolt it out of its rut. It's been stuck in a world that's long gone. It's time for a change."

So the slow business wasn't just because it was a Tuesday, she thought to herself.

"Tell me you can do this again tomorrow," Charlie said.

Renee's heart expanded again. "I'll bring double tomorrow."

And she did.

CHAPTER 15

"Don't even think about her," José said, pounding a nail into a four by four as if it were a stick of butter.

"Easy for you to say," Mateo said, leaning against the frame of their newest renovation project, a small fisherman's cape along the main strip. The customers allowed the brothers to post their sign in the front yard, which had already yielded two new bids. "She's everywhere."

"I could take over at the job," José reminded him.

Mateo shut up. He'd stop complaining. He wasn't going to quit the job. He loved working on the Roses' house. He just wished Harper wasn't there all the time.

"You need to get over yourself," his brother said bluntly.

"She wants to start the cottage next," he said. He couldn't wait to see how this next project turned out. "So I'd like to get the framers out here as soon as possible."

José opened his phone. "Do you have the plans set?"

Mateo nodded. Evelyn had given her final approval that morning at the house. He had arrived at the house early, wanting to congratulate Renee, but she had already taken off before he came, and that's when he'd run into Harper.

"She approved the widow's peak." Mateo almost said I told

you so but declined. José's face showed he was impressed with his baby brother.

"I got to hand it to you, Teo, you really did good with this one." José patted him hard on the back. Even though Mateo was the boss of the business, José would always be the boss of the brothers. Having his big brother's approval meant everything to him.

"Would you mind me inviting a friend for dinner at your place?" Mateo asked.

"You want to invite Harper?" José asked.

Mateo shook his head. "No, Evelyn's daughter, Renee."

"The pregnant one?" José looked concerned.

"The pregnant one." Mateo made a face back at him as José shivered. "I thought it might be nice to meet another mother who lives on the island."

"I'd be careful with that one," José warned him. "I mean, where's the father?"

"Is that any of our business?" Mateo changed his mind. Maybe he shouldn't bring Renee to his brother's place. "Remind me again how you got Julia to marry you?"

"I have no flipping clue." José slapped his forehead with his hand. "All I'm saying is to be careful. You're stepping into something that's already a little messy."

"She's just a friend."

"Sure," José said. "Whatever you say."

Mateo didn't have time to argue with José about it. Besides, after hanging his heart out there on the line with Harper and being rejected, he had no reason to go out searching for anything at this point.

But an hour later, his brother called him as he left for a bid in Oak Bluffs. "Julia invited Renee over for dinner."

"What?" He couldn't believe it. "Renee?"

"Yes, I guess they met at the bookstore today, and Julia bought a bunch of her pastries." José sounded as surprised as Mateo felt. "She's coming for dinner tonight."

Mateo couldn't believe the coincidence. "Did you say something?"

"I mentioned you had the hots for her, but I didn't know she had invited her over."

"I don't have the hots for her!" Mateo wished he could reach through his phone and deck his brother. "She's the daughter of *our* biggest client."

"She's coming tonight, so I'd be ready by six." José hung up before Mateo could argue against his attendance.

Something told him that his brother would most likely say something completely idiotic.

And he was right. Just as he arrived at the house, José yelled from the front door. "She's already here!"

Mateo should've called her before coming. Warned her of his brother who had social hindrances. Julia stood next to him, a pillar of beauty and common sense. He kissed his sister-in-law on the cheek as he walked into the house. He handed over a plant he'd dug out of the garden.

"Thanks for including me," Mateo said.

"What's this one?" Julia asked, kissing him back. She held up the sedum. It was Mateo's favorite at this time of year. It's dark burgundy color stood out against the yellowing leaves in his garden. The cooler nights didn't bother the fall perennial yet.

"It's called Autumn Joy," he said. "Plant it in the south end by the cherry tree."

She lifted it up and turned behind her. There stood Renee. "Mateo, you know Renee."

He walked over to her, and like he had with his sister-in-law, he kissed her on the cheek. "How are you doing, Renee?"

He hoped to God his brother wouldn't say anything embarrassing or hadn't already said something in front of his young nephews.

"I met Julia at the bookstore with the kids this morning," Renee said. "I didn't know she was your sister-in-law."

He looked to Julia, whose attention was on his four-year-old nephew as he hung on her. José, on the other hand, had a smirk and a quip ready to go, Mateo was sure.

"When's dinner?" JJ, his nephew, asked.

"In just a minute," Julia said, her shirt hanging halfway off her shoulder.

"You said that a minute ago," JJ complained.

"Have you had her pastries?" Julia asked Mateo, ignoring her son.

"They're amazing, right?" Mateo said.

Renee smiled, but her eyes were on JJ as he fell to the floor. All four limbs hung out from his body.

"I'm going to starve to death," JJ said.

"He's four?" Renee asked Mateo, out of earshot from the rest.

Mateo nodded.

"Children look a lot harder at dinnertime," Renee said quietly.

"Hanger is a real thing," Mateo said, even quieter.

She let out a big belly laugh, rubbing her stomach. One thing Mateo knew for certain was that José was wrong about Renee. There was nothing messy about her.

"Can I get you something to drink?" Mateo asked, hoping to drum up conversation.

"I have water already," Renee said, and they stood in silence. Then she leaned over, covering her mouth and whispered, "Is Sandy here?"

A laugh escaped him, and said, "She left yesterday."

Julia whisked Renee away into the kitchen, which left Mateo manning the grill outside with José who wore a *kiss the chef* apron.

"You're making burgers for our biggest client?" Mateo looked behind him at the women inside the house talking as the kids played on the kitchen floor.

"I just found out she was coming for dinner this afternoon," José said. "What do you want me to do?"

Mateo suddenly felt the metaphorical blue collar hanging around his neck when they sat for dinner. The Rose household never had just cheese and crackers as an appetizer. Evelyn always had something fancier. What had Renee made the other night? Some homemade pasta with expensive fresh fish.

"This is exactly the kind of night I miss," Renee said, sitting at the kitchen table. "I love a burger."

Conversation halted as everyone ate their burgers, which to José's credit, were delicious.

"José," Renee said out of the silence. Everyone looked over to where she sat. "This is an amazing burger."

Mateo could see a shift in José. He no longer saw a mess in Renee, but a woman who knew a burger, which in José's opinion meant more than her financial status. "I grate the onion into the hamburger." José explained the rest of his recipe to Renee, who seemed to be taking notes.

"At my restaurant, I used a prime cut of dry aged La Frieda ribeye." Then she added, "No cheese."

José shot Mateo a look across the table. His brother was impressed.

All three children behaved like angels the rest of the night, including José, which was a huge relief. After dinner, Julia and Renee sat in the kitchen and didn't stop talking about pregnancy and motherhood and all things women, while José and Mateo took the kids on a walk to the beach.

"She's like... cool," José said as they followed the kids to find shells.

"She's nice." Mateo liked Renee, but José had been kind of right. She had a lot going on, and some of it probably was messy. Mateo had never been divorced, or even married for that matter. He didn't have a child on the way. He hadn't even been in a serious relationship. But he was certain this was not the time to get involved with her.

"What's her story?" José asked.

Mateo shrugged. "I don't really know much."

"Julia will know everything within a half hour." José called out to the kids, who ran ahead. "We should take these rugrats in for a bath."

By the time they returned, Renee was saying goodbye outside.

"You're leaving already?" Mateo asked.

"I'm exhausted," she said, waving again to the kids. "Thanks for the invitation."

"Let's go to the beach with the kids before the weather turns," Julia suggested.

"Sounds great."

Renee got into her car and drove off.

"Bath time!" José called out, and all three kids ran inside.

"I should probably head out as well," Mateo said.

"Have you heard what her ex-husband did to her?" Julia asked. It had taken her all of forty-five minutes to find out.

He wasn't sure if he wanted to know. It felt like he was learning a secret he didn't have permission.

"He tried to pay her off." Julia looked indignant. "Can you imagine finding out you're pregnant and your husband wants nothing to do with you or the baby?"

His stomach dropped at the thought of Renee being tossed aside. "What kind of man does that to someone?"

Julia shook her head, her hands on her hips. "I know you joke about your brother," she said, looking up the staircase at the bathroom door where José had turned on the faucet to the tub in the kid's bathroom, "but he's one of the good ones."

Mateo smiled at his sister-in-law.

"Just like you," she said. "Harper will figure it out. You just wait."

The name surprised him, because he was almost certain she would've said Renee.

Maybe he had been thinking too much.

"Yeah, I don't think Harper's going to change her mind with Gerard in town," he said. He had overheard her talking to Bitty about the artist who stayed during the summers and went to Portugal during the winters.

Mateo knew an artist like Gerard was most likely a trust fund baby. Not many artists got to travel back and forth to two of the most expensive islands in the world.

"Maybe you two aren't meant to be together," Julia said.

And that was his cue to go.

He waved at Julia. "Thanks again for everything," he said, opening up the front door. "See you tomorrow, guys!"

"Mateo, I'm sorry," Julia said as he walked out. "I just meant that you're a great guy, and there's someone out there for you too."

He left, smiling to himself. He'd had fun. And until up a minute ago, he hadn't thought about Harper. When he got home, he looked in the garage and found some cedar, but not enough for a whole chair.

The next morning, he headed out to the lumber yard straight away. He ordered a hardwood white oak for four chairs. Something that would last for years with multiple tourists getting in and out of them. They would look sophisticated and have the soft feel only wood could provide. They'd take a few days, well, nights, since that was his only free time lately.

And for the next few evenings, after leaving the Roses' house, he worked on the chairs, cutting and assembling, sanding and painting. Something in him wanted those chairs to come out even better than he'd first intended. Something told him they'd draw even more people to the bookstore and to Renee's baked goods. Something told him that these chairs would make a difference for her.

And for some reason, that seemed really important to him.

CHAPTER 16

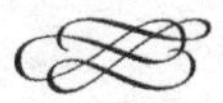

A new routine ensued after that first day Renee had sold her pastries at the bookstore.

Now, each morning, Renee woke at three and started baking. She felt like the man in the old Dunkin' Donuts commercial, drudging out of bed, mumbling, "Time to make the donuts" in a sleepy haze. She'd rise before the sun, come downstairs, and turn on the ovens. Then she took everything out of the fridge to sit and wait.

After the first week, she expanded her selection, made different varieties of each item, and packaged them all up with a sticker. She had no idea what her name would be. She was still thinking, but nothing really stuck. She liked Sweet and Savory, but it wasn't very original. She bet there were others registered under that name already in the state of Massachusetts.

She also hadn't figured out what exactly she was selling. Was she a pastry chef who specialized in small treats for the moment? Or was she an occasion baker who created birthday cakes, seven-tiered wedding cakes, and anything else people celebrated? Would she sell only pastries or specialize in a certain delicacy? Suddenly even coffee seemed complicated and too much to decide for her future.

One morning, when she arrived at the bookstore, she found Charlie standing out front with Mateo. They stood, both with their arms crossed against their chests as they looked at four Adirondack chairs.

"What's going on?" she asked as she walked up to them.

"Mateo made these for the store!" Charlie's arms spread out at the chairs. "Can you believe it?"

Renee's hand immediately covered her gasp. "You made these for the store?"

She couldn't believe it. She rushed to a chair and rubbed its smooth surface with her palm. The edges were rounded.

"They're beautiful," she said. There were two tables sitting in between the chairs with potted flowers on top.

Her eyes immediately moistened, and without thinking, she walked over to Mateo and hugged him. "Thank you so much."

He laughed and wrapped his arms around her. "My pleasure."

She could've blamed it on the hormones, but she couldn't fight back the tears that escaped at his gesture. Her emotions swelled up so fast that they got the better of her, and she couldn't contain them. No one had gone to such trouble to help her out like that before. Not even her husband. The chairs showed so much of who Mateo was as a person, his kindness, his thoughtfulness. She couldn't help but wish Harry could be as great a man as Mateo. Whoever did catch Mateo's heart next would be one special woman.

For a split second, she just let the feeling of his embrace wash over her. For that split second, she felt safe and happy and secure. But as he let go of her hold, she noticed where he gazed off.

Harper stood there watching the two of them. As Renee wiped her eyes, she noticed Harper hadn't greeted anyone as she'd come from behind the store.

"Hey, Harper," Renee said. "Did you see the chairs Mateo built?"

Charlie sat down in one of them. "They're perfect. Mateo, this is way too nice. Let me at least pay you for the materials."

Mateo shook his head. "It's the least I could do for all the recommendations you've given me over the years."

Renee shook her head. "Charlie's right. This is too nice."

Mateo didn't budge. "No, this is a gift."

He broke his stare and gave a nod to Charlie. "I should get back to work, but I knew you'd all like them."

"Like them?" Renee said as she slowly lowered herself into one. "We love them."

As she leaned back, realizing she would be stuck without help, she promised that one day, someday soon, she'd repay Mateo for his kindness.

For the rest of the day, the chairs were full of couples and friends, men waiting for their wives, and families enjoying a treat. Even Charlie and the girls spent their afternoon coffee klatch in them.

Renee continued to sell out day after day. And soon, she started knowing her customers. An elderly man named Tom liked a chocolate croissant in the morning with a coffee as he browsed the books. He came right when she delivered the goods and waited with Charlie. A pair of women came in every midmorning after their walk, and each got a crème-filled donut. Renee had been in so much turmoil about her whole life that she'd forgotten one very important piece of it that always brought her back to the center: the gift of serving others pleasure.

"It actually melts in my mouth," Alice said after she finished her donut. "It's delectable."

"Thank you," Renee said. She had been hanging out at the store more and more these days. Charlie had removed another full section of shelves to make room for more customers to sit inside, which was a good thing, too, as leaves were just beginning to fade from their summer green.

The next time the women went into the city, Renee made a stop at a farmer's market.

"Are you looking for something in particular?" Evelyn asked

as they walked the rows of stalls of produce and other locally made products.

Renee nodded. She was looking for the one thing she knew would be the best way to thank Mateo for the chairs. "I'm looking for something that's called chiverre, but it's not in season. I might be able to find some made like a honey or jelly in a jar."

She combed through the market for what looked more like a melon to her. As she hunted, she came across locally roasted coffee beans which she bought for the store. Then some fresh picked apples from Vermont and huge blackberries. At the very end of the market, she almost skipped the last stall, but then she saw a jar with the word chiverre on it.

"Excuse me," she said to the vendor. "Is that miel de chiverre?"

"Si," the man said, pointing to jars full of what looked like a marmalade. "Would you like one?"

"I'll take four," she said, pulling out cash.

The man grabbed the jars, then leaned over the table for the money before exchanging with change from his apron.

"Gracias," she said, taking the jars of chiverre from the man's hands.

The next morning, she made the dough for the empanadas, making sure to follow the traditional way of folding it together. As the chiverre empanadas baked in the oven, she got ready for the day. Cinnamon rolls, donuts, crème puffs, scones, apple cider donuts, and the rest. She had quadrupled in sales since she started a few weeks back and still didn't have enough at the end of the day.

"Good morning." Harper came through the side door in sunglasses and her hair braided down her back. Renee noticed she had started coming earlier and earlier each morning. Today, she carried her laptop.

"Hey," Renee said as the buzzer for the oven went off. "You're here early."

Her mom hadn't even come downstairs for her morning coffee yet.

"Evelyn and I are going to do these things called writing sprints." Harper turned on her computer. "It's when you try to write as fast as you can in a certain amount of time. Your mom's going to kick my butt."

Renee couldn't help but laugh at the truth. Evelyn would kick her butt with word count.

"Isn't it about improving each time?" Renee pointed out. "Writing seems like a competition with oneself, not a competition with a thirty-year career author."

Harper pointed at her. "You're right. I've been freaking out that I'll only write like five words and your mom will have like twenty thousand. But it's all about having six the next round."

Renee wiped her hair out of her face, ready to start feeling jealous of this woman standing next to her, but she didn't. Harper had her own things, things Renee had no idea about, and who was she to judge or compare? Why did anyone have to feel inferior or superior?

"How's the book coming?" Renee asked.

"Ugh." Harper slouched into the stool. "I am a bit overwhelmed by the daunting task of editing and still thinking it's halfway decent. Most of the time, I'm thinking it's a bunch of donkey manure."

Renee shook her head at Harper's choice of words. "I'm sure it's not donkey manure."

"Are you ready for Lamaze tonight?" Harper asked, sliding her computer closer to her.

Renee groaned silently to herself. After she had "agreed" to Lamaze, Bitty and Harper had found a class at the clinic. They'd signed her up for classes without even asking if she could go. "Not really."

"Oh, we're going to have so much fun," Harper said cheerfully.

Renee almost came back with a sarcastic reminder that Harper was only playing a role, whereas this was Renee's actual life, but she held back. She'd only sound sour when she wasn't. When she looked down at her belly, no longer did she feel her stomach tighten in fear of the future. Instead, she was excited to finally meet her baby.

She looked down at her belly, which seemed to get bigger by the second. She could no longer see her toes. And by the end of the day, she didn't recognize her ankles at all. She had stretch marks in places she'd never even known could stretch, she no longer slept, and all she wanted was a huge grinder of sandwich meat. But mostly, she just wanted to hold George in her arms.

"Thanks again for coming with me." Renee had been grateful for the offer. Her other option was going with her mother, and that seemed a bit pathetic.

The timer went off, and Renee pulled out the empanadas.

"Those smell so good," Harper said. "What are they?"

She set the baking sheet down on the counter and used the spatula to remove the pastries one by one onto the cooling rack.

"They're a pastry Mateo's grandmother made in Costa Rica."

Harper gave her a look, lifting her eyebrow up. "He has a grandmother in Costa Rica?"

Renee shook her head. "No, he said she passed away when he was fifteen, but this was his favorite dessert of hers."

Harper squinted her eyes as if she were studying Renee. "He's really himself with you."

Renee didn't know if that was a good thing or what, but she waited for Harper to finish her thoughts.

"I mean, he's..." She paused, looking as though she was contemplating what to say next. "Different with you."

This did not help her figure out what Harper was trying to say, but she didn't have time to think about it all. She had to bake. Soon, her mom and Bitty were up. Evelyn and Harper headed out to the porch. They all let Wanda sleep.

"I have a shake in the fridge for when Wanda gets up," Renee said, getting ready to go to the bookstore.

Evelyn picked up a basket full of pain au chocolat as Harper carried out another basket full of cookies to the car. "Tomorrow night, the writer's group is coming for dinner."

Renee didn't remember these plans. "Do you need me to cook?"

Evelyn shook her head. "No, it's all taken care of. But I would like you to join us."

If it had been a few weeks ago, Renee would have refused like she had the last time, but this morning, the idea of having dinner with the company of her mom and Charlie's friends seemed like fun. They were the people who frequented the bookstore and bought her pastries. Hank was known for picking up a half dozen of anything for him and his partner. Anita came each day to get a "special" treat for herself and another for her mother. In fact, most of the customers lately didn't appear to be tourists but locals, and she still couldn't bake enough inventory.

"You should invite Mateo to dinner," Renee said. She still couldn't get over the fact that he'd built the chairs for Charlie's store. She couldn't imagine the time and energy he put into the Adirondacks. This may have been the main motivation why she'd suggested including Mateo, but there was a little part of her that wanted to figure out what Harper had meant. How did he act differently?

Was it because he didn't have to worry around her and could act more naturally? Maybe it was the fact that he was always in his element at the house, working on what he did best, and was able to show off his talents. She realized that over the past few months, Mateo had turned out to be a good friend to her, and Renee needed as many of those as she could get.

"Speaking of which," Renee said. "I made some empanadas for him if you wouldn't mind giving them to him when he comes this morning."

"Sure," Evelyn said. "And I'll invite him to dinner."

Renee left for the bookstore after that. Charlie met her at the back door as she pulled her mother's Volvo in backward.

"This has been my best month in years!" Charlie said as she

got out. "I did the books this morning, and my business rose thirty-seven percent, and tourist season is slowing down."

"Really?" She had been wondering how business overall was doing but didn't know how to broach the topic. Had the pastries and coffee helped his bottom line? It wasn't hard to notice the stale titles that had been sitting on the shelves. She also noticed Charlie hadn't restocked all that much with new inventory as the old stuff moved out. Shouldn't he order more to keep the momentum?

"I wondered if you have been thinking long term?" Charlie asked, grabbing a couple bins of pastries and following her into the bookstore.

Renee had. With staying with her mom and making money each day from her pastries, she hoped to earn enough within a year or two to find a place to rent on the island and start her own bakery. They walked to the back room, where she had a table permanently set up for her pastries and coffee.

She placed the bins down and looked at Charlie. "What do you mean?"

"What if you stayed here?" Charlie handed over a leather journal. The words Books and Bread were engraved on the front cover.

She looked up at him. "Are you serious?"

He nodded. "Very serious. I've been looking into what airports carry for books and magazines. They have limited space, so they only carry hot titles." He expanded out his arms as if he were a conductor in front of a symphony. "I could do the same here by cutting down the inventory to a fourth of what I carry now and give you the room to expand into a real bakery."

The shock hit her like a Mack truck at sixty miles an hour. "But this is your bookstore."

"And I'm going to lose it if I keep going the way I have been—the way things have been for years." He heaved out a long sigh. "I'm a great writer, and I love books, and reading, and everything that goes into this business. I'm just not good at business."

She didn't look at him, afraid the truth would sit in her eyes like a puddle you couldn't avoid. Charlie *wasn't* good at business. He loved books, but he had to think beyond the books he sold to make the store successful. "But what about Harper?"

He let out a laugh. "I love my daughter to pieces, but she wants nothing to do with this place."

"But have you discussed this with her?" Renee didn't want to assume anything. Maybe deep down, Harper did want to be part of her family history.

Charlie shook his head. "I haven't talked to anyone, not even your mother. I wanted to run this by you first to see if you're even interested."

She looked him over. "You're really serious about this?"

He leaned closer to her. "This place has been in my family since it was a fish market back eighty years ago. I've grown up here, raised my child here; it's where I wrote my first novel. I can't just sell it, but I don't have it in me any longer to make it successful."

The circles under his eyes looked suddenly heavier than she had noticed before. "What about your retirement? I mean, don't you want to sell to be able to do what you want and not continue working."

"I'm not ready to stop yet, but when I am, maybe you'll be ready to take over?"

Her heart pounded inside her chest.

"So?" Charlie asked, his eyebrows lifted. "What do you think?"

"What's in it for you?" She really didn't see the upside for him. "I'm not bringing anything to the table."

"You're bringing customers!" He laughed out the words as if she couldn't see the obvious answer.

The excitement of the possibilities grew inside her but also a consciousness that she may have signed the divorce papers, but taking this opportunity on the island would forever change things.

"Okay," she said. "Let's do it."

CHAPTER 17

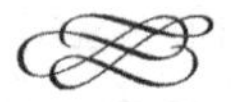

Evelyn could feel a shift in the weather when she got up that morning. New England mornings usually held a coolness, but the humidity of the summer heat had disappeared, and a crispness had entered.

Evelyn couldn't describe the shift, but she felt it. Her writing didn't flow like it had been throughout the summer, Wanda seemed especially drained and quiet, and Bitty seemed tense about the summer ending.

"If at any time you need me, you just call," Bitty said for the second time that morning. "I can easily get a ticket and come right back."

Evelyn couldn't believe Bitty's time at the beach house was coming to an end in less than a week. "I'm so sad the summer's over."

"Oh, girl, don't I know it." Bitty sat down in her seat across from Renee's, which had become her spot at the table. Wanda sat on her left and Evelyn to her right. "I've had such a blast."

"You do know you can stay as long as you'd like," Evelyn reminded her for the second time. "And you will always have a room to stay in."

Bitty tapped her fingernails against the table. "I'm afraid I need to figure some things out back home."

Evelyn felt the shift again. Bitty didn't expand on the subject, which felt different.

"Everything okay?" Evelyn asked.

Bitty shrugged. "It'll be fine. Just need to get home and settle some stuff."

She didn't press it, but Evelyn knew what fine meant, and it didn't mean fine.

Wanda glanced over at Evelyn and caught her eye. She'd noticed the shift as well.

From outside, she heard a car pull into the driveway. She could see Renee hobble out of the driver's seat and bound up the steps, holding her stomach as she came inside. Charlie followed behind her.

"Guess what?" Renee said, interrupting their conversation. Her whole face expanded in her smile. She looked as though she had big news to share and couldn't wait to let it out.

Evelyn let out a laugh at Renee's excitement. "What's going on?"

Evelyn noticed Renee looked to Charlie for confirmation, as though he knew the news as well.

"Charlie just asked me to be his partner!" Renee said to Evelyn.

"What?" The shift turned into a shove.

"He asked me to work with him at the store, but, like, open my own part with my own bakery." Renee appeared over the moon by the news.

Evelyn vaguely remembered Charlie talking about going into a partnership with another business owner. "Renee's the person you were talking about the other day?"

He pointed at her like she'd figured out a clue to a riddle. "Yes, she was."

Evelyn looked back at her overjoyed daughter. "What about

the baby? What are you going to do? You can't continue baking the way you are with a baby."

Renee's joy immediately extinguished.

"Women with babies work all the time." Renee sounded put off, and Evelyn couldn't blame her. She could feel her body tensing for no good reason. She should be happy her new boyfriend had offered her daughter a place to work.

"She could bring the baby to the store, and we could watch him," Charlie said.

"You haven't taken care of a baby in twenty-eight years," Evelyn reminded him. "A baby is a lot of work."

Charlie looked like he was about to say something, but he stopped himself and began to study her as if her reaction confused him.

"What if things don't work out?" She didn't want to sound heartless, but the truth glared them in the face.

"Then we cross that bridge when it comes up," Charlie said nonchalantly. "This is a win-win for everyone."

But Evelyn could feel the walls closing in. Charlie thought she meant his working relationship with Renee, but she had been thinking about her and Charlie's relationship.

What if *they* didn't work out?

They had only been dating for a couple of months. She loved him, that she was sure of, but was it the forever love? Did she want to go back to a full partnership? She finally started to enjoy being on her own. Never in her life had she been able to choose things just for herself by herself. She could eat what she wanted when she wanted. Travel where she wanted and how. She could live anywhere and with anyone she chose.

She had loved every minute of being married to George, but a happy marriage had a lot of give and take. Their marriage included a lot of sacrifices on both of their parts. Did she want to go back to having to give up? And was she selfish for thinking this way? What did that mean for their relationship?

The conversation kept going without her as everyone poured over all the new things that would need to happen.

"We're going to call it Books and Bread," Renee said proudly.

Evelyn remained quiet.

Doubt seemed to spread faster through her than happiness. By the afternoon, all she could think about was her relationship with Charlie and how she needed to figure things out before Renee finalized any plans. If things shifted in their relationship, would that create consequences for Renee and Charlie's partnership?

Evelyn watched from the dining room window as Renee and Charlie sat out on the back porch, both buzzing with excitement about all the new possibilities. Charlie had a sketch pad out, drawing up plans for a whole new store.

"We could have Mateo build a counter that holds refrigerated glass cases," Charlie said.

Charlie was right. The business idea was a win-win for both Renee and him. Evelyn had noticed the glaring problems with Charlie's bookstore. Not that she could've done better inheriting an overstocked, overstuffed bookstore that was dead on arrival. Charlie made no bones that he'd kept it because it was his only option when Tanya had left him. His career had hit a slump in Hollywood. But going into business with her daughter?

"You're not joining in on the celebration?" Wanda asked from the kitchen, holding up a tea bag. "Want some?"

"Yes, thank you," Evelyn said, walking to where her friend stood. "Is it wrong that I'm not joining in on the excitement?"

Wanda turned on the faucet and hung the kettle underneath, her hand shaking by its weight. "Is something bothering you about it?"

Evelyn thought carefully before she spoke. She almost wished she could write it down before she said it out loud, because once she spoke the words, her hidden thoughts would be out in the universe.

"What if Charlie and I don't work out and that affects all of them?" Evelyn didn't want to see her daughter crumble again. The last few months had been heart crushing enough to see Renee go through this messy divorce. She wouldn't be able to see her lose her one true love for a second time. All that cooking Renee had done when she arrived, all those pastries... Her need to have to cook and bake had broken Evelyn's heart. Harry not only broke her heart but took away the one thing that would break her soul.

Cooking.

"Why does it have to end?" Wanda asked, placing the kettle on the stove and switching on the burner. She met Evelyn at the island with an empty mug. "Maybe it only gets better from here?"

"Things are good now." Evelyn didn't want to say it, but the truth was, nothing could last forever. "But things don't always stay the same."

"My oncologist had said one time that worrying is like fantasy," Wanda said. Her eyes looked tired and red. "It's not real. It's only made up in your head. Focus on the present moment, which is the only real moment."

Evelyn knew she should take Wanda's advice. She hadn't seen Renee this happy in so long. But by the time Harper arrived back at the house that evening, she secretly hoped Harper would raise her own concerns. The store was her inheritance, her family history, not Renee's, but Harper was thrilled with the idea.

"It's about time things changed at the store," she said. "It's been in need of something to bring it into the twenty-first century. That's awesome."

A knee-jerk reaction made Evelyn say, "You should think about hiring an attorney to set up certain agreements."

The lines between Charlie's eyebrows creased.

"The first thing you should do is come up with a business plan." Wanda jumped in from the other side of the porch. "You're also going to want to hire a lawyer to help register the business."

Wanda sat under a blanket on the porch. She had started wearing Evelyn's scarves around her head. The seventy-degree day was the first time Evelyn could feel the fall air blowing in from the west as the locals had said it would and she wondered if Wanda needed another blanket.

Harper and Charlie stayed for dinner, and the conversation naturally shifted to other topics, but when Renee and Harper left for Lamaze, the whole situation consumed her thoughts.

"You okay?" Charlie asked as they cleaned up in the kitchen together. He stood at the sink and washed dishes as she dried.

"Yes," she said, then quickly, "no. I mean, I don't know."

She set the dish down on the counter and let out a breath.

"Uh-oh." Charlie shut off the water. "That's your concerned face."

"I am concerned, actually," she confessed. She knew the moment she said it, there was no turning back. Wanda's advice blared in her head.

"Are you worried about the store?" He took her hands into his. "Renee's going to make it a success, and when she's established and has the customer base she needs, I'll back out and the place can be hers."

"It's your store, though," she said. She wanted to hit herself. Here was a guy who was willing to help her daughter, who was in a tight situation, and she was balking at it. She just couldn't help herself.

"I have no doubt that Renee will be able to buy me out in a matter of a few years." Charlie seemed to have no problem with the future.

"But what about the meantime? I mean, what if you need the money and need to sell. What then?"

"I don't need the money," he said. "I just want the place to stay in the family."

"But she's not family." Evelyn said the words before even really thinking about what she was saying.

The comment hit Charlie like a slap in the face.

"Oh." Charlie loosened his grip but didn't let go.

Evelyn intertwined her fingers in his loose grip and played

with them, keeping her gaze on his fingers instead of looking at his eyes. "We've only just reconnected."

She had so many questions that logistically needed to be answered. She didn't want to be a Debbie Downer, but she had been through enough business partnerships throughout her own career to see the simplest things could damage a company.

But silence permeated around them. When she finally looked up, she could see the wheels spinning in his head.

"You're worried we're not going to make it, is that it?" he asked, his eyebrows furrowed.

She let go of his hands and wiped her palms down the sides of her hips. "I don't know. Yes, I guess I am. But I'm also worried about Renee's situation changing and how that will affect our relationship. What if she wants to go back to Chicago?"

He just kept looking at her. So she filled the silence.

"What if things fall apart with the store? Will that affect our relationship? Mixing work and relationships can get messy fast." She straightened her posture, feeling more like a jerk by the second.

He leaned against the counter, facing across from her, crossing his arms. "What exactly are you worried about, Evelyn?"

He looked upset. She knew the things she rattled off weren't exactly what was bothering her, and even though warning signs flashed, she couldn't stop herself.

"I just wish you had come to me before talking to Renee about all this," she said.

He opened his mouth as though he was going to say something but then stopped, and she could feel him shift, like the plates under the earth's crust, sliding against one another. "Would you have discouraged me from asking Renee?"

"Well, I think I'd have asked you to wait, at least until the baby was born." Evelyn could list off a dozen different reasons why.

"Right." He looked at the sink as dishes floated in bubbles. "I guess I should have. I'm sorry."

Evelyn's stomach dropped.

"I don't mean to be harsh," she said, wishing she had just kept quiet. What good did it do now? He had already asked Renee. Bringing this up only made him feel bad, and what would the ripple effect be? Their relationship would suffer. Renee's dream would be crushed, Harper's energetic friendship extinguished.

But as he stood there, his face contoured as though questioning her. "Have you thought maybe this is the best thing for Renee?"

The suggestion hit her like a ton of bricks. "Yes."

He nodded. "So this isn't about Renee. It's about you?"

Ouch. "I don't want us to have a falling out and Renee be affected by it."

There. The truth. Renee wasn't like Evelyn. She hadn't built a career on her own. She had worked for Harry and built his career and got *nothing* in return.

"Evelyn." His tone became serious. "I'm not asking Renee to bake for me because she's your daughter. I'm asking a talented chef to give life back to my store."

He made complete sense. She was being irrational. "I want Renee to be successful for herself."

Charlie stared at her. "It's really hard to move forward when you're stuck in the past."

"What's that supposed to mean?" she asked.

"You're judging me on my twenty-year-old self and that's not fair," he said.

His statement threw her back. "I'm not judging you."

He snorted. "You just suggested I'd ruin your daughter if we broke up."

"I didn't mean it like that," she said, but she had. "I'm expressing my feelings. I would have liked to be involved, that's all."

"Evelyn, she's an adult who can make her own decisions."

"Thank you," Renee said, suddenly standing in the doorway with Harper.

"Renee," Evelyn said, turning around to see the two girls. "Harper."

"What's going on here?" Renee asked, her arms crossed against her chest, resting on top of her baby bump.

Evelyn dropped her head back and looked to the ceiling. "I'm just worried about everything. I should've stayed out of it."

"It's fine." Charlie feigned a smile, but his eyes didn't reach Evelyn's and her heart dropped. "I should go."

"Charlie, please wait," Evelyn said after him, but he was already walking out of the kitchen. She went after him as the girls stayed in the kitchen. "Charlie, please."

He didn't turn when he spoke. "It's fine, Evelyn. I just think it's best I go."

"Charlie." She stood by the door as he opened it. "Don't. Let's talk. I make mistakes, too."

He stopped, holding his hand on the doorknob. "Too?" He shook his head and pulled the door open. "Good night, Evelyn."

And he left.

When Evelyn returned to the kitchen, Renee's face was red.

"What is your problem?" Renee said immediately.

"My problem?" Evelyn took a second to remind herself that Renee was pregnant and emotional and tired. "I'm actually looking out for you."

Renee's mouth dropped. "No, you're looking out for yourself."

"Renee, that's not fair," she said, her hands beginning to shake. "I'm just being rational here. What would happen if Charlie and I broke up?"

Renee cocked her head to one side. "What do you think will happen?"

Evelyn knew what she thought. Charlie left when the going got tough.

"I'm sorry you're upset," Evelyn said.

"No, you're not," Renee shot back.

"Be reasonable for a second," Evelyn said. "All I'm saying is you have to think of all the different possibilities."

"I heard what you said," Renee said. "I heard you say you would've discouraged him from asking me. What kind of mother does that?"

Renee shook her head in disgust, and Evelyn's heart shattered. "Come on, Renee. I'm just trying to protect—"

"Control," Renee cut her off. "You try to control everyone. Why do you think Samantha's across the ocean in another country? Wanda can't leave the house without you telling her to use the bathroom. You try to make everything work for you." Renee's eyes brimmed with tears. "What's worse is that you knew how important this was for me."

"I just want you to make sure you think before you jump into things," Evelyn said. "Look what happened to you with Harry."

Renee looked like she had been slapped across the face.

She opened her mouth as if to say something, but she shut it closed quickly and stormed out of the room.

Evelyn looked out the window at the dark sky, wishing she could rewind time and go back and fix this catastrophe. She rubbed her thumbs hard inside her palms. She had really messed things up this time.

"You okay, girl?" Bitty asked from the other side of the kitchen.

Evelyn kept her back facing Bitty and nodded, holding in her emotions as she said, "Yup, I'm fine."

CHAPTER 18

"Dad?" Harper knocked on his bedroom.

His daughter had no boundaries. "Yes, Harper."

"Do you want to talk?" she asked as if he were her teenage girlfriend who'd been dumped in tenth period.

"No, I'm good." But as he sat on his bed, still in his clothes with Stan lying beside him, he wasn't good.

God, he was a fool.

"Dad?" she said again.

Exasperation filled his voice. "Yes?"

"I love you," she said.

His throat closed from the lump stuck in it. He rubbed his knuckles hard. "Love you too, kid."

But she didn't move from the door. "What happened?"

"Harper, I'm going to bed now, okay?"

The words stumbled out, not wobbling from sadness but strong from tension. Harper seemed to get the gist.

"Okay, good night," she said. "Call me in the morning."

He listened to her footsteps. Stan's ears perked as the car rolled out of the back driveway. He looked out the window into the black night. The days were getting shorter. He had even noticed the change of wind at the beach and color on the trees. Fall wasn't just approaching; it had arrived.

He had looked forward to the fall. He had even booked a minivacation to New Hampshire with Evelyn. They would've stayed on Newfound Lake, leaf peeped all day, and stayed in with a cozy fire at night.

Now, he wasn't so sure.

He had imagined the holidays with the combined families. Meeting the infamous Samantha. Baby G would have arrived by then, and they would all be together. Christmas had never been a big affair for Harper. It was usually only Martha and him or Harper and Tanya. Though, he couldn't remember the last time Harper had spent time with Tanya.

When was the last time Harper had talked to her mother?

Charlie didn't sleep that night. By four, Stan was restless from his restlessness and wanted to wake up. When he turned on the lights and turned on the coffee, he heard footsteps on the back staircase leading up to the apartment. Then a knock.

Stan ran to the door but didn't bark. Was it Evelyn? Or was Harper back? He looked at the time. Harper wouldn't wake up this early.

He noticed the long, blonde hair pulled back. Renee stood with her back toward the window.

"Charlie?" Renee said.

He wasn't ready to talk. He couldn't even begin to think about the store at that moment. But he also couldn't let Renee down. He had brought this whole thing up, so he opened the door.

"Good morning, Renee," he said, wondering how she was feeling about all of this. Had Evelyn continued the conversation after he left? Had she talked to Renee, convinced her what he did wasn't right?

"I'm really sorry about all this," she said.

He shook his head, waving his hand at the kitchen table that sat in the middle of the room. "Come in."

He walked to the cabinet and pulled out two mugs. "Tea?"

"Sure, thank you." She sat, her hand holding her belly.

They didn't speak as he fixed her a cup of hot water, then he passed her a box of assorted teas. "Not much of a tea drinker."

She picked around and pulled out a lemon ginger. "I've been drinking mostly chocolate milkshakes."

He smiled at the joke, glad she tried to lighten the mood. "I should be the one who's sorry."

He had thought asking Renee first had been the right choice. Boy had he been wrong. *Men are certainly from Mars*, he thought.

"I love my mom," she said. "But you have nothing to be sorry about."

She opened the packet of the tea and dropped the bag into the water before pulling the string like a fishing line up and down in the water.

"I should've run everything by her first."

"I want to do it." Renee put the string down and faced him. "I want to make Books and Bread happen."

He wanted time before he had to answer. He was a man of his word. Yet, he'd be betraying one of them by keeping his word.

"I want to invest my own money," she said.

He cocked his head. "You want to invest?"

She nodded. "I'm calling my attorney this morning and telling him I'll accept Harry's offer."

He shook out his hands. "I can't have you do that."

But he could feel her resolve as she sat across from him. Her big eyes were determined to make this work.

He understood why Renee wanted to turn down Harry's offer. Tanya's child support payments hardly covered her portion for food, and like a faucet, the payments had stopped as soon as Harper turned eighteen, even though she had still lived at home, had still attended high school. As far as Tanya was concerned, she'd been done being a parent.

"The money will just end up with the attorneys if I don't agree," she said. "I want to go in on this with you, fifty-fifty." She placed papers on the table. "I researched the property values around the area, along with the payment for your brand." She pointed to a number circled at the bottom of the spreadsheet. "I want to be a partner and have a voice."

He understood the need of being an equal, but he couldn't ask her to risk her savings. He had proved he wasn't that strong of a business partner. "What does your mother think?"

"I don't think business partners ask their mommies what they think." Renee crossed her legs. "I know this business. I can put Books and Bread on the map."

He smiled, then immediately frowned. "I believe you could."

"But?" she said.

"You're here, not your mother." He took in a long breath before saying, "And that's a problem."

Renee's head slanted to the side. "She's upset, I get that. But she's wrong."

He didn't want to speak about Evelyn, especially without her.

"I feel as though everything and everyone should be included in the conversation so no one feels left out." He was sure of that more than anything.

Renee uncrossed her legs, adjusting her position in the chair. "I know she's trying to protect me, but this is my business, not Evelyn's. I don't intrude on her writing business." She sat back. "The fact is, I need this. I can't live in the garage with my son and be fine with that. I need to find a job. I need a place to live. I need to be working to be a good mother for my son. Charlie, I need this."

Her eyes pleaded with him.

He believed in Renee and had no doubt she would make the place a success. But he also knew if he agreed to this, Evelyn would be even more upset.

"I'm afraid I can't, Renee. I'm sorry."

CHAPTER 19

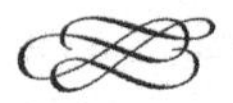

Renee walked out to the car as soon as Harper pulled up to the house in her MINI Cooper. "Thank you so much for coming with me."

Renee clicked her seat belt and Harper pulled away. "No problem."

Renee didn't deserve the friendship Harper was so willing to offer after her behavior this summer, but she appreciated it nonetheless. "This whole thing shouldn't take too long."

The excitement and butterflies she felt earlier when thinking about her new possibilities had now turned to wasps as they drove toward her attorney's office. Well, her mother's attorney's office, who she'd be able to pay once she cashed in Harry's guilt money.

"I just have to sign the papers and we can go," she said flatly. She pictured Harry's face when the papers arrived at his office in midtown Chicago. He'd probably leave them to his assistant like he usually did with all things relating to her. As much as she loved Harry Winthrop, she also equally despised him.

"Maybe your mom's right. Maybe you should think about this before you commit," Harper said.

"Do you want to continue to live off your father?" Renee's

question was rhetorical because she knew dang well Harper wanted her own independence more than she did.

"Tell me how to get there," Harper answered.

Renee smiled. Never in a million years would she have imagined that she would think of her mother's boyfriend's daughter as a sister, but Harper had been the one she'd confessed her plans to regarding her future. Harper had been the one who had encouraged her to go for her dreams. And Harper was the one now who walked her through the next phase of her life: complete independence.

"Take a right at the end of the road," Renee said.

It took twenty-five minutes to get there and find a parking spot. It may have been mid-September, but Oak Bluffs was still crowded with tourists. Renee paid the parking fee and went back to the car.

"I'll be fine by myself." She said this as a casual request, but if she was going to sign this agreement, she would have to do it on her own. Not with her mother, not with a friend—just her. "It should only be a few minutes, but I can meet you at the square if you want to walk around."

Harper put on her sunglasses, looking down the street.

"I'm going to go find a bench to sit and read." She patted her burlap bag that crossed against her chest.

"I'll see you in a bit," Renee said, walking up to the office's door.

Like most of the buildings in Oak Bluffs, the office resembled the Victorian clapboard that was so prevalent around the island. Yet inside, sleek modern furniture filled the very updated interior.

"Ms. Rose?" the front secretary asked as she walked in. "Ms. Parker is waiting in her office."

The secretary walked her down the hall and stopped outside the door. "Can I get you anything?"

Renee shook her head. She wanted to get this over with. "No, thank you."

She entered the office and Ms. Parker stood up. "Renee, it's good to see you."

They shook hands and Ms. Parker waved her hand at a table set up in the office. "I have everything ready for you to sign."

She walked Renee to the papers all lined up with a pen. "This is the agreement your ex-husband has proposed with his attorneys."

Renee looked at the black-and-white legal papers; everything appeared formal and final.

"A trust fund will be set up for the child after its birth," the attorney said.

She continued rattling off the key points of the divorce agreement. Harry, on paper, sounded like a very generous father. In the agreement, Renee would be taken care of and baby George would be given plenty, even up until adulthood. All she had to do was sign.

Renee picked up the pen, the lines blurring as her eyes watered. Ms. Parker handed her a box of tissues. She grabbed one, dotting her eyes. "Thanks."

She inhaled, nodding as she continued to stare at the spots marked by an *X*.

"Can you give him something with the papers?" she asked.

Ms. Parker looked curious. "Sure."

Renee opened her purse and pulled out her journal she had started carrying around with her. Inside, from her last ultrasound, she had a 3D picture of baby George. The image showed baby George so lifelike and real that she could count his little toes. She handed the attorney the photograph. "I'd like that to be delivered with the papers."

Renee leaned over the table and signed every single *X* in a flurry. Then she dropped the pen on the table.

"Thank you for handling everything for me," Renee said to the attorney.

Ms. Parker reached out her hand. "I really do believe this will allow you and your son to live comfortably."

She nodded but didn't say anything more. Instead, she put the journal back into her purse and walked out of the office. Her head spun from the significance of that one tiny moment.

She pulled out her phone and dialed the number.

"Are you okay?" Samantha said right as she picked up.

Renee didn't say anything at first but focused on a crack in the sidewalk. "I will be."

She wasn't sure, though.

"Mom's been calling me all morning," Samantha said.

Renee didn't care what Evelyn thought at this point. She had interfered like she had promised not to do. She had promised to be supportive. She had promised to go with whatever Renee wanted to do. Until it wasn't what she wanted her to do.

She could've expressed her opinions and left it at that, but instead, she had made the whole situation about her.

So what if Charlie didn't discuss his business idea with her? Did Evelyn involve Charlie with her business? Did Evelyn involve Renee?

No, she didn't.

Renee understood Evelyn's concerns, but sometimes meaning well and doing the right thing were two separate issues. Her opinion didn't make it right.

The fact was, Renee *could* make the bookstore more successful. She had devoted hours into studying the island of Martha's Vineyard and what it had to offer in the way of baked goods. The island had a dozen or so cafés and bakeries throughout the ninety-six square mile island, which seemed like a lot if someone scaled that to another area in the state of Massachusetts, even Boston. But as she studied each bakery, she realized she and Charlie had something different to offer. Most places were about grabbing a bite and going, but Books and Bread would be about grabbing a bite and staying. She didn't need to make huge profits. She wanted to create a community spot where people could come together and *be* together. It would be a refuge where people could take a break from the busy. A place to slow down and enjoy a sweet treat with friends and family. Charlie had already made that community. Now she would nourish it, and Renee knew she was good at that.

Even if Evelyn couldn't see it.

"This is good," Samantha said, almost as if feeling her doubt through the phone. "I promise, Harry Winthrop didn't make you Renee. *You* made you. And you helped make him into what he is now. He owes you this."

Renee had never missed Samantha more than she did right then. Only her sister would understand exactly how she felt. Could she do this all on her own? Be a mother, start a business, and be a great chef?

She inhaled a wobbling breath to steady her voice. "You're coming for the birth, right?"

She prayed Samantha would keep her promise.

"Yup, I'm planning on being there before the baby's born,"

In other words, Samantha wasn't making any promises. "I really want you to be here, Sam."

Renee could hear traffic in the background. Samantha had been in and out of London the past month, but her backpacking sister had been known to travel to a completely different continent without telling someone.

"I promise." But Samantha's promise felt empty and forced from Renee's pressure.

Renee could see Harper down the road, sitting on a bench, and she waved when she noticed Renee.

"I'm headed to a dressmaker on Prince Street downtown in the fashion district," Samantha said. Renee could hear Samantha hurrying to her next fabulous London adventure. "I'm meeting this woman who worked with Stella McCartney."

"That's awesome." Renee tried not to be neurotic. This wasn't about her. She didn't have to compare herself any longer. She had her own path, and today she chose it for herself. "I can't wait to see her work," she said back.

"I'll send you pics tonight." Samantha said goodbye with her usual promise to call, but Renee knew it would be her calling.

"I love you," Renee said before she hung up.

"I love you too."

Just as she went to put her phone back into her purse, a text from Evelyn popped up.

Call when you're done with your appointment.

She dropped her phone into her purse. She wasn't trying to be a jerk or make a statement by ignoring her mom's texts. She just wasn't ready to have that conversation.

She waved back to Harper and walked over to where she sat. "Do you mind if we just sit for a bit?"

Harper shook her head. "You okay?"

Renee sat on the bench and put her purse in her lap before taking out her journal. She held the book in her hands. "Yes, I'm going to be okay."

Harper wrapped her arm around Renee's shoulders and leaned into her. "You are going to be great. This is the right decision for you and George."

Renee held her breath, waiting for the tidal wave of emotions, but this time, the swell was only of one feeling... freedom.

Harper loosened her grip, and Renee opened the journal, taking out the pen stuffed in the binding. She turned to a clean page and wrote the date, then titled the page: My next adventure.

She turned the page.

"There's something I need to tell you," Harper said, looking up from her phone.

"What is it?" Renee looked at her, not sure if she could take more news.

Harper's face twisted as she started to speak. "You know, if you need some space, you're always welcome to stay at my place."

Renee wished she could take the offer, but she needed to follow through on her end. She didn't want to fight with her mother and run away from their problems. This had been a long time coming. They had swept everything under the rug for way too long. They both needed to face the fact they hadn't really grieved their old lives.

Renee planned her speech the whole drive back to the house. She loved Evelyn with her whole being—she was the greatest mother a girl could've asked for—but she needed to back off. Her job as a parent was over, whether she wanted it to be or not. Renee needed to break out on her own and not have to ask for permission from her mother in order to live.

Harper dropped her off. Even Mateo, who waved from the garage, didn't come out like he usually would, almost sensing she needed to be alone with Evelyn.

When Renee walked inside, through the side door into the kitchen, Evelyn stood there behind the counter.

"I owe you an apology," Evelyn said right away.

Her words made Renee stop in the doorframe.

"I should've stayed out of your business."

"You're right," Renee said.

"But your business with Charlie *is* my business," Evelyn said. Her point throughout their argument last night.

"So, this isn't an apology?" Renee shook her head. Her mother apparently hadn't thought about her side yet.

"I am sorry." Evelyn held the counter. "I know you are going to be wonderful at whatever you do in your future, especially with baking. You've just developed into this master chef."

"Then what's the problem?" Because Renee really wanted to know. "I don't understand."

Evelyn slanted her head to the side but looked like she was having trouble saying the whole truth.

"Are you afraid Charlie isn't going to follow through?" Renee really wanted to see her mother's side, but every excuse she came up with didn't make sense.

"No." Evelyn slumped onto a stool. She let out a long breath. "The truth is… I'm not sure if I want the same thing as Charlie."

This was news to Renee. "Are you saying you want to break up?"

Renee hadn't even thought of the possibility that her mother didn't want to continue the relationship with Charlie.

"Of course not, but..." Her mother hesitated, and for the first time in Renee's life, she looked vulnerable.

"He keeps talking about things I'm not ready for," Evelyn said. "Marriage, retirement, things like traveling."

"That sounds wonderful," Renee said. Didn't the women and her talk about that stuff all the time? Her career was based on writing happily ever afters. "You seem so happy together."

"Yes, but"—Evelyn hesitated for a moment—"I'm scared." For the first time in Renee's life, she saw fear in Evelyn's eyes. "If things don't work out, I could lose him, but I could also lose you too."

"You won't lose me." Renee sighed, regretting saying what she had about Samantha, because Samantha wasn't only running from Evelyn. She was running from Renee and their father's death too. "I shouldn't have said what I did."

"It's got to be slightly true," Evelyn said. "I've hardly heard from the two of you these past five years. Now, I got you back in my life, and I don't want anything to ruin it." Evelyn took Renee's arm and squeezed it. "I'm sorry. I don't want to fight, but I'm just scared."

"I'll figure something out," Renee said. "I could probably find a rental on the mainland somewhere close."

"Let me help you find something on the island," Evelyn said, but Renee started shaking her head immediately.

"I appreciate everything you've done for me," Renee said, holding up her hands as Evelyn opened her mouth to argue. "But I need to do this on my own."

"Do you want to stay on the island?" Evelyn asked.

Renee did want to stay. She wanted to raise her son around her family, to live in a community where people took care of each other, celebrated each other's accomplishments. She wanted her son to breathe in salty air and fall asleep to the quiet roar of the waves coming into shore.

"I want to, yes, but that's not really an option anymore." Renee didn't want to leave. She had nowhere else to go.

"What do you mean?" Evelyn asked. "What about the bookstore?"

"Charlie doesn't want to do it any longer." Renee didn't blame him for pulling back his offer. He loved Evelyn and didn't want to upset her.

Evelyn rested her hand on Renee's arm. "Let me talk to him."

Renee didn't want to get in the middle of the two of them. "No, I don't want to be the reason you don't work out."

Evelyn got off the stool and stood in front of Renee, holding her elbows in the palms of her hands. "I will support you with whatever you want to do."

"I thought you two were really happy?" Renee didn't understand the sudden doubt.

"We are." Evelyn looked around the room. "But why move so fast and change things that are working? I like that my daughter is living with me and my friends. I like that my boyfriend comes for dinner and stays for a movie but goes home to his apartment. I like our big dinners with everyone around the table in my house. I like things the way they are."

Renee looked around her mother's kitchen. The gourmet range and stove could handle her daily baking no doubt. She could watch the baby while she baked at home, with the help of the women. There wasn't a ton of room. She'd have to be creative with her time, extremely organized, and willing to work long and hard. The truth was, she could run a successful business with or without Charlie.

"Maybe I could do some sort of catering thing here." Renee patted the counter. "Start small. Build it up over time."

Evelyn held Renee against her.

"Oh! I felt the baby kick!" She held Renee's belly with her hands. "Oh! There he is again."

The two laughed as George kicked again.

"He'll be George Rose, Jr.," Renee said, realizing he wouldn't take the last name Winthrop.

Evelyn smiled, but her worry lines returned. "It's going to be wonderful having another Rose."

"You and Charlie are really good together," Renee said. Charlie was perfect for her mother. "I know if you told him how you feel, he'd be understanding."

Evelyn shook her head. "How do I tell him that I want to slow down without hurting his feelings?"

"You just tell him the truth." It really was that simple.

"Shouldn't I be the one giving wise advice?" Evelyn asked, hugging Renee again.

"The apple doesn't fall far from the tree."

Renee felt like she could hold on for good. She had forgotten how safe she felt inside her mother's arms. At four, or sixteen, or twenty-eight, she'd always feel safe in her mother's arms.

"Go talk to him," Renee said.

Evelyn walked to the key holder and picked up her phone and car keys. "I'll be back."

Renee watched her pull out of the driveway just as Bitty came into the room.

"How'd it go today in town?" Bitty asked, referring to the divorce papers.

"I signed everything," Renee said, pulling out her journal and dropping it on the counter. She walked to the pantry and started pulling out the ingredients she needed to prep for tomorrow's inventory. "I'm officially divorced."

She tried to laugh and ease the worry on Bitty's face.

But Bitty stopped her, placing her hand on her shoulder. "Someone told me a piece of advice when I divorced my first husband, which was: your journey may look different than everyone else's, but it's yours." Bitty paused to let it sink in. "Live the life you want to live."

Bitty dug in her pocket and handed over a blue piece of sea

glass naturally forming the shape of a heart. "Let's go throw that into the ocean."

Bitty led the way outside, down the back porch to the edge of the lawn, and down the wooden-planked path to the beach. Renee squeezed the piece of glass in her palm, then rubbed its dulled edges with her thumb. She looked out at the water, white-caps foaming for miles out to sea.

She would chase her dreams and choose her own path.

Renee stopped at the top of the waves, opened her palm, and looked at the piece of glass.

"Think of all the things you want to let go and toss them with the glass into the ocean." Bitty squeezed her hands together, prayer style. "Let go of the past."

She thought about when she had first met Harry. How young and naïve she had been. She hadn't known her talents, hadn't known her strengths. She thought she needed Harry to be successful. Needed him to move her career forward in *his* restaurants, under *his* guidance. She thought her loyalty to his brand was building a business for *their* future. But it was all a ruse. Harry Winthrop had only cared about himself and his career. No one else. She had thought his possessiveness for her work was love. She thought his control was to protect her. And like a business deal, he had negotiated what worked best for him.

"I'm only moving forward from this point on," Renee said out loud. She pulled her arm back, then tossed the piece of glass into the water. A small splash on the water showed where the glass landed as it instantly disappeared into the gray sea.

Bitty gave out a holler and a "That a girl."

But Renee had no idea how freeing the whole experience was going to be. The weight lifted off her, the burden floating away with the waves.

She was free.

CHAPTER 20

Evelyn met Charlie at the pier. Stan sat on the concrete in a patch of sun as Charlie looked out at the harbor. It was practically in the same spot where they'd first broken up as twenty-year-olds. The world had been at their fingertips—Charlie leaving for Los Angeles; Evelyn leaving for graduate school. Things immediately and forever changed after they had walked away. She wondered if he had planned it that way. He loved his symbolism.

She didn't wait for him to talk, didn't even wait for him to acknowledge her presence, just went straight into things. "I'm sorry I freaked out about everything, and I wish I had taken a cue from everyone to let go and trust you, but I got scared."

"I should've talked to you about things before I went and offered anything to your daughter."

The acknowledgement wasn't as satisfying as she had wanted it to be. As she stood there, she wished she could've done everything over, behaved completely different.

"No, I was projecting my own fears onto the two of you," she said.

Recognition flickered in his eyes. "You're not the only one afraid, Evelyn."

And like the clouds over her head, her thoughts began to untangle.

"I wake up thinking about you and go to bed dreaming of you," he said. "I want to move forward, and I'm ready for the next steps, but I can be patient."

How could she tell him she might never be? "I can't make any promises."

Charlie leaned his elbows on the railing, looking over the water. "I never asked you to make any."

Her breath caught in her throat, when just then, a seagull floated out in front of them, gliding in the sunshine, flying just above the water's surface. And she started seeing the situation as if she were looking from the outside in. Charlie had been nothing but open about his feelings. Yet, she had been the one worried. Why didn't she trust him? "You're right. I am judging you for back then."

He didn't say anything, and the silence between them made her swallow her pride and finally admit the truth. "I'm afraid that you'll see through this shiny exterior, the fancy beach house, and see the same insecure girl who wasn't exciting enough to stay with."

"That's where you're wrong. You were always exciting." Charlie paused for a long moment, but Evelyn could tell he wasn't done speaking. "I love you, Evelyn, but I can't fix something my twenty-year-old self did. All I can do is be the fifty-five-year-old man who has learned from his past mistakes."

She could feel her emotions rising. "That's the man I love. The man who would do anything for those around him, including his girlfriend's daughter."

He turned and faced her. He wrapped his arms around her waist and pulled her into his embrace, then kissed her on the lips, long and with everything he had in his body. He showed her that his love was very real. Her fingers reached into his hair, tangling them in his curls, pulling him closer to her, taking in his lips with hers as he kissed her.

She pressed her forehead against his as they regained their breath, intertwining her fingers into his.

"Be patient," she said in a whisper. "I'm still figuring out who I am."

He kissed her lips softly, lightly. "I'm going nowhere."

CHAPTER 21

Renee sat in the waiting room at Wanda's infusion. Her mother had to get ready for the writer's group, so she agreed to bring Wanda. Bitty sat next to her, reading a home décor magazine.

"Your momma's house is prettier than all of these," she said, flipping the page.

"My parents' house back home is very modest," Renee said, almost wanting to show their humble beginnings. "A two story. Nothing fancy. Nothing like Sea View. Our house doesn't have a name."

"Will you two go back?" Bitty asked.

Renee adjusted to her other hip. Sitting had increasingly become more and more uncomfortable.

"I'd like to go back before the baby." Renee wondered about her mother's next step. Would she hold on to the house? Was there a point without Daddy? Would Samantha want it? Renee didn't want it. But she didn't want to let it go either.

"I think that'd be good for your mom," Bitty said. "I think she has some ghost to reckon with."

"My dad?" Renee knew the answer but wanted Bitty to go

deeper. "Do you think that's why she's so worried about everything with Charlie?"

Bitty nodded. "That and everything else. I think your mother is learning to become someone new, but she's reached a point where she can't get any further without letting go of the person she was in the past."

Renee saw how instead of dealing with the loss of her father, she had gone straight into a relationship with Harry. Besides him being her superior, Harry was also fifteen years older than her. He had been established in his career, owned businesses, houses, properties. He had found success already, and she was able to join along under his guidance.

But her age was something Harry frequently used against her, chalking up her youth as a hindrance. She had less experience, less knowledge. He would make comments about her success as though it was luck or his help that got her there, though he did nothing to support her. What Harry never understood about his wife was what she brought to the business.

She knew her customers. Did she really want to serve big Kobe beef burgers in her gourmet kitchen? No, but high-ego businessmen liked burgers. Did she want to have forty-three draft beers and barely a dozen wines on her wine list? It absolutely broke her heart at times that she had Dr. Pepper shots being chugged at the bar, but she knew that's what the bar crowd wanted on a Thursday night before they did. That was Renee's superpower. She could read what people wanted.

Her thoughts drifted from one to another quickly. One minute she was thinking about learning to ride her bike with Samantha and being scared. Then she thought about teaching Baby G on his bike, and if she'd be like her dad and let go or be like her mother and never loosen her grip. She thought about Charlie and her speech about why she would have made a great business partner. She thought about the offer she'd given him—half of the money she was getting from Harry. The guilt money, the payoff, the I-don't-have-to-be-a-father debt he'd given to her. The rest of his money would go to her baby. The lump sum, including payments until he turned eighteen. Harry had given her a generous settlement—even Samantha had told her to take it—but a little part of her wished she hadn't. She wanted to let him live with the guilt. Let him remember he'd done absolutely nothing for his son.

Evelyn warned her that he might change his mind. He might have some epiphany and suddenly want to become a father. She wanted it in writing that he'd have nothing to do with him. Ever.

"When will you come back?" Renee asked out of the blue, her thoughts suddenly wandering again.

Bitty clicked her tongue. "Honestly?"

Renee smiled at first, thinking Bitty was her usual upbeat self, but she fiddled with the back of her earring. Her foot bobbed up and down.

"Richard's children want me out of the house," Bitty said, pulling on her earlobe now.

"What?" Renee couldn't believe it. "I thought you said they would let you stay as long as you can afford the payments."

She nodded. "His youngest now wants it for himself. And since he's the estate's owner, he can legally have me evicted. He gave me two weeks from the day I return."

Renee couldn't believe it. "I thought you got along great with Richard's son?"

Bitty shrugged, but her eyes stayed focused in front of her.

"Stay with us," Renee said.

"Your mother is in love with a man who wants more than to just be neighbors. And I don't think he wants her homeless friend staying in the guest room."

"Evelyn and Charlie are not getting married anytime soon," Renee said. "Stay with us. You can be here to help me with the baby."

Renee hoped she'd reconsider the idea. She would love to have a nurse down the hall with a newborn.

Bitty's anxiety didn't seem to dissipate. Her worry lines only deepened as she sat there.

"The worst part is..." Bitty paused. "I asked my son to stay with him and his family until I find a decent place, and he told me they didn't have the room."

"Oh, Bitty." Renee couldn't imagine how Bitty felt hearing that.

Bitty clasped her hands together over her knee, her foot bobbing more intensely. "After all I did for my son, and he can't spare me a couch."

Renee leaned over the wooden armrest separating the seats. She slipped her arm under Bitty's and hooked on, sliding close to her friend. When she first met her mother's friends, she would've never considered them to be *her* friends too. Now she couldn't consider living without them.

"Stay, Bitty, Stay." Renee caught Bitty's eyes. "Stay with us. We're your family, too."

Bitty shook her head. "Your mother never intended for me to stay past this summer."

"There's plenty of room."

Bitty narrowed her eyes. "What if she wants to be alone? Or get married?"

"Then we'll move out." Renee wasn't going to let Bitty go anywhere else now that she had nowhere else to go. "We'll find a place."

"You want to live with a sixty-year-old?" Bitty now looked bewildered. "Don't give up that easily Renee. You're a beautiful girl. You're going to find happiness with someone very soon, believe me."

"First of all, I like living with everyone right now." Then Renee rolled her eyes. "Besides, no man in their right mind wants to date a woman who's pregnant with another man's baby."

"Never say never," Bitty said, her eyebrow raising to the ceiling.

Renee shook her head, ready to change the topic, when she remembered what she had wanted to ask Bitty in private.

"Have you noticed Wanda's hair?" Renee asked. She had noticed Wanda wearing the scarves more and more, with large sun hats. Her visor with the open back she loved so much had been sitting in the mudroom.

Bitty nodded. "It's beginning to fall out."

"But she's wearing the cooling cap." Renee felt horrible. Wanda had been so stressed about losing her red curls. She felt devastated for her.

"Stay, Bitty." Renee couldn't drop it. She knew what being stubborn could do. She took Bitty's hand in hers. "You should stay for the winter at least."

"I can't afford to live here on the island." Bitty's face fell. "I'm not sure where I'm going to live. I might have to go back to work."

"Stay with me. I need someone to take care of the baby, and then there's Wanda." Renee squeezed Bitty's hand. "Stay. At least until you figure things out."

Then just as Renee was about to beg, Wanda walked back into the waiting room. Her face looked paler, the bags under her eyes hung lower, deeper in color.

Wanda didn't look well today.

Bitty patted her hand and got up to meet Wanda. "You ready?"

Wanda looked worn down and exhausted but pretended as though nothing beyond a normal procedure happened down the hall.

"I met someone who is originally from Texas," Wanda told them as they walked out.

Renee didn't know why, but she felt like calling her mother and telling her about how she told Bitty to stay, like a kid who got an award for doing something good at school. When she had first heard Evelyn opened her house to Bitty and Wanda, she wasn't surprised. That was just who Evelyn was. When Renee had won her softball tournament, Evelyn had invited the whole team to the house. Evelyn would always allow sleepovers, family to stay, big dinners for friends, and always joined community events. Evelyn believed in including everyone and always showed how much she loved them by opening her heart to them.

And as Renee stood by the elevator, rubbing Baby G with her hands, everything suddenly clicked. All this time, she had been so worried that she'd never be as good of a mother as Evelyn Rose. Or as good of a career woman as her mother. She feared she wouldn't be able to build a business while also raising a child. She felt like a failure who had lost a husband. She assumed if the same ingredients weren't there, she'd never make herself into Evelyn.

But she didn't have to follow the recipe if she had the foundation. She could veer off, do her own thing, and be true to what Evelyn had taught her all these years: open her heart to others, accept help, practice self-forgiveness, and never give up on your dreams. She had everything right in front of her the whole time to be a good mom—her mom.

After pulling out her phone, she texted Samantha. **I think I found a nanny and a roommate.**

Me? she replied with a laughing face emoji. The comment surprised Renee. Hmm. Did Samantha want to return to the States?

No. Bitty.

Dots flashed across the bottom on Samantha's side of the conversation. **Mom's Golden Girl friend?**

Yes. Renee looked up to see if Bitty or Wanda were paying attention to her text, but the two were talking about Wanda's sandals. Renee began to type again. **Besides, she's my friend.** Renee sent a kissy-face, winky-face emoji back. **But seriously, get your plane ticket. Baby G's coming sooner than later. I'm huge.**

The dots flashed but suddenly disappeared. By the time they reached the car in the parking lot, Samantha hadn't texted back.

Renee tried to shake the sinking sensation that Samantha

wasn't going to come. She thought about how she could confront Samantha, who was known to be the most sensitive of the Rose family, but also convince her to come out. She tapped the steering wheel without thinking.

"You okay?" Wanda asked. She looked even more petite in the passenger's side next to the tubalub Renee felt like.

"Yes, just thinking about my sister."

"Samantha?" Wanda asked, though Samantha was Renee's only sister.

Renee nodded. "I think she's going to miss the baby's birth."

"Well, if she does, we'll be here for you," Bitty said as she rubbed her back with her hand. But instead of feeling sorry for herself, Renee focused on the exact word Wanda did.

"We?" Wanda turned to face Bitty in the back seat.

Bitty looked out the window. "I've decided to stay until the baby comes and maybe stay while I figure some things out."

Wanda slapped her hands together. "Well, I think that sounds like a marvelous plan."

Wanda closed her eyes the rest of the ride to the ferry. Even though she smiled and seemed interested throughout their conversation, she was more distant and quieter than usual.

When they finally reached the house, Renee was so lost in her worries about Wanda that she didn't pay attention to all the cars lined up along Cliffside Point Road. She even recognized some of the cars from working those few weeks at the bookstore. Maybe people were at the beach? When she saw the other cars parked along the driveway, they were regulars like Mateo, Hank, Harper, and Charlie, so she wasn't suspicious.

Maybe it was baby brain or the fact she had been thinking about Wanda and Bitty and Samantha, but she didn't even notice the sign saying *Welcome, Baby George!* Or the blue balloons hanging off the lamppost and the railings to the porch. Only once she walked into the house did she realize something wasn't right. She didn't hear anything.

"Surprise!" People jumped out of the corners, from behind the furniture, and from out of the dining room.

"Ahh!" She held her stomach as though the shock might send her into labor.

She looked around the room, and she noticed the person in the corner.

"Nobody puts Samantha in the corner!" Renee ran to her sister and hugged her with everything in her body.

"Look at your belly!" Samantha pulled out of Renee's embrace to see her transformation. "Look at your ankles."

Renee pointed to her swollen feet. "I know! I grew two shoe sizes."

The sisters hugged again as the crowd gathered around them. Everyone welcomed Samantha while also congratulating Renee.

"Samantha! I can't believe you're here." Renee squeezed her sister again. Tears floated on her eyelids. She hadn't realized how much she had missed her sister. Once people moved around the room, talking to each other, and Renee had a second alone with her, she said, "I'm so sorry."

Samantha gave her a side glance, her eyes narrowing with doubt.

"I was a total jerk." Renee had never meant to upset Samantha. She'd never meant the words that came out that day. She just hadn't needed advice; she needed her sister.

"I know, you loser." Samantha squeezed her back. When Samantha released her, she looked down. "Me too."

Renee could feel her heart swelling as she looked around the room. She rested her head on Samantha's shoulder before joining the group and said, "I'm so glad you're here."

CHAPTER 22

Mateo didn't know how he ended up being Harper's assistant for the afternoon, but there he was setting up for Renee's baby shower, blowing up balloons, draping blue and white streamers from one wall to the next, and arranging the crib exactly where she told him to.

The conversation stayed on the weather and about her book's release and her directions.

"Did you hear that Renee finalized her divorce?" Harper said.

He shook his head, sad for her suddenly. "She okay? Should you even have this shower?"

Harper looked over, pausing to think about her answer. "You know? I think she is okay."

He nodded but wondered if that was just Renee. With everything life had thrown at her, he had to admit Renee had been extremely resilient through it all. He was most certain none of it had been easy. He'd never forget the look on her face at Prayer Cove. But the cliffs on Martha's Vineyard stood tall even after years of being pounded by the waves. And in his opinion, the cliffs' perseverance made them even more beautiful. Just like Renee.

"I guess he offered a big settlement, and Renee now has the

money to maybe start her own bakery." Harper put her hand on her hip. "She wants to partner up with my dad. They'll need to renovate it. It's going to be a lot of work."

He didn't want to assume Charlie and Renee would want him and his brothers to work on the project, but he could take Harper's hint.

"She knows where to find me," he said, non-committal. But working on a store on Harbor Lane would be a whole new ball game. He'd been in the major leagues. Lots of street cred as Elias would say. Showing the rest of the businesses on the harbor that the Perez Brothers could do interior renovations. That would elevate everything.

"Isn't that great? That means she's staying here on the island."

He suddenly noticed this had been the first time since the kiss that Harper had seemed comfortable to talk to him again. Would he have taken back the kiss? It had changed everything. But, if he hadn't kissed her, he'd be following her around, begging for her attention, wishing he had kissed her, not knowing exactly how she felt.

"That's great news," he said. "Have you heard much about her ex?"

It wasn't his business, but curiosity got the best of him.

She shook her head. "Just that he was willing to pay a lot of money to get out of any responsibility."

Mateo could feel a burn inside his chest as he hoped he'd never meet this guy.

"This is going to be so cute," Harper said, arranging the stuffed animals on top of the new sheets he'd put on.

He wondered if Harper wanted children. He had never really asked her. Their conversations weren't usually deep. They usually talked about working, writing, and anything to do with the island. They never really mentioned stuff around relationships and family and what they wanted in the future.

"I thought I'd have a gaggle of kids by now," he said.

"Gaggle?" She laughed at his choice of words, plucking up an octopus and placing it in the crib.

"It's what they call geese babies."

"I know, but I just can't see you with a goose." She winked at him. Then, she adjusted a stuffed whale in the corner. "I don't even want children."

"Really?" Mateo said, surprised. Harper had always been so over the top when she saw his niece and nephews when they were babies. "You squealed when you saw the crib."

"I'm not afraid of the baby. More afraid of being a bad parent." Harper's eyes floated away from his. She bit her bottom lip and moved to the dining room table, shuffling the decorations around and fixing a diaper tower.

"You'd be a great mom, are you kidding?" he said from the crib. "But I don't think everyone needs to be a mom or a dad." Being a parent wasn't the only choice in life. "Being an uncle is the coolest."

"I don't have any siblings," Harper reminded him.

"You'll be auntie to my kids." He gave her a smile. A truce.

She tilted her head and her lip moved up. She understood the olive branch had been extended. "You mean your gaggle?"

"I mean someday," he said to her as she walked back into the living room. He tried to shift the conversation and pointed to the stack of tagboard game cards. "Baby bingo?"

"Do you have anyone in mind for this gaggle?" she asked, passing by him, but he could see her eye follow him. She wanted to see his reaction.

He shook his head.

He stopped and studied Harper. Her magnetism was undeniable. Her beauty, like the island itself, so gorgeous it could sweep the breath out of your lungs. But as they stood there, they were a complete juxtaposition, two adults with two very different paths. He realized this would be the closest he'd ever be with Harper, friends, and he was okay with that.

"How's the guy?" he asked. "Gerard?"

She shrugged. "Okay."

He nodded, noticing her silence, and he didn't push the subject further. He'd just be there when she needed a friend. "You two should come for a barbeque at the house."

"Really?" she asked, not holding back her surprise.

"Yes, really," he said, stuffing his hands into his pocket, but it sounded like a horrible idea.

Harper's eyes narrowed and she studied him for a moment. She smiled mischievously and asked, "How do you feel about Renee staying on the island?"

"I'm glad she's figuring out what's best for her and the baby." Which was the truth. Mateo wanted nothing more than for Renee to find happiness on the island. "I loved growing up here. It's safe. It's got everything a kid needs: water, sand, bike paths, everything."

"It was a great place to grow up." She looked at him and gave him a half smile. "You did a beautiful job on the crib."

"Thanks. I'm glad to do it." He had enjoyed it. The hours he'd spent working on the crib had been something he had looked forward to at night. He enjoyed creating something that would be special for Renee and the baby. He liked using his hands, his mind focused on the task, not all the extra stuff floating in his head.

When people arrived for the shower, Charlie came with Evelyn to finish setting up, and Mateo was relieved he wasn't going to be the only dude there. Better, Hank and Marty came around the same time, walking in together. Some of the other members of the writers' group came, but he only recognized his old English teacher, Anita White. Evelyn made everyone comfortable and collected drinks. Julia came next, surprising Mateo. Harper even included his nephews and niece, who were already eating from the table of food set up.

Harper suddenly froze, waving her arms at Evelyn. "She's here!"

When Mateo looked out the window to see Renee, he saw

someone who could be considered her double but wasn't pregnant.

Harper slapped him with the back of her hand on the chest. "That's Samantha, Evelyn's youngest daughter."

Walking into the house was a shorter and slightly different version of Renee. Mateo watched as the room introduced themselves to the newcomer.

"Welcome to Martha's Vineyard," Hank said, shaking her hand.

"It's gorgeous. I'm so glad I'm here," Samantha cheerfully said back to him. The rest of the crowd welcomed her to the festivities.

"This is Mateo," Evelyn said as she led Samantha to him. "He's the brilliance behind the renovations."

"I've heard all about you." Samantha looked him up and down as she held out her hand. "You've done an amazing job."

His eyebrows wondered how the Rose women described him. "Nice to meet you."

"Renee told me about your house," Samantha said. "She said it was really beautiful. I actually run a blog where I showcase fine art and living. I'd love to showcase your work."

"You two should come by and see it for yourself," he said, but then he felt silly as he talked to her. Just like her sister, her beauty was mesmerizing.

She smiled. "I'd like that."

Samantha moved to another one of Evelyn's guests as he stepped back into the background, wishing he could be anywhere but a baby shower.

"She's really beautiful." Harper craned her neck to get a better view of Samantha.

"How long is she staying?" he asked. He hadn't heard anything about her visit.

"She's leaving in a couple days," Harper said.

Mateo suddenly felt sad for Renee. He'd wanted his brothers and sister-in-law around when he had his first child. But as he watched Evelyn walk Samantha around the room, he realized how many people were there for the island's newest local. Renee hadn't been here more than a few months, and the house was full of people supporting her.

"She's here!" Charlie shouted and everyone scrambled to a hiding spot.

Evelyn stood in the foyer. Harper snuck behind a door. Anita crouched behind the dining room table. Others hid on the back deck. He could see Renee coming up the walkway with Bitty and Wanda. She looked good, smiling, radiant. An energy inside his chest warmed as she came inside, and he could feel his heart speeding up, excited for her to see the crib he'd built for her.

"Surprise!" they all shouted out as she walked through the door.

"Ah!" She grabbed her stomach. The celebration suddenly became silent, not sure how to respond until she laughed out loud. A jubilee rang throughout the room as Renee hugged her sister and then Evelyn.

Mateo hadn't been to many baby showers, if ever, but he enjoyed himself as the village of Eastport all mingled. And it wasn't all women either. Mateo stood on the back porch talking to Marty with Hank for a while.

"You really delivered through Hurricane Irene?" he asked, impressed with the honor of duty that Marty had.

"Rain, sleet, or snow," Marty said.

From behind him, Harper grabbed his elbow and whispered in his ear. "She's about to open the presents."

Harper pulled him into the house, where Renee sat next to Samantha on a couch. He stood in the back, leaning against the frame of the opening to the dining room.

One by one, she opened gifts from the group. Hand-knitted blankets, baby books, diapers, and adorable clothes that made all the women *oh* and *ah* over. Just when he was thinking of a reason to bow out, Harper gestured her hand like Vanna White toward the crib.

"That's Mateo's gift," Harper said to Renee, but Harper's eyes were on him.

He looked away from Harper's gaze to Renee's reaction. She stood up from the couch and walked over to where the crib sat in the corner of the room. She covered her face with both hands, then looked at Mateo. "You built the crib?"

She walked up to his handcrafted crib, framed with a knotty maple. It looked exactly like the image she had shown him but better.

"Mateo." She stopped in front of the piece of furniture, rubbing her hand against the railing. "It's beautiful."

Mateo had even purchased a mattress, and the nautical sheets and stuffed sea life were all shades of blue and orange. He'd found a stuffed Green Monster that he stuck among the other stuffed animals. What if the kid wanted to play baseball someday?

She rubbed her belly, and only when he looked hard did he realize she was crying. "Oh no. Do you not like it?"

She wiped her eyes, then before he could take hold of his stance, she hugged him, taking him in her arms, stuffing her belly against him in a full bear hug.

"This is the nicest gift anyone has ever given me," she cried in his shirt. "I love it."

The whole room awed and laughed at the same time. People got up from their spots to see the crib themselves, since the presents were done. Once Renee let go of him, a buzzing feeling filled his whole body.

"I can't believe you built this," she said, her attention back on the crib. She didn't seem to notice his body temperature rising or the fact he couldn't stop staring at her.

He wanted to explain how he'd chiseled the decorative indentations by hand as she brushed her fingertips over them, or how he'd built it to scale for her height and had followed every safety procedure, but he stayed silent as he watched her check it out.

"It's just gorgeous." She picked up the Green Monster and

squeezed it against her chest. "It's the perfect way to begin this new chapter of my life."

A sense of relief moved through him because he realized she looked like she was finally at peace. As though her life finally found harmony that had been missing.

"I heard you're opening up a bakery with Charlie," he said.

She shrugged. "Well, maybe. It's not definite. But I am going to open a bakery. That I am definite about."

How could someone divorce her?

"You're incredibly brave," he said.

"Or incredibly stupid," she said, laughing to herself.

Mateo couldn't imagine becoming a parent now, but never could he imagine starting everything over and becoming a parent alone.

"No, just brave." Something twitched in his chest when he looked at her, like a flutter. He was too young to have heart palpitations, right? But every time he looked at her, running her hand along the crib's headboard, he couldn't help but stare. She was no longer just glowing in his eyes. She was the most beautiful woman he had ever laid eyes on.

She walked the perimeter of the crib and came back to his side, and he suddenly started overthinking everything, and cold sweats entered his swagger. What was he doing? She was someone else's wife up until yesterday. She wasn't looking for anything other than a business.

"Let me know if you need any work done for your bakery," he said, stepping back, putting some space between the two of them. "I'd love to help any way possible, especially if you make those empanadas."

She held out her hand to his, holding it in hers as she stayed focused on the crib. He wondered if his palm was sweaty.

"Thank you, Mateo," she said, holding it. She looked up at him. "Thank you for everything."

If the two of them weren't standing in the middle of a crowd, he was certain he would've kissed Renee. Thank God, Harper came, but not before she saw the look on his face when she returned. The smirk on her face said it all. She knew what he was thinking.

And it wasn't about the crib.

Her smile grew in recognition, and he needed to get out of there. "I should probably head out. I have a ton of work to do."

"Aren't you staying for food?" Renee asked.

He flashed a look to Harper, who now stood with Evelyn and her sister. "No, I've got work."

He took off as Harper was about to say something. He didn't even say goodbye.

What had gotten into him?

First, he kissed Harper and that ended up being an epic fail. Now, he almost kissed a pregnant woman who was the daughter of his biggest client?

Get yourself together. He smacked his forehead with his hand before jumping into the cab of his truck. He took off down the drive, out of Sea View and onto Cliffside Point, and headed back to his place. He needed to get his head straight before he messed even more things up.

CHAPTER 23

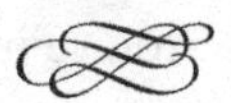

Renee lay on the couch in the living room and stared at the crib in the dark. Even with half of her mother's decorative pillows stuffed under her belly, they still didn't help her get comfortable. Nothing made her comfortable anymore. And she still had two full months of this?

She sat up and looked at the clock. Two thirty-six a.m. After turning on the lamp, she grabbed her journal and portfolio, or whatever she called her business plan, and opened it up to her massive to-do list. No sleep meant time to build her business plan. Put everything into place so that nothing could go wrong.

Vendors, equipment, and materials were just a few things on her list this morning. She needed to buy wholesale for some items. Ingredients were another issue. She wanted nothing but the best, but that would take more time. She needed to research and find local organic products for her baked goods. She expected to hire a few extra hands, but she'd be the only baker at the beginning, which, with a baby, posed some real obstacles. Could she keep up with the demands of a bakery with a newborn?

She looked at the crib.

She'd just have to do it. She'd have to keep up and make the bakery a success. She had no other choice.

As she turned on the light, she heard someone coming down the stairs.

"Wanda?" Renee looked at the clock to make sure she was right. "What are you doing up so early?"

"I'm ready," Wanda said. "You've inspired me to face my fears. I'm going to cut my hair."

"I inspired you?" Was Wanda being sarcastic? She was the one fighting a deadly illness. How did little, well, large young Renee inspire tiny, wise Wanda?

"You're very brave in my book," Wanda said.

She kept hearing it, but nothing inside her felt brave. "What did I inspire?"

"Well, I was sort of hoping you'd help me." She lifted a plastic container and opened it. Inside sat an electric clipper and all its accessories.

The first thing Renee wanted to do was suggest waking Evelyn up. She'd know what to do in this situation. But she didn't. She removed the electric clipper. "What length would you like?"

She was about to tell Wanda she'd never cut hair before, but she assumed Wanda hadn't picked her for her haircutting skills, and instead, she pulled out her phone. She threw on her mom's favorite album she'd often played when she and Samantha were little.

Carol King sang in the background. It felt cheesy—she almost apologized right then and there—but Wanda took hold of Renee's hand and held it there, singing a verse. Renee took off the scarf around Wanda's head. She had some thin patches on her scalp. Wanda's hands immediately began to itch her head.

"I just want a buzz." Wanda smiled. "I'll look like my brother, Tommy."

"Does Tommy live near you in Palm Springs?" Renee asked,

taking out a hair tie and pulling Wanda's hair back into a ponytail. She'd save what Wanda had left if she wanted.

"No, Tommy passed away some time ago." Wanda's fingers felt the tail. "Let's do it on the porch. I read somewhere that birds will use the hair for their nests."

"Don't you want to keep it?" Renee asked, following Wanda out onto the back patio.

"To remind me of who I was?" Wanda shook her head, her focus on the ocean off in the distance. "No, I like to look forward."

Renee called the whole hair cutting a surrendering.

Wanda let go of who she was and allowed who she was becoming to come out, like a butterfly breaking from its cocoon. Cutting her hair was her way of breaking her cocoon. Whatever it was, Renee took the clippers as the familiar prickle of uncomfortable anxiety ran up her arms and began cutting Wanda's hair.

With each stroke of the clippers against Wanda's head, Renee watched as Wanda shed her most prized possession. The fiery curls fell upon the patio, the sun's rays rising from the horizon.

Renee continued to shave Wanda's head in silence. She didn't think too much about why Wanda chose Renee to do this with, but she felt proud she had been the one.

First, Bitty's confession at the hospital. Now, Wanda asked her to cut her hair. Maybe it was baby George, or maybe being pregnant made her feel less threatening, less judgmental. But she felt a big responsibility to be exactly the person they needed at that moment.

"You look beautiful," Renee said, holding up her phone to show Wanda's image through the camera.

Wanda took the phone, rubbing her fuzzy head with her hand as she stared back at herself. "I think this will be just fine."

But Wanda's chin trembled, and her eyes began to water as she held the phone, looking back at her head. Renee dug her tooth into her cheek to hold her own emotions back and said, "Have you seen what's out there nowadays?"

She took the phone from Wanda, opening up her favorites to a wig website she found the other day. An image of a petite woman close to the same age as Wanda popped up on the screen. "It's called melted ocean."

The wig's curls started dark at the roots and blended into light and deep blues with light lavender tips. It was gorgeous.

"I love it." Wanda expanded the image to get a better look. "But would it look good on someone like me?"

"You'll look incredible." Renee showed another image of the woman walking with sunglasses along the street. "That'll be you soon."

Wanda nodded as she looked at the photo. A big wind blew in from the water, and Wanda's old curls scattered around the patio and into the yard. Birds swooped in the air above them.

"Thank you, Renee," Wanda said, getting up out of the chair. She tied the scarf around her head, the way women did in the sixties to cover their hair from the rain.

Renee pressed buy on the website. She'd get the wig for Wanda. She'd also get a blonde wig for good measure. Maybe she could convince her mom and Bitty to get one too, and they could all go out with wigs on one night for dinner.

She looked up and saw Evelyn meet Wanda at the door to the kitchen. She hugged her and looked beyond at Renee. She mouthed the words, "I love you."

Renee gave her mom a nod but couldn't say it back this time. She kept biting her cheek to hold in her emotions as she watched the women she admired so very much embrace.

By six, Renee was in her usual spot behind the kitchen counter, making breakfast for everyone. Bitty had her overnight oats, and Wanda, her ginger protein shake. With the apples that Phil had dropped off from the mainland, she'd made apple-cinnamon tarts that smelled divine coming out of the oven.

"What's that?" Samantha asked as she came into the kitchen.

Renee looked at her little sister in just an oversized T-shirt and remembered how skinny she had once been too. Would she be that woman who never lost the baby weight? The books said breastfeeding made the weight disappear, but Renee had a feeling she'd have to breastfeed for years to get all the baked goods she'd eaten throughout this pregnancy off.

"Did you channel June Cleaver?" Samantha asked as Renee placed a cup of black coffee in front of her.

"Ha ha," Renee said, but she dropped the sugar down with a spoon. "How'd you sleep?"

"Great." Samantha stretched her arms out as she yawned big and loud. "Where is everyone?"

"Walking," Renee said. "They walk every morning."

"Even Wanda?"

Renee nodded, not mentioning the hair cutting. "Sometimes she stays behind, but most of the time she tries to walk."

Samantha studied her for a moment, then asked, "How are you?"

Immediately, the word fine came to mind, but she looked across the counter to where her little sister sat and said, "You know that saying, 'What doesn't kill you makes you stronger'?"

"Now you're Kelly Clarkson?" Samantha smiled.

"All this with Harry has just made me more determined to start my own bakery than I ever was with him." Renee rolled her eyes at herself. "I don't know. I just don't want to hide in my mother's kitchen anymore. I want to chase my dreams, even if I'm on my own."

"Did he cheat on you?" Samantha asked.

Renee shook her head. She almost wished he had, because admitting the truth stung worse. "He just didn't love me."

Samantha's eyes didn't hold the pity Renee had come to recognize when she talked about her situation. Instead, she reached across the counter, taking Renee's hand in hers, and said, "Well, isn't he a big sack of—"

"Good morning," Mateo said. He stood in the doorway.

Renee's face immediately flushed with heat. How long had Mateo been standing there?

"Good morning," Samantha said back, flashing her brilliant white pearls at him.

Renee watched in awe as her sister charmed the contractor. Even in a T-shirt, Samantha didn't seem fazed by a man in the kitchen. In fact, she looked like a beach babe with her long messy hair down around her shoulders.

Mateo blinked a few times as he noticed Samantha had no pants on, her long, slender legs on display. "Um, sorry, I didn't know you were..."

He turned his back to her.

"Maybe I should go get dressed," Samantha said. She scooted off the stool and skittered away up the stairs.

"Coffee?" Renee poured a cup before he answered.

"Thanks," he said as she passed it to him. His vision was still focused away from where Samantha had been sitting.

"She's gone." She hadn't baked anything that morning. Her mind was consumed with spreadsheets, figures, and lists. "I have store-bought bagels if you want them."

He shook his head. "Thanks, but I'm good."

"What are you working on today?" Renee asked.

"I'm meeting with the electrician about the guest cottage," he said.

She made a new mental goal. She wanted to find her own place before the cottage was finished. Otherwise, she'd never leave her mother's house.

"How long do you think it will take to finish it?" Renee asked.

He shrugged. "With winter coming, and the lack of full-year help, a few months at least. Plus, your mother has a few other projects she wants to finish in the main house first."

"Mostly carpentry stuff, right?" she asked.

She knew her mother wanted to make the front sitting room into a library where she could have an antique desk and a few comfortable places to sit and read, but also all the walls full of shelves for her favorite books. *Very similar to Mateo's own front room,* she thought to herself. Her mother's room had an original fireplace that no longer worked, which she was certain Evelyn wanted to restore.

"I still can't believe you built the crib." She had an idea Mateo had talent, but she'd had no idea to what extent. "It's the most beautiful piece of furniture I've ever owned."

"I like working with my hands and doing those unique pieces," Mateo said.

Her eyes went to his hands, which made the mug look small. "You could open another business selling furniture."

"You are very talented," Samantha said, bouncing into the kitchen in an itsy-bitsy bikini that wasn't yellow but could catch the whole island's attention. She was better covered when she wore just the T-shirt. "The house looks amazing. You've done an incredible job."

Samantha, unlike Renee, could capture the whole island's attention even if she wore a habit. She had a charismatic way about her. She could captivate even the orneriest person, steal any man's heart, and make you feel good in return. Always the extrovert, she could talk to anyone. In school, Samantha had only been two years behind her, but she had more friends and a higher social status than Renee, who could hardly say more than a sentence to most boys.

Renee could barely speak when someone as attractive as Mateo came into the room. It didn't help that she was the size of a minivan, but even before baby George, she could never strut through the house in a bikini and hold a serious conversation about woodworking. But unlike most men, she noticed, Mateo didn't seem to get all googly eyes or tongue-tied. He seemed like, well, Mateo.

"I'm here for a couple days at least," Samantha said, leaning on the counter, closer to him. "Where do you all hang out around here?"

That's when Renee could feel her heart skip inside her chest. Was Samantha asking Mateo out? And why did it bother her that her glamorous sister asked out someone as kind and as wonderful as Mateo? Wouldn't she want that for her sister? What kind of sister didn't want that for her?

That's when she saw Mateo flash a grin, and she could see he was hooked. Like with all men, Samantha dazzled him with her loveliness. She sparkled and bedazzled, her golden blonde locks, her olive tanned skin, her polished nails and jewelry. Where did she get such expensive jewelry?

Renee took hold of the diamond tennis bracelet. "That's quite a bracelet."

Samantha twisted the diamond jewelry around her wrist. "A friend found it in an estate sale in London."

A friend?

"Do people go out around here? Or are we the only ones under sixty?" Samantha looked serious, which made Mateo laugh and made her feel lame.

"Don't people go to that hotel on the beach for drinks?" Renee said, hiding the fact that all she did was hang out with people over sixty.

"The Wharf?" Mateo asked.

Renee hadn't gone out on the island at all since she arrived.

"So, Mateo," Samantha said, tilting her head just enough to have her hair fall over her smooth shoulder. "What do you think of our mom's new boyfriend?"

Mateo burrowed his eyebrows, apparently surprised by the question. "Charlie?" he shook his head. "I think of him as a friend. He's the nicest."

Samantha looked at Renee. "And you?"

Renee looked back to Mateo, then agreed. "He's great."

Samantha leaned her hand on the counter. "I like him too."

Renee smiled at that. She didn't know until then that she wanted Samantha to like him. She wanted her to like Harper too.

"And his daughter seems super cool," Samantha went on. "She's got fabulous style."

Renee shot a glance at Mateo to see if talking about Harper, and how cool she was, would make him uncomfortable. She could tell there was still tension with the two of them, but Mateo only nodded while listening to Samantha compliment her. Renee's heart swelled up again, and her emotions stuck in her throat. God, being pregnant could throw her through an emotional whirlpool. She opened her portfolio instead of looking at them, otherwise she would cry.

"Are those your plans?" Mateo asked, pointing to the name. "Books and Bread—that's a good name."

"I know, right?" She pulled out her vision board, fabric swatches, interior colors, refrigerators, furniture, and built-ins.

"This is genius," Samantha said, leaning over the plans.

"I can do all this," Mateo said, pointing to the photograph of a Parisian boulangerie she had seen on Pinterest. Dark woods against soft earth tones, white marble counters, brass hardware—retro meets French country.

"I want to make the customer feel at home while they're there," Renee said.

"What's the space like?" Samantha asked.

"You'd love it." Renee knew her sister would adore the old bookstore as much as she did. The building had been one of the original structures in the little village of Eastport. The gray clapboard exterior, the wide twelve-inch pine floors, a large picture window with white square grilles facing the harbor.

She had to change Charlie's mind. "Do you think Charlie will go for it?"

She directed her question to Mateo. He ran a successful business, and he knew this island better than all of them, but it was Samantha who answered.

"He'd be crazy not to. Your bakery will draw the kind of clientele that will buy a vacation read as they pick up a gourmet coffee and scone. It'll be part of the experience."

Mateo snapped his fingers. "Your sister's right. Go talk to him. Show him your plans."

Renee looked down at the portfolio and felt childish. Who did she think she was? Bringing in a vision board wouldn't change

Charlie's mind. What did a few pictures from Pinterest show him about her business skills? All night when she made her proposal, she kept wishing she could get a reference. Have Harry call and talk about her as an employee, not his wife. Tell Charlie how she ran a forty-plus staff for the front and back of the house. How she handled scheduling, ordering, most of the management, along with running the line, and was only considered a cook. But without Harry, she had no real references for the past five years. How could she have been so stupid? How could she just let a man come in and have that much control?

Because she wanted someone to take control for her. Losing her dad, not having that one person to cheer her on, made her go looking for some sort of weird approval from Harry. If Renee had met Harry Winthrop today, she'd tell him to bug off, because she would never allow herself to be that constrained to anyone.

"You should go talk to Charlie," Samantha said. "There's no harm in telling him how you'd like to go into business with him."

"Do you think he'll still want to work with me?" Renee had tried to talk to Charlie after the shower, but with everyone around, she could never really find the appropriate time.

"I do," Mateo said, looking to Renee for her response.

"Yes," Samantha said.

The rest of the morning, Samantha stayed with Renee as she finished up her proposal to Charlie. When Mateo wasn't working with his electrician, he'd come and give his two cents, which turned out to be very helpful.

By the time she left for the bookstore, Samantha and Mateo were in a full-on conversation about what it was like to live in Barcelona for a year.

"I've always wanted to go to Spain," Mateo said.

"It's amazing." Samantha flipped through her photos to dozens of perfect photographs of her in the streets of the city, among the people, dancing in clubs, visiting museums, her picture-perfect life.

"You hungry?" Samantha asked Mateo. "I'm dying for one of those famous lobster rolls you have out here."

"I can take you down to The Wharf," Mateo said like a puppy dog. "They have a beer on draft that goes great with their rolls."

"Perfect."

"We can drop you off to talk to Charlie," Samantha suggested.

Renee's excitement of starting the business suddenly receded as her sister was getting cozy with Mateo, the one friend Renee had, and Samantha was going to break his heart, which would make everything weird. Now, she understood where her mother was coming from.

"Have fun you guys," Renee said. "I'll head over on my own."

She organized the last of her notes and put them in order in her portfolio. Her energy was so pumped up that when she called Charlie to ask to come talk, she danced as she heard the phone ringing.

"Hey, Charlie," she said enthusiastically as he picked up the bookstore's phone. "It's Renee."

A short bit of silence fell, and Charlie then said, "It's good to hear from you."

Her excitement was immediately snuffed out. "I was hoping maybe we could have a conversation about the bakery?" she asked, her words hesitant as they came out.

Another bit of silence, then a breath. "Sure. How about tomorrow morning?"

"That sounds great," she said, but it didn't. She wanted to run over there now. She didn't think she could wait. "I'll come when you open."

"Perfect," he said.

But now her perfect plan didn't sound so perfect.

CHAPTER 24

Mateo was having a real nice time with Samantha at The Wharf. She seemed to like the same things he did—food, good beer, traveling, and books. She had read everything.

"I fly a lot, so I read a lot." Samantha shrugged as though most people flew across the oceans to exotic places like Indonesia and Argentina.

"Do you ever want to settle down?" he asked.

"Yes." She had said it quickly, faster than he had expected a travel blogger to say. "I liked growing up in a neighborhood with neighbors who'd give you a cup of sugar if you ran out."

Mateo nodded. "I have a Mrs. Wilson next door."

"That sounds nice." Samantha spun her glass of a local pale ale. "I miss that routine. Dropping your keys in the same place, always having a good sound system, a place to escape away from the world."

"You sound like your mom," Mateo said.

Mateo had gotten to know Evelyn in a weirdly intimate way. She had shared the most intimate details of her lifestyle through building with him. The way she had lived and the way she wanted to live. The things that mattered to her and the things that weren't worth it. Evelyn splurged on a lot, but never for vanity items like others requested in the big beach houses. She put her money in the details—the woodworking, the built-ins, rebuilding the original architecture, and making every inch of the house part of the show.

"I'd love to be like my mom," Samantha said, resting her elbows on the table as she stirred her drink. "She's worked so hard to get where she is."

He didn't know much about Evelyn's career besides that she was successful, but he saw the work ethic in Renee. "Is it a Rose woman trait?"

"What?" Samantha swept her hair behind her shoulder, reminding him of how Renee's hair fell. It was strange how similar the two sisters looked and acted, yet they were totally different.

"You all chase after what you want."

She tilted her head and shrugged. "Sometimes, I guess."

She frowned for a second, then perked up more than before. "Let's get another drink."

As they ordered another round, Samantha took videos and photos of the drinks, the surroundings, and the menu. Mateo enjoyed his time with her but felt weird spending time with her without Renee. The conversation stilted every once in a while, and he'd try to ramp it up, but Samantha seemed to be lost in her thoughts a lot, and the conversation dragged out. Back at the house with Renee, they had no problem talking, laughing, and enjoying each other's company. He wouldn't have agreed to go out if he'd thought Renee wasn't coming with them, but when she suggested it, he assumed she would join.

"Are you like Renee?" he asked. "Always working?"

She snorted, shaking her head. "If you mean always shutting out the world around me, then no." Samantha held her beer in her hands. "My family calls what I do, playing."

He instantly heard a different tone. Clearly, there was something deeper to her comment than he understood.

He nodded, but he could tell Samantha was studying him, which made him feel even more uncomfortable.

With her fingers, she wiped the condensation off her glass. "Have you met Harry?"

"No." He answered quickly from the whiplash of change in conversation, but when she didn't elaborate, his curiosity crept in. "What's he like?"

She shrugged, looking out at the crowd of people hanging at the bar. Mostly the last of the summer people, those who owned homes on the island but didn't stay during the winter. The fall weather had crept in even during the days, and the cool nights no longer allowed the crowds to hang outside on the patio.

"Commanding," she finally answered. "He had a way of making his presence known."

He didn't know what kind of person Renee would fall for, but commanding wasn't what he'd expected. Talented, driven, powerful maybe, but not commanding. Commanding didn't sound equal; commanding sounded imposing, dominating.

He had so many questions floating around in his head. Was she surprised the marriage had failed? Or had she been surprised at how he'd left Renee while pregnant? Because he had a feeling Samantha hadn't been.

"Seems to me like he's more into disappearing than anything," he said, mostly mumbling to himself as he grabbed his beer.

This made Samantha study him again, her eyes narrowing as her lips curled up on one side. "You'd hate him."

He let out a chuckle. "I already hate him."

This made her laugh too, and like her sister, her soft pitch came out melodious. She leaned on the table. "You know, they were having serious problems even before she found out she was pregnant."

Something shifted—a line that hadn't been there before, but one he felt very strongly he couldn't cross. He knew Samantha meant well, that it wasn't gossip in her world, but talking about

Renee's relationship, intimate details she hadn't ever mentioned to him, felt wrong.

"Seems to me she's better off without him," Mateo said, and he quickly changed the conversation. "Where are you headed next to play?"

She pulled back her hair behind her ear and leaned closer, almost perched in her seat as she got a good look at him. A smile grew on her face. "I like you, Mateo."

Her comment made him wonder if her second drink had been a good idea. "You're pretty cool too."

"I like how you've helped my family." Her stare became hard and objective. "I like how you treat people."

"Thanks." He didn't know where this compliment was coming from, but if it got the subject off Renee and her marriage, then so be it.

Her hand went up as a waitress walked by their table. "I'll take the check."

Mateo reached in his back pocket immediately. "Let me take care of the bill."

She had a plastic card out before he could scramble to open his wallet, and she handed it to the passing waitress. "I'll charge it to my business account."

He had heard Samantha's travel and fashion blog—or vlog, as Samantha had corrected him earlier—was how she earned her money, but he didn't really understand how all that stuff worked. He did admire the work she put in after seeing a couple of her videos. But he wasn't about to let her pay.

"I've got this," he said.

"Can't a woman pay?" Samantha's lips pursed in a straight line.

"Yes." He believed in modern views of women. He didn't want to be condescending, but his mother would kill him if he let a woman pay or even walk into a building without holding open the door. It wasn't about being a man but being polite and respectful toward a woman. "Look, my mother raised me to be a gentleman. Please, just let me pay for at least my portion."

Samantha shook her head. "You're the real deal, huh?"

"Excuse me?" He threw down enough cash for a generous tip.

Samantha leaned over the table closer to him. "Look, Mateo, I haven't seen my sister this happy in a very, very long time."

"That's great," he said, looking away from her stare. He had seen Renee go through tough times and was glad she'd come out stronger in the end. "She's worked hard to get where she is."

She started laughing and it felt directed at him. "I mean, the two of you are totally ridiculous, you know that, right?"

Now he was confused. "What?"

She threw her head back in even more laughter, as though he said the punch line to a joke.

"Thanks for getting me out of the house," she said, still chuckling, but Mateo had no idea what was so funny.

CHAPTER 25

"I really like them," Samantha said in bed.

Renee was reading her *What to Expect When You're Expecting* pregnancy book for the umpteenth time, but her thoughts were completely elsewhere. She couldn't pay attention to the already highlighted notes, as her mind raced about how Samantha and Mateo went out for hours at The Wharf.

She had seen the posts on Samantha's social media feed before he had dropped her off. From her position in the kitchen, she'd seen there was no good night kiss, but she stayed in his truck long enough for a sweet goodbye.

"I need to eat way more vegetables," Renee said as she tried to read about brain development during her stage of pregnancy.

"I really like Charlie and Harper," Samantha said again.

"Hmm," Renee said, flipping to the next page, wondering why her sister wasn't talking about her night.

"I think she should marry him," Samantha said.

"What?" Renee couldn't believe, of all people, that Samantha thought their mother should get married. "Why?" She didn't understand. "She's so happy with everything right now." Their mother had said so herself. "And you hate commitment."

"I know, but they're, like, totally in love with each other." Samantha placed her hands on her chest. "They're adorable."

"Let them figure things out on their own." Renee could see her little sister sticking her nose where it didn't belong.

"What's with you and Mateo?" Samantha asked.

Speaking of noses.

"What do you mean?" Renee asked. She glued her eyes to the words at the top of the page, trying to appear completely neutral.

"I mean, the two of you seem to like each other, but no one will admit it."

"We're friends." Renee said it louder than she'd expected, and quicker. She let out a laugh about the absurdity. "He's Mom's contractor."

"Who's wicked hot and wicked into you." Samantha exaggerated her words with a Boston accent.

Renee rolled her eyes. "He went out with you."

"Only because you bailed." Samantha dropped her head, eyebrows raised, eyes up at Renee with that exasperated look she did so well.

"What?"

"You like him."

"I was married five seconds ago." Renee wasn't hearing it. She didn't have time for relationships. "I'm about to have a baby."

"Mark my words, big sister. This is your happily ever after," Samantha said, adjusting her pillows. She reached out her arm to the light beside the bed she shared with Renee and turned off the light. "Good night."

Renee sat there in her lamp's light, completely dumbfounded. "He has a thing for Harper."

Samantha pulled the covers up under her arms as she lay down on her side and tucked her hands underneath the pillows. "I think he has a major thing for you."

Samantha closed her eyes, but Renee knew well enough that her sister was waiting for Renee's reaction. "He doesn't. Believe me. He's just a nice guy. Besides, he wouldn't want to date someone who's pregnant."

"Why not?"

"Because I'm literally walking around with my baggage." She counted with her fingers the many reasons why Mateo was not into her. "I'm seven months pregnant. I recently signed my divorce papers. I haven't gone back to my apartment to pick up my stuff after I left without telling my ex-husband. I have no job. I live with my mom." She was running out of fingers. "Besides, I have no time for that kind of stuff." She continued with the argument inside her head. She didn't have time to worry about anyone besides the people in her life now. She liked having him as a friend, and anything more than that was ridiculous.

"Maybe you do have time," Samantha said, her eyes still closed.

"Do you think I sit around and eat bonbons all day?" Renee could feel her irritation grow. Samantha had made comments before about living off their mother, but was she saying Renee was just full of free time?

"Chill out, Renee." Samantha opened her eyes. "All I'm saying is that you should find time to make *you* happy, and if Mateo makes you happy… find time."

"I'm already happy," Renee countered quickly.

Samantha gave her a look that said, *yeah right*.

"I am," Renee said.

Samantha reached out her hand and rubbed Renee's belly just as Baby George kicked. "Ow, little man's got some kick."

Renee placed her hand beside Samantha's. "I'm so glad you're here."

"Me, too." Samantha sat up on her elbow. "I think you should go for him."

Renee looked down at her belly. "No, I want to focus on George and only George."

When Renee finally shut off her light, Samantha had already fallen fast asleep, but Renee couldn't get her mind to slow down.

Charlie had agreed to talk about her business proposal the next day, but now she wondered if she should after all. What if being in business together caused stress to their relationships? What if it made things change? Made them awkward?

Or what if it turns out like she thought it might? A place where they could watch each other's backs. A place where both could grow and build a business that was greater together than as separate pieces?

By four, she got up, unable to sleep any longer, and headed down to the kitchen. She prepped Wanda's smoothie and Evelyn and Bitty's oatmeal. When the clock hit six, she left out the back door. Dawn's pale light broke the darkness of the early morning. The waves sounded closer than usual. The crisp fall air magnified the sounds, and she pulled up her collar as she walked to her car. Just as she hit the unlock button on her keys, Mateo's truck pulled up the drive. She looked at her watch.

"I thought I was up early," she said as he got out.

He handed over a set of rolled-up papers. "I did some sketches."

She immediately pulled off the band holding them together. "You drew out the plans already?"

He nodded as she opened the papers and placed them on the hood of her car. She pulled out her phone and turned on the flashlight as the sun's light slowly crept over the valleys of seagrass.

She could see the exterior structure of the bookstore, but the inside had a whole new space. She had imagined almost two separate areas in the store, a bookstore and a bakery, but in Mateo's drawing, it reminded her of one big, great room. In the back of the store was a kitchen with a long island counter, which were refrigerated shelves. Along the back wall, he'd placed another long counter.

"There will be open shelving above," he said, pointing to where she was studying. "And the books will run along all these walls."

His finger traced the rest of the store. Shelves ran along the perimeter, and the seating was placed in the middle of it all. "And if the city permits it, I can put a gas fireplace here."

"This is amazing," she said, staring at the plan. "I can't believe you did this in one night."

"I'm not an architect, but I'm confident this will work." He pointed to the kitchen. "I made enough room for oven racks, as well as a double unit in the back."

The back room where Charlie's office and storage room was now had been converted into another kitchen area with large sinks, refrigerators, and a walk-in pantry.

"How can I ever thank you?" she said, staring at the design.

He took her hand in his and squeezed it. She felt a rush of electricity running through her from his touch, reverberating in her chest. "Now knock it out of the park with Charlie."

She squeezed his hand back. She was so pumped up after seeing Mateo's designs that she almost woke the house as she left for Charlie's store. When she arrived at the bookstore, she parked in the back and climbed the back staircase to the apartment door. After knocking softly, she could hear movement inside. From working with him those few weeks, she knew he'd be up.

"Good morning," she said as he opened the door. She held out the basket of his favorite banana-nut muffins.

"Good morning," he said, his arm extended into his kitchen. "Come in."

She came inside and passed him the booklet she had created. Books and Bread was printed on the cover.

"Renee, there's something I should say first," he began, but she cut him off.

She held up her hand. "Please, let me talk first."

He sat down at the kitchen table as she turned the first page over to the table of contents of the proposal. He'd see how very serious she was about her business plan.

She pointed to the chapter titled "Estimated Profits," where she had placed a blue post-it. "Turn to page six."

He flipped to the page, and she could see his eyes expand in surprise. "You believe this is what we'll make by next year?"

She nodded. She was almost positive. From her research and her observations over the last few weeks, along with the years of working in the industry, she had a real solid estimate of what it would take to make it work. And she could make it work, but only if she had the location and the customer's trust that Charlie had created with his bookstore.

"I want to take your idea of the airport bookshop but make it more like a vacation stop." She turned to the eighth page, the one with her images of the interior and Mateo's estimated time of building. She then opened Mateo's designs.

"This can be done by spring?" He sounded doubtful.

She nodded. "Mateo said he thinks by the end of April."

He looked at the plans again, then began the arduous task of flipping through her thorough booklet, page by page, not uttering a word and showing no emotion whatsoever. Renee was slowly dying inside as she waited for him to finish.

"Well?" she said, not able to take it any longer.

"Well, what I was going to say is that I think we should be partners."

She ran to him at the chair and wrapped her arms around his neck, squeezing him in his seat. "I think this is going to be great!"

He squeezed her back but also coughed as though she were choking him. "Okay, easy goes there."

She eased up and sat in her own chair. "But I want to make sure that I won't get in the way of you and Mom, because Samantha and I just love you two together, and we love Harper and—"

"Renee," he said, "I can't wait to start this next chapter with you."

He held out his hand and she reached across the table to shake it vigorously.

"I'll make you so proud."

He took his hands and wrapped them around hers. "You already do."

The words sounded like those of a father, and as the tears formed, and just when she was about to blubber on, Charlie said, "Let's go see your bakery."

Charlie brought Renee down to the bookstore and showed her around the back.

"This was my aunt Martha's place before me, and my grandfather's fish market before her, and my great-grandfather's before that," Charlie said with a look of pride.

"You're kidding." Renee looked around the space, imagining fish from a table of ice being weighed on a scale, wrapped in paper.

He shook his head, looking around the room and sinking into a wooden swivel chair that reminded her of what a newsroom would have in the fifties.

"I could never lose this place, but Harper doesn't want it, and knowing that you and the baby might stay here..." Charlie smiled. "I'd love to let another family grow up here and keep this place going."

"It's here!" Harper slammed open the door and held up a copy of a book in her hands. Harper Moran was written in large print on the top of the cover.

"It's your book," Renee said, looking over Charlie's shoulder at the cover. It was beautiful, one of those covers that would pop off the shelf. Renee watched as Harper flipped the pages in front of her dad, but Charlie beamed at his daughter, not the book. Renee's hands immediately went to George. "That's wonderful, Harper."

"Well, let's make room in the store," Charlie said.

It took only an hour to clear room for the new display. Charlie packed up an old display of mysteries, and Renee made a new sign of chalk art saying, "Coming soon!" Harper placed a tagboard poster of her cover.

"Let's celebrate tonight," Renee suggested. "I can make dinner and invite everyone over."

Harper wrinkled her forehead. "Would you mind if I invited someone?"

Renee shook her head. "Of course not. Bring whomever you'd like."'

Renee wondered if Mateo knew and if inviting him would be a good idea.

Once she got home, she started cooking right away, with Wanda as her sous chef. Evelyn and Bitty ran errands and gathered supplies for the celebration, and Samantha did the table setting on the patio.

"Everyone is coming," Evelyn said to Renee as she and Bitty walked inside the house. "Even Marty."

"He's been coming a lot more frequently these days," Bitty said, winking at the women. "I think he may have a little crush on somebody."

Bitty's Oklahoma accent came out heavy as she swung her hip at Wanda, whose face turned to shock.

"You couldn't be saying Marty is crushing on me," Wanda said to Bitty. Her hand landed on her chest in dismay. "He couldn't possibly."

"And why not?" Renee said at the same time the timer went off from the oven. "Oh, my mini cheesecakes are ready."

"Because he..." Wanda stumbled for words. "Because he just doesn't."

Samantha's words from the night before blared in Renee's head. *Why not?*

"Wanda, people fall in love with the whole person, even the bad and scary bits," Bitty said.

Wanda made a face as if Bitty was being ridiculous. "Well, I have a lot of scary bits right now."

"But you also have a lot of cool bits too," Renee said, jumping into the conversation. "Like how you moved across the country to live with two strangers and a pregnant girl on the beach. Or how you fight your cancer head-on like a lioness. Or how you take care of those around you by listening while always showing tremendous strength through everything."

"You're sounding like your mother," Wanda said.

Renee looked over to Evelyn, who smiled back at her. Suddenly, moving out didn't seem so important. She'd miss these moments and these women.

"Oof!" Evelyn said. "Something just beeped."

As Renee watched the scene in front of her, Evelyn pulling trays of appetizers out of the oven, Wanda plating it all for the guests, Bitty and Samantha setting the table making homemade centerpieces of shells and candle votives filled with sand, she felt a great wave of gratitude fill every part of her body. It wasn't traditional. It wasn't how she was raised. But as she watched everyone laughing and talking, she had never felt so much love in one room.

"I just have to finish the artichoke and crab dip and a loaf of bread," Renee said. "Charlie said he'd make kabobs."

"I'm going to run to the ladies' room before everyone arrives," Wanda said, leaving the kitchen and leaving Evelyn and Renee alone.

Evelyn walked over to Renee, whose hands were in oven mitts, and hugged her. "I'm really proud of you, and I know Daddy would be too."

Renee hadn't realized how badly she'd needed to hear that, but the minute she did, it was like she could breathe fully again. "Thanks."

The breath came full, but on the back end, so did the emotions. She missed her father so much. The idea that baby George would never know the man he was named for broke her heart. The man who had made Renee confident and crazy enough to think she could run a business and raise a strong man at the same time. The man who had been her hero her whole life. The man who never got to finish teaching her everything he knew. How much knowledge had she missed by his years being cut so short?

Evelyn brushed a tear as one escaped from Renee's eye.

"You're going to do great at whatever you set your mind to. You always have," Evelyn said. "Even when you were little, you'd do whatever it took to get whatever you wanted."

"Thanks for standing by me." Renee knew so many parents that hadn't. She had known friends whose parents let the relationship go for far less.

"I'm always going to be there for you," Evelyn said. "Always."

CHAPTER 26

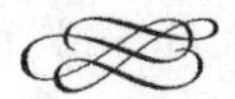

Thunder exploded outside the bookstore as Evelyn stood along the last of the shelves, boxing up the titles she had picked for the retirement home up the road. Martha's Mystery Book Shoppe was officially going out of business. Weeks of clearance had made a good dent in Charlie's inventory, but there were still thousands of books unsold.

With help from those of the writers' group, slowly but surely the books had been either sold, given away, or donated. The last of the unwanted books that remained, Evelyn had decided to box up and take to local shelters and retirement homes.

The bookstore officially closed its doors for good the first week in November, just as Mateo and his brothers finished the third floor and the rest of the bathrooms upstairs in Sea View.

"I'm so glad they're keeping the original structure," Mrs. Johnson said, taking a pile of books on scrapbooking. The former schoolteacher had taught Harper and Mateo at the local elementary school and offered to take some books to the rectory in town. "The church will love these."

"It's nice to see Charlie moving with the times," Hank said to Evelyn as he tossed aside dated almanacs. "This is exactly what this place needs. A whole new face-lift."

Evelyn enjoyed listening as Anita gave her opinion while taking measurements for the windows. She had promised Renee to make curtains that looked like a pair from a Parisian market Renee had seen once. "I've found this great material that will go perfectly in the space."

The biggest contributor to the space was Samantha. She drove throughout New England the month she stayed in Martha's Vineyard and hit every flea market, antique shop, or consignment she could find on the East Coast. Exeter, Andover, Worcester, Chichester—strolling down the aisles of dusty things. And though it looked like junk to Evelyn, Samantha would discover its treasure. She found a beautiful set of floral China dinnerware on the cheap and silver at garage sales for the customers who stayed to eat. Baskets and antique trunks and furniture that fit perfectly in the room. She'd bring the item back to the house and clean it up, paint it, reupholster it while videoing everything, posting it all on her vlog.

Soon people started peeking in the windows, but Renee didn't mind. In fact, Renee, at nine months pregnant, invited onlookers inside to taste her recipes. She'd offer free samples and a cup of coffee. Families with children came for her free chocolate chip cookie for the kids and a coffee for Mom and Dad. Renee asked for nothing but kept a glass jar on top of the table.

"She's making more money in donations and tips than I did with actual prices on my inventory," Charlie said from behind his computer.

Evelyn smiled to herself as she placed the last book from the shelf in a box. "I think this is it."

She stood up slowly, stretching her back out carefully so she didn't pull anything. Another crack of thunder rumbled outside. A flash of lightning illuminated the store. She looked at Charlie, who got up to check out the storm.

"Looks like it's going to be a doozy later," he said, peeking out of the front window.

Evelyn groaned as her spine cracked. "I feel old."

"I feel young again." Charlie grabbed hold of her waist and twirled her in his arms. "I feel like so much weight has been lifted from my shoulders."

She kissed him sweetly. With her thumb, she brushed his beard and kissed him again.

"Why don't I take the last of the boxes to the retirement home?" Charlie said, taking the box in his arms.

"Okay."

Charlie kissed her goodbye and took off toward the door.

"Be careful out there!" Evelyn called out after him as he left. He blew her a kiss as he backed out the door.

She looked at the empty shelf in disbelief. When she had come into the bookstore that past summer, the space was crammed and jammed with stuff. It felt stuffy and sticky. But as Hank started taking apart the last of the shelving units, she could see a new vision for the space, and it was going to be great.

As Evelyn went to another pile of books, she noticed Samantha marching down the sidewalk toward the store. The wind tossed her hair in her face as pellets of some form of rain and sleet and slush dropped from the sky.

Samantha had spent most days editing her videos at the house, which turned out to be a lot more work than Evelyn had imagined. Hours upon hours of editing on her laptop just to make a sixty-second video. The end product made all her hard work look so simple and satisfying. Samantha's followers started following Books and Bread on Instagram, which Samantha helped create content for. Luckily, though, at nights when it was dinnertime, when people congregated at Sea View to eat, Samantha always joined them.

Those were the nights Evelyn enjoyed the most. When everyone sat around her table with full bellies and full hearts. Her heart felt completely full, especially with Samantha back with them.

She noticed a seagull sitting on a street bench, watching

Samantha walk down the pavement. What was he doing out in this kind of weather?

"Is Charlie here?" Samantha said as she came into the store. She looked like she was on a mission. She wore a parka with big puffy arms, and it reminded Evelyn of when she was little.

"He ran some books to the retirement home," Evelyn said, wiping her dusty hands on her jeans. "Why, what's up?"

'I'm going back to Europe." Samantha said it quickly. "Scotland, actually."

"But why?" Evelyn couldn't hide her shock. She didn't want to be selfish, but Samantha had stayed for so long that Evelyn had expected her daughter to stay up until the birth at this point. "Why not stay until the baby comes? Why leave now?"

"There's something big that's come up." She looked down at her phone. "I have a flight out in a few hours from Boston."

"What?" Evelyn didn't realize how serious she was. "You're leaving now?"

"Yes, basically. Can you tell Charlie I said goodbye?"

Evelyn's heart dropped. "Have you talked to Renee?" She had known the two girls had gotten into something when Renee became pregnant, but knowing them, this could start World War III.

"Yes, and she understands," Samantha said, but her youngest was being cryptic.

"But what's the rush?" Evelyn just didn't understand. "Besides, there's a storm coming. You shouldn't go out in that storm." Evelyn waved her arm toward the window. The sky looked dark beyond the harbor. The ferry certainly wouldn't travel in a storm, would it?

"That's why I have to leave now," Samantha said impatiently.

Evelyn's face must've screwed all up in confusion, because Samantha answered before she even asked.

"I just have to get back for work." Samantha looked at her phone. "There's an event I need to attend."

"Will you be able to make it back before the baby?" Evelyn

wanted to understand, but she didn't, and she felt like Samantha was leaving out important details like why she needed to go so badly.

"Come on, Samantha." Evelyn couldn't control her annoyance. What was the immediacy? And in a storm to boot. "Your sister is about to have a baby."

Samantha looked at her watch. "This is really important."

"Important enough to miss your nephew's birth?"

Samantha's face twisted. Evelyn immediately felt bad saying it, but it had to be said. What was so important that she'd miss the birth of the newest member of their family? And for what? Pictures to post on a blog? Videos showing how cool she lived?

"I'll be back," Samantha said. But she didn't look at Evelyn. Instead, she pulled back her hair into a tie. Then she kissed Evelyn's cheek.

"Is this really that important?" Evelyn wanted to ask Samantha to make her understand, but she knew that'd only start a fight.

Samantha's lips pierced at first, as though she had to force her mouth to stay shut, but then she said, "It's about a guy."

Evelyn stood and blinked. This completely shocked her. Samantha had been here for over a month. "There's a guy back in London?"

"Scotland, actually." Samantha still didn't make eye contact. "I just need to be somewhere. Can you stop giving me a guilt trip? I'll be back."

Evelyn could feel her body turn rigid by Samantha's urgency. She didn't wake up this morning thinking her daughter was leaving. Now she was going just like that?

Samantha looked down at her phone.

"Who is he?" Evelyn asked.

"He's just a guy I met while doing a photoshoot." Samantha got a text, and she looked at it as dozens of questions rolled around in Evelyn's head. What was this guy's name? Where was he from?

Evelyn wanted more. She wanted more information, more time to hear it, but mostly, she wanted more Samantha.

But Samantha was no longer a teenager, and Evelyn could no longer make her do anything she didn't want to.

Evelyn reached out and hugged Samantha, holding her close like she would when Samantha was a child. Samantha had been her little shadow, pretending to type like her mom in her office back home and wanting to be involved in whatever Evelyn was doing—knitting, sewing, needlepoint. Samantha would always be by her side. But now, as she forced Samantha a look, something felt distant between her and her daughter. And Evelyn felt left out.

Samantha held her tight but let go before Evelyn was ready. "Please tell Charlie I said goodbye."

"We're just going to miss you so much." Evelyn said this not to make her feel guilty but so that her daughter understood how much she loved having her there. "You filled my cup."

"I'm going to miss you too, Mom." Samantha squeezed Evelyn up off her feet. "Tell Charlie he has my blessing whenever he decides to ask you for your hand in marriage."

"Don't you go starting that again." Evelyn shook her head. Turned out, Samantha had become Charlie's biggest fan.

"And let Harper know she can come stay whenever she wants," Samantha said.

"But you're coming back," Evelyn repeated.

"Yes, I'm coming back," Samantha said in exasperation.

Evelyn took in a deep breath. After grabbing an umbrella and her winter coat, she walked Samantha to the ferry's dock. Its engine powered in the water, ready to head out to the mainland. "Come back as soon as you can."

Samantha paid for a ticket and hugged Evelyn one last time. "I will."

Evelyn stepped away. She clenched her jaw. She had forgotten the feeling of letting her girls go. Each time they had returned to school or left for new places, the feeling in her stomach never really went away until she saw them again. Samantha got on the ferry and Evelyn stayed standing on the harbor's dock as sleet and slush splatted to the ground. She watched until the ferry was completely out of sight.

When she returned to the store, she saw Charlie sitting in one of the chairs Samantha had found, writing longhand in his notebook.

"You're writing," Evelyn said, walking over and sitting on the arm of the chair next to him.

He moved over, putting his arm around her, and slid her into his lap. They fit perfectly together.

"I now have the time," Charlie said. "I don't have the workload I had before."

She hadn't thought about the stress Charlie must've had all those years, running his aunt's bookstore, which had already been full of junk, and failing. What free time did he have when he took care of his aunt and was a single parent?

"I've taken your idea about the treasure maps," he said.

"Oh?" She didn't think he had remembered what she had said all those months ago. How he should use his aunt's treasure map stories in his next book.

"I'm writing from the point of view of the treasure from where it began to where it ended, as a metaphor of a person's journey," he said, his hands animated, and she could see the excitement on his face.

As he explained his draft, she could see the twenty-year-old she had fallen in love with. The guy who had loved her before she was Evelyn Rose. The one who had gotten her to write her deepest, darkest secrets but let the hero always win in the end. She'd fallen in love with him the minute he'd let her read his writing on the beach that first time. But now, as his eyes glimmered with new ideas, she saw so much more. A man who had stood by her through her new self-discovery, a man who loved her children as much as their father had, and a man who welcomed everyone to be part of his community.

"Evelyn?" Charlie stopped talking. "You okay?"

She realized she must have drifted off in her head for a moment. "Yes, sorry. It's just that Samantha left."

"What?" Charlie looked as surprised as she had been. "She left the island? Was the ferry still running?"

She nodded, wondering if she should have made a bigger fuss about it all. "Will she be okay?"

Charlie nodded. "Yes, they take the weather very seriously."

But the weather started to look more serious by the minute. "Do they have plows here on the island?"

Evelyn had stayed all those summers on the island as a young adult working, but she had never stayed the winter.

"It's a very modern island, you know." Charlie pretended to be offended. "Why did she leave?"

"To go back to London." Evelyn still didn't understand. "Scotland, actually." Did Renee know what was going on? "She thinks she'll be back, but I don't know. Renee might have the baby any time now."

"It must've been important if she had to leave," Charlie said.

"Yes, I suppose so," Evelyn said, but she couldn't help but feel a little upset thinking more about it.

"If she said she'll come back, then she'll make it back in time," Charlie said rationally, logically.

She adjusted her position to meet his eyes. Was she ready for the next step? Was she just holding back the inevitable? Will she regret wasting time not being with him?

"I love you," she said.

He smiled at her, holding her face in his palm. "I love you too."

Never in a million years would Evelyn have thought she'd be this happy again after she'd lost George, but here she was in Charlie's arms, with a newer and bigger family. She didn't want whatever they had to end. Ever.

"I say we go back to my place and make a big fire and roast some marshmallows," she said.

When she heard the back door open, Evelyn popped out of the seat and saw Renee walking in.

"Did you hear?' Evelyn asked right away.

Renee nodded. "About Samantha?"

Evelyn waited for Renee's reaction, but there was none. "Are you okay?"

Renee shrugged, then her hands went straight to her belly. Was she not upset? Her face didn't show much of any emotion, which for Renee these days was extremely unusual.

"I guess whoever this guy is, he's important to her."

Evelyn waited for Renee to say more. A dig, or a "I can't believe Samantha did this," but Renee seemed to completely understand.

"What did she tell you?" Did she know more than Evelyn? Those two had been thick as thieves the past few weeks.

Renee shrugged. "She said that he's Scottish and comes from money. His name is Hamish and he's a lawyer over there."

Nothing about this made any sense. "What's the urgency?"

Renee made a face, then let out a long sigh. "She said he's getting married."

"What?" This whole thing was making no sense at all. "She's in love with a man who's getting married?"

Renee sat suddenly. Her mouth blew out, making an *O* with her lips. "Ugh."

"You okay?" Evelyn had been noticing more cramping, more Braxton Hicks than normal.

"I'm fine. I just can't even breathe anymore," Renee said, blowing out another long breath. Then she got back to her feet. "I've got a few more biscuits I need to make before Mommy and Me Tea, but with this storm, I think maybe I should cancel."

"Who's coming?" Evelyn asked.

The morning tea had been Renee's idea. A small group of mothers who lived on the island gathered for tea and sweet treats at the store. She always had children's toys and books and yummy healthy treats for the kids, and on the side, lots of delicious sugary treats for the mommies.

"Julia and her sister, Catherine; Ray and Ian; and Megan, the woman who recently returned from living abroad."

Mateo's sister-in-law had not only included Renee in her group of friends but they seemed to act like old friends gossiping about the people around town. The two reminded her of Bitty and Wanda. The great thing about Julia was that she seemed to know everyone on the island, or they knew her. Julia was invited to everything and had started including Renee, which pleased Evelyn. She had worried Renee wouldn't be able to find a group of young moms on the island. Julia turned out to be a perfect friend for Renee.

"Hank." Renee turned in her seat as Hank came through the front door of the store with his toolbelt on. She got up from the chair and walked over to where Hank took down the last of the old metal shelves. "You did a fabulous job."

"It took no time at all," Hank said. "What can I do next?"

"Get home before this crazy storm comes in," Renee said to the retired fisherman.

Evelyn made a mental note to discuss Samantha's mystery man further with Renee.

"You know," Hank said. "I was thinking this place should hold an open mic night." Hank held a box of books with guitar music inside. "Pass out these books to kids interested in learning music."

"Have you ever thought of running one?" Evelyn asked Hank. She knew Hank liked to write poetry and had been in a band years ago when he was younger. He'd be perfect to run the event.

He looked around the room. "I could help, I suppose."

"That would be fun, for sure," Renee said to Hank, then patted him on the back. "Thanks again for offering to bring these books to the school. I really appreciate it."

Evelyn's pride grew every time she watched Renee run her business. Turns out, she knew more about building a bakery than

Evelyn had given her credit. She knew exactly what she wanted and told Mateo and his brothers so in the walk-throughs. She knew what appliances she wanted, their model numbers, the measurements, the delivery services, the trash pick-up, the paper distributor, the graphic design company. She had everything under complete control.

"Why don't you listen to your advice and go home?" Evelyn said. She'd try talking to Renee about this Scottish mystery man later.

Renee made a face. "I've got to figure out a few things, and then I'll take off."

"Please be careful," Evelyn said as she kissed Renee on the cheek. "See you later."

"Love you," Renee said.

"Love you more," Evelyn said back, and she realized even if she didn't know what was going on with her youngest, her heart was still full.

CHAPTER 27

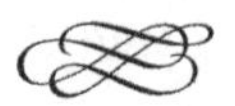

Mateo hadn't done demolition in a long time, but it felt good to get in the bookstore and pull out the old walls. He didn't tell his brothers all the extra work he had done on the side for Renee and Charlie, and luckily, they didn't ask, otherwise he was sure his brothers would give him a hard time.

Leave it to Harper to do the job for them. "When are you going to just admit you like her?"

"I'm just her friend," Mateo said to her, but mostly to himself. Lately, he even had a hard time believing himself. The truth was, he couldn't stop thinking about Renee. He couldn't stop worrying about her either. He started coming earlier to the store and staying later each night. If he was honest with himself, he'd even say he had fallen for her.

"You're ridiculous," Harper said as she grabbed a box of books in the back where Charlie had his office.

"Need help?" Mateo asked, although he knew she wouldn't accept his help. Harper could handle anything.

She shook her head, but her focus stayed on Renee on the other end of the store, out of earshot. "You know the night you kissed me?"

Mateo's face warmed thinking about what an idiot he had been that night. "What about it?"

"I swooned after," she said. She held the box on her hip, her focus directly on him.

What did that even mean? Mateo wanted to know more but also wanted to make this conversation stop.

All those years in high school on the island, wishing he could be like all the other boys with the names Jack, Tyler, and John, whose fathers worked in finance and banking and management. Instead, he got teased relentlessly about being a son of the help. Even the parents were no better. Many asked if he was illegally in the country, even though his parents were both US citizens. Girls like Harper didn't even notice him, and they certainly didn't swoon.

"You're a great kisser," Harper said to him, taking his silence as a sign to continue.

"Harper, please stop."

"Seriously, Mateo. Kiss her."

He grabbed the box from her hip, swooping it out of her hands, and walked it out the back door. "Where are you parked?"

The right side of her mouth lifted in a grin, then a simple shake of the head. "I'm glad we're talking again, you know?"

He held the door open with his back for her. "I'm glad too."

He followed her to her little car and dropped the box in the back seat. Snow had started to accumulate on the ground. "You sure you can drive in this?"

"I'm an islander," she said, as if that proved her driving skills in inclement winter weather.

He wondered if she was still happy with Gerard. "See you soon."

She waved as she jumped into the driver's side.

As she drove away and as he walked back to the store, he couldn't help but smile. He made Harper Moran swoon? *Well, I'll be.*

As he walked back into the store, he saw Renee frozen, standing in the middle of the store, her face white as a ghost.

"You okay?" he asked, almost laughing at her stature, her legs were wide apart.

"I just heard a pop," Renee said, and she looked down to the floor. "Then a swoosh."

His eyes fell at her feet too. On the old pine floors was a puddle of water.

"Is that your…?" he stared at the pinkish-tinged water that he was certain wasn't water.

"I think I'm in labor." She looked startled and scared.

His heart immediately started pumping. "Oh, geez, let me get Harper." He was about to run to the back door where Harper had been parked, when Renee held up her hands.

"Stop, Mateo!" She looked down. "Can you help me sit?"

He reached out for her hand and led her out of the puddle to a chair in the middle of the room. "I'll take care of the mess, and I'll grab some towels for you."

Her forehead creased. "I need to call my mom."

He nodded, holding his hands under her arms as she sat down.

"I have to write down the time." She pulled out her own phone.

"Are you okay?" He wished he had read some of those maternity books he had seen lying around their house. He knew nothing about labor other than what happened on farms. "Is there anything you need right now?"

Renee shook her head. "No, I'm fine."

"Isn't this early?"

She nodded, and he noticed a look of panic across her face. "By a few weeks."

"Should we call an ambulance?" he asked, now panicking himself. He didn't want to waste any time.

"It's okay." Renee's face held concern, but her voice remained calm, which made him feel a bit better, but his anxiety was revving as she continued to just sit there.

She looked up at him, her eyes big and round, and she smiled. "This might be my son's birthday."

A tear fell down her cheek, and without thinking, he grabbed it off her chin with the back of his hand. She wiped another tear that fell, sitting straighter.

"I knew there was going to be a storm." Renee shook her head, her gaze out the windows. She kept shaking it back and forth, and soon her bottom lip began to tremble. "How am I going to do this all alone?"

She covered her face with her hands, and he knelt in front of her, placing his hands on her knee, his eyes waiting to see hers. He could try and deny all he wanted with Harper, but at that moment, he had never been more certain of his feelings for anyone than he did right then for Renee. All he wanted to do was take her in his arms, do whatever he could to protect and take care of her. Harper was right. He was in love with Renee.

"You have all of us," he said, but it was a cop out. He needed to speak the truth. He needed her to understand that she wasn't going to be alone. He'd never let that happen. Mateo would be there for her.

She coiled in the chair, sending her hand to her back as a contraction must've dug into her. The pain whipped her head forward, and Mateo pulled out his phone.

"Should I call 911?" Mateo said, ready to press the numbers.

"No, my mom." Her face twisted in pain.

He dialed Evelyn's number right away. As soon as she answered, Mateo said, "Renee's in labor."

"Oh!" Evelyn sounded just as surprised by the turn of events as they were. "Okay, do you know how far apart the contractions are?"

He heard Renee moan again. "No, but her water broke."

"Already?" Evelyn's voice became less excited and suddenly serious. "Okay, Mateo, I'm coming to the store right now."

"Why don't you meet us at the hospital?" Mateo heard Renee groan louder from the chair. "I can get her there in less time."

"Okay, tell her I'll bring her overnight bag," Evelyn said, then he hung up.

Mateo turned to Renee, who was panting "hee-hee, ho-ho" furiously while focusing on her phone's screen of a video of the beach. "It's my happy place."

He smiled but put on his game face, hiding the fear happening inside him. "I'm taking you to the hospital now."

She immediately looked frightened. "What about my mom? I want Bitty there too."

"They're going to meet us there," he said, making his voice as soothing and as calm as possible.

She nodded, but he could see she wasn't sure of this new plan.

"Your mom's going to bring your overnight bag," he said, reassuring her with more details.

"Does it have four-wheel drive?" she asked.

"Yes," he said with a smirk. "Don't worry. I've driven in this kind of weather many times."

She nodded again, but her whole body tensed as another contraction hit. "Are you sure you want me in your expensive truck? I can wait for my mom."

"I want to get you to a hospital." He took her hand and began to help her out of the chair, when she stopped him. He thought she was having another contraction, but she looked up to him, her eyes meeting his.

"Thank you," she said.

The truth sat on the tip of his tongue. He wanted to be there for her. He wanted to help her. He would always want that. But instead, he chickened out and said, "Anything for you, Renee."

CHAPTER 28

Renee watched baby George breathe on her chest. He'd slept skin to skin all night long. The seven-hour labor had been quite the feat, but just like the books said, she couldn't remember a bit of it as she stared at her baby boy. She lifted his little hand and breathed in his smell, resting it on her lips and kissing it. His little legs stretched out as he nestled in closer.

The night nurse came in for her two-hour vitals check.

"You should get some rest," the nurse said to Renee again.

"I will," Renee said, but she couldn't imagine missing any of this. She wasn't going to be able to close her eyes now that George was finally here.

Samantha stirred as she slept in the pullout chair next to her. At first, Renee hadn't wanted to tell her sister about being in labor. She didn't want Samantha to have to choose between the man she loved and her nephew, but somehow, Samantha showed up at the hospital just before he was born. She looked like the proud auntie, just like it said on the shirt Bitty and Wanda had given her.

"Hey, you're still awake?" Samantha said groggily, yawning and stretching in the plastic upholstered chair. "Do you need anything?"

Renee kissed George softly on the forehead, "Thank you for coming back."

Samantha turned on her side, facing Renee and the baby. "I wasn't going to miss it for a silly boy."

"Who is this man?"

"An egotistical aristocrat who chose an outdated traditional lifestyle over happiness." Samantha played with her perfectly manicured nails.

"I'm sorry." Renee could see through her glossy exterior. Inside, Samantha's heart was breaking.

"Yeah, well, I hope he's happy sneaking around and playing games." Samantha flung her hair behind her shoulders and reached out toward the baby. "When do I get to hold him for a bit?"

Renee inhaled the sweet scent of George's head, not ready to let go. "Alright, I should probably get up and move around."

Samantha's eyes widened with delight as she softly clapped. "Come to Auntie Samantha."

Opening her nightshirt, Samantha sat on the bed. Renee slowly got out of it, gently keeping George in a tight bundle, and transferred him to Samantha's chest. He didn't even stir.

"He's such a good boy already," Samantha said, his head resting in the crook of her neck. "So, what's it like becoming a mother?"

Renee tried to think of the right words to explain everything that was going on inside her, but the emotions overwhelmed her as she sat there staring at her baby in her sister's arms. She had worried so much over the past nine months if she'd be enough for him, but this was enough. Her family was enough. She was enough for this little human being. She felt more sure of this than anything in her life.

A tear fell. "I feel complete."

The left side of Samantha's mouth perked up, but the worry lines on her forehead creased. "Do you regret you and Harry not working out?"

Renee did a double take at the mere mention of his name, because she hadn't been thinking of him at all. "No. This sounds so cheesy, like something mom would write in one of her books, but all that grief and struggle I went through with him made this moment, right now, an absolute blessing."

Samantha smiled at Renee's newfound aphorism. "Good, because we need to talk."

"About what?" She lay back down on the bed, a soreness radiating throughout her body, but it only reminded her of the strength she had. She'd given birth to a human being. The most precious human being on earth. She created a perfect baby boy, and she would raise a man—all by herself. She was a warrior.

"About Mateo being here all night," Samantha said.

"Mateo's here?" Renee'd had no idea. Hadn't he gone home with everyone else?

Samantha nodded. "He's out in the waiting room, waiting."

"For what?"

"You!" Samantha whispered loudly. The two women froze as George cooed. Then when he settled, she said in a quieter tone, "He's been there all night."

"Really?" Renee wondered why.

"Why are you so surprised?" Samantha shook her head. "He's obviously crazy about you."

Renee couldn't believe he'd stick around this long. "Tell him to go home."

Samantha yawned, kissing George's head. She closed her eyes and said, "You tell him."

Before she could argue, Samantha fell asleep with George. It wasn't until the nurse came back in that she decided to send him home.

"Can I get a large coffee?" she asked the nurse. "For a friend?"

"I'll be right back."

Renee got up slowly. Her body had never felt so mangled and bruised, but a liveliness radiated throughout her.

When the nurse returned with a coffee, she gently nodded Samantha awake.

"I'll be back," Renee said.

"Mm-hmm," Samantha said, her eyes still closed.

Renee grabbed the cup and walked slowly to the waiting room. Mateo sat in the corner, his head up against the wall, asleep, using his coat as a blanket. He was the only one in the room.

"Good morning," Renee said as she sat in the open seat next to him. She gently rubbed his arm under the coat.

He jumped awake, but immediately, a smile broke across his face. "Renee." Then he panicked. "Should you be out of your hospital room? Is everything okay?"

She nodded, handing him the cup of coffee. "Here."

His hand snuck out from under the coat and took the cup. He sat up, rubbing his face with his other hand. "Thank you."

"You stayed all night?" She couldn't help but smile at his chivalrous act.

He took a sip, nodding. "I wanted to be here in case you needed anything. How's George?"

"Perfect." A lump grew in her throat at the simple yet profound gesture. "I wish I could tell you how much I appreciate you staying without my emotions taking over."

She was already crying before she finished her sentence, but it was so nice, so thoughtful. He stayed the whole night, for her?

"Ugh, I can't stop once they start lately." She remembered how she used to be so tough. Now, since George, she couldn't hold it together.

Mateo let out a soft laugh. "It's okay, really. Here, this is for you." He picked up a small package wrapped in pink paper that sat on the chair on the other side of him.

She pulled off the paper, and in a box was a set of unicorn tights. She looked up at him. Her mouth opened wide in amazement. "You remembered."

He nodded.

She couldn't believe he had heard her, like really heard her.

"I wanted to give them to you for your opening, but I figured this was as good a time as any," he said.

Her throat tightened more, and as she tried to get more words to come out, her emotions swallowed her voice. Mateo tossed his coat aside and set the coffee on the table in front of him. Then he gently cupped her chin in his palm. Her hand went straight to his.

He stared at her for a moment but then said, "I'm falling in love with you."

And she took in a breath, like she would if she were about to jump into a wave, and she leaned in and kissed him. Their lips pressed together softly, barely touching, but it sent heat throughout her body.

He pressed his forehead against hers. She could feel his heartbeat and smell his aftershave.

"I'm here," he whispered, so close she could feel the moisture off his breath "You just let me know what you need."

She kissed him softly again, letting her lips gently pull away. "Why don't you come and meet baby George?"

He smiled, taking her hand in his as she guided him down the hospital hallway. She looked behind her shoulder and saw a smile across his face, and she could feel her breath release.

Emotions took over again with his reaction to baby George in Samantha's arms. He gave the baby his full attention, his face full of enthusiasm, his voice high and soft.

"He's perfect," Mateo said, staring at George.

"That's what we've been saying," Renee said, staring at Mateo.

"Hey, Mateo, you think you could stick around so I can run home and shower?" Samantha asked, but she winked at Renee.

"Sure, yeah. That's no problem at all." Mateo's full attention was on George.

But Renee knew it wasn't as easy as he made it out to be. He had a business to run, employees and subcontractors that needed his attention, but he chose to stay for her and the baby.

Was all of this for real? Could Mateo really be that nice of a guy? Did he really feel something for her? Was this too good to be true?

The rest of the day was a whirlwind of visitors, but the one constant was Mateo. He stayed all day at the hospital, doing whatever he could to be helpful. He'd quietly ask if she needed time alone, but she'd always refuse. She didn't want him to leave.

When Evelyn came to stay the night, that was when Mateo decided to go.

"I'll be at the bookstore if you need anything at all," he said, kissing her and baby George on the foreheads.

"Go home and get some rest," Evelyn said, acting like the mother hen as usual as she walked him out of the room. When her mother returned, she had a look on her face that said exactly what Renee was thinking. "Is there something between the two of you?"

Renee held George against her chest and looked down into his tiny, perfect features. "I think maybe there is." She couldn't stop staring at George. "I can't believe he's mine."

Evelyn walked over to the bed. "I thought the happiest moment of my life was the day I gave birth to you and your sister, but yesterday, when George entered this world, that was the best." Evelyn lay down on the bed beside Renee, baby George between the two women. Renee rested her head on Evelyn's shoulder and finally fell asleep.

The next morning, she got discharged from the hospital. Bitty parked the car at the front door of the hospital with Samantha in the passenger's seat in back. It took about fifteen minutes to make sure her six-pound, seven-ounce baby was safely snug in his car seat.

"I'm not supposed to be able to loosely stick my finger between the baby and the strap," Renee explained to Samantha as the two of them adjusted the seat.

When George was set and secured, they took off. Even though nothing appeared different on the drive back to the house, Renee felt completely different. Her whole perspective on the island that had once felt isolating and dangerous, now felt safe and connected. She felt more a part of the tiny village than she had ever felt in her own restaurant back in Chicago. She never had felt like she belonged there, always trying to prove herself, and she wasn't wrong. No one came looking for her.

No one.

George gurgled a noise, and she grabbed the burp cloth from the diaper bag. When she looked up, she noticed signs and balloons as they pulled into the driveway. Marty stood on the porch with what looked like the whole village of Eastport.

"What's Marty doing here?" Renee suddenly wished the sweatsuit set from Walmart hadn't been her choice to leave the hospital in, but she shouldn't have worried. Everyone's attention was on George.

Charlie videotaped everything on his phone as Harper took more pictures. Hank opened the door to the house, and everyone stepped aside as Renee walked into Sea View with George for the very first time.

"Oh, Renee!" Wanda said, who had stayed home from the hospital. "He's precious."

"Let's get him in your lap first," Renee said, moving through the crowd.

But that's when she saw Mateo standing in the middle of everyone. Clean-shaven, with his hands stuffed in his jeans pockets, he looked even more handsome than usual, and she wished she could be back in the hospital room with him, alone with baby George.

The crowd congregated in the kitchen. As the winter breeze cut across the Atlantic Ocean, whipping the flag against the pole, inside felt warm and cozy. The fireplaces were lit throughout the bottom floor as warm drinks and soups were served for everyone.

Even though Renee was exhausted, she enjoyed having everyone there to welcome home George. She listened as Mrs. Johnson told her a story of having her first child in the church sanctuary during mass. She watched as Charlie snuck kisses to Evelyn and laughed as he made silly faces at George. She passed George off to Samantha while she ate and made sure Wanda got to hold him while he slept. The crowd was boisterous and joyful, and Baby George slept through it all. After two hours of socializing, Bitty sent Renee to bed after she finished her soup, but it was Mateo who walked her to the staircase.

"I'm going to rest, I promise," Renee said, though he looked as though he didn't believe her.

"You better." He walked behind her, gently edging her along ahead of him. She tangled her fingers with his as her other hand reached for the handcrafted newel post he had replicated.

She stopped at the bottom step and faced him, catching a glimpse of her reflection in the hallway mirror. She had expected a nasty rat's nest on top of a tired and drained face, but her cheeks blushed a rosy color, and her lips wore a natural rouge. Her happiness shined out of her.

"Thank you for staying at the hospital," she said to him once again.

He stepped closer to her. "I'll always be here for you and George."

She stayed on the step, her eyes on him, her hand in his, and she had never felt so much love in her life. She had her family, who chose her over everything else. She had a community that stood behind her. She had a man willing to stand beside her. Her journey had just begun, and she couldn't wait to see what came next.

CHAPTER 29

At six months, George turned out to be a genius. Yes, he was her son, but Renee had never heard of a six-month old as smart and as fast a learner as George.

"He really is a smarty-pants," Wanda said as she tried feeding him the peas. "He knows they're yours and not the jar stuff."

"They put sugar in the jar stuff, that's why," Renee said from behind the kitchen counter, gathering up the last-minute items before the opening. "Wanda, are you sure you don't mind watching him?"

"Of course not." Wanda leaned toward George in his high-chair and kissed his pea-stained nose. "Hmm. Yummy."

"Seriously, I can ask Julia," Renee said as Mateo walked into the kitchen with another travel bag for Renee. She took it as she kissed him on the cheek.

"No, it's everyone's big day." Wanda waved her hand at them. Her hair just started coming back with an even tighter curl than before. "Let me spoil my grandnephew for the day."

George slapped the tray with his hands and almost made Wanda lose the peas.

"Almost, little man," Mateo said. "You almost got rid of those peas."

"Hey," Renee said, scolding Mateo. "Don't encourage him. Those peas are healthy and nutritious."

"I think it's more that you're feeding him them at breakfast. Who wants peas for breakfast?" Mateo asked this to George, who banged the tray again.

"I want coffee," Samantha said, dragging into the kitchen. "Where's coffee?"

"There's plenty of coffee at the store, so let's get going," Renee said, clapping her hands at her sister.

"Those are cute," Samantha said, pointing at Renee's unicorn tights.

Renee looked at Mateo when she said, "Thanks."

All those months ago, she would have never worn tights like these or even thought of doing so. She hadn't stood out; she'd blended in. She hadn't taken chances. She'd played things safe. She'd fallen into grooves. She'd hid in life, and it had gotten her nowhere and with nothing.

Mateo caught her looking at him, and he leaned over and kissed her on the cheek. "You're going to knock 'em dead today."

"Thanks," she said, but her heart pounded in her chest.

This was it. This was her moment she had been working toward her whole life.

She quickly ran to George one last time and kissed him hard on the cheek, making huge kissy noises in the process that made George squeal in delight.

She kissed Wanda next. Another big, exaggerated kiss just like George's, which made him giggle even harder deep within his belly.

"Oh, goodness me!" Wanda laughed out. "I'm going to tinkle before you go!"

Renee sat in Wanda's seat, scooping up the peas and choo-chooing them into George's mouth. But as soon as the spoon came close, he sealed his lips tight and threw up his chin as a defensive mechanism, which worked.

"He's brilliant," she said to Mateo, who stood behind her, looking down at George.

"He's the smartest baby ever," he said back to her, his hand on her shoulder.

She patted it with hers and nodded. "Totally."

"Alright, I'm back," Wanda said as she came into the room.

The spring weather on the island had been warmer than usual, and it had given Wanda a new bounce in her step—along with the cocktail of medications that her doctor had prescribed. Wanda said she had never felt better, but there were still days she looked worn from the disease, tired of the treatments that continued after, and unsure of herself. That's when one of them would step up. Evelyn and Bitty made sure she continued to go on walks. Charlie kept finding her books and knitting supplies. Renee continued making meals that she liked. But if someone were to ask what brought Wanda most happiness, it would undoubtedly be George.

George was the biggest and brightest part of everyone's day at Sea View. Every new stage was cuter than the last. Every movement, smile, and giggle brought joy to everyone. With the women and Charlie, along with Mateo and his brothers, there was always someone helping with George.

"Now scat," Wanda said to Renee and Mateo. "You're going to miss your own party."

"Okay, call if you need anything," Renee said. "I'll be back in a couple of hours."

"I'll be fine. Besides, Marty's stopping by."

"Oh," Renee said, her eyes meeting Mateo's right away. "Great."

They said their last goodbyes and hightailed out. They didn't say a thing until they closed Mateo's truck's doors.

"Marty's coming over?" Renee said and laughed at the casual way Wanda had brought it up.

"Remember the last time they watched George?" Mateo asked.

She shook the image of Marty, the mailman, and Wanda kissing on the couch, with George in his playpen watching.

"God, I hope not," she said.

When they reached the store, her mother and Charlie were already inside.

"Where's the baby?" Evelyn asked, looking for him.

"It's too much this morning," Renee said. She had changed her mind a dozen times. "Wanda said she'd watch him for a couple of hours."

Evelyn smiled. "Good, you should enjoy this."

Renee looked at the room. She had painted the space a baby robin's shell blue; so soft, yet a complete contrast to the darkly stained shelving Mateo had designed for the kitchen space. Like a piece of furniture, her refrigerated cases housed most of her pastries, macarons, individual tarts, quiches, custom mini cakes, and gourmet sandwiches. It had been framed with wood and given white marble countertops. On top, she had placed different pieces to showcase all the items for sale. Freshly baked biscotti stood tall in a clear glass jar with a blown glass decorative tip. In a glass cake stand, she had piled different types of handmade donuts. In baskets, sat loaves of artisan bread.

Renee's favorite decoration in the store was the chandelier Samantha had found somewhere in a grand estate.

The whole back end housed the bakery, like a kitchen in a house, and the rest of the store was floor-to-ceiling bookshelves with all of the newest and best sellers, which also included a whole section of Evelyn Rose. Renee made sure Evelyn Rose came to the opening and told her fans to come visit.

"I've got your table set up by the register with Charlie." Renee pointed to the table with two chairs. Evelyn had pre-signed books, and a stack was piled, ready to go. "I have a seat for Harper next to you."

Renee had two solid hours to work before she had to race home and feed George. After which, she had an interview with the local paper about the grand opening. She also had to make sure there was enough inventory for the tourists on top of the Evelyn Rose fans and keep her sanity the whole time.

Julia helped work the counter with Renee and took over when she ran back to throw more cookies into the oven. Everything was selling; even the sandwiches she'd had doubts about.

When Renee ran home, Bitty swapped with Wanda to watch George, and Wanda and Marty came to the store to see how things were going.

When the newspaper arrived, they took photos of Renee behind the counter with Samantha, then of Evelyn and Harper signing books, and of Charlie behind the register talking to the tourists. Then they took a picture of the kitchen Mateo and his brothers had completely renovated for the space.

By closing, Renee's feet and back killed her, but she didn't want to stop. The day had been exhilarating.

"You ready to close up?" Charlie asked her.

She nodded, looking at the empty trays of food.

"It's time, right?" Samantha laid her head down on the counter. "I'm exhausted."

When the doors finally closed and the closed sign went up, everyone who had helped seemed to empty out. She finished washing up some of the dishes in the back kitchen sink as Samantha kissed her on the cheek.

"Relax," Samantha said to her.

"I will," Renee said, but her sister knew she had no plans to slow down. Her energy was racing. There was so much to do before tomorrow. Prep work, cleaning from the day, and she wanted to look over the numbers to prepare for the next crowd.

As she walked back to the floor from the back room, she noticed the place had emptied out, leaving Renee and Mateo alone.

"Are you headed out?" she asked him, removing her apron from around her neck.

He shook his head. Suddenly, she heard background music being played. She looked around and noticed candles, and their shadows danced against the walls and ceiling. The gas fireplace was lit and glowing.

"What's going on?" she asked, narrowing her eyes at him suspiciously. What romantic gesture did Mateo have up his sleeve now?

He stood in the middle of the room and held out his hand. As she walked toward him, she noticed he wasn't wearing his usual work boots or his regular hoodie, but leather dress shoes and a button-up with khakis.

Her heart skipped in her chest as he took her into his arms, holding her close to him as he looked into her eyes.

"I feel like everything in my life, all the trials and tribulations, all the work and choices I've made, led me to this moment with you." He held her elbows with his palms, his arms resting underneath hers, their bodies together. Every cell in her body pulsed as he took her in with his eyes. "I never knew I could live with purpose and with passion until I met you."

She bit her bottom lip as a tear fell. "I never knew I could be so happy until I met you."

Her emotions took over once again, and as if on cue, he handed her his handkerchief, and she laughed at what a sight she must be.

"I must look disastrous." Renee pushed back the loose strands of hair falling out of her messy ponytail.

"You're gorgeous," he said, his eyes focusing on hers, unbreaking.

Then he let go of her arms and dropped to one knee. She let out a gasp as he took her left hand.

"Renee, I want you and George and me to be a family," he said, looking at her, holding her eyes. "I want to marry you and help raise him with you. I want to be a father to him and love you as your husband. I want us all to be together forever."

Renee dropped to her knees, placing her hands around his jaw and looking deep into his eyes. The man who knelt before her could never understand how she felt in that moment. He'd never fully comprehend the pure blessing he had become to her.

"Mateo, I want you in our lives forever too."

Renee kissed her prince and began her happily ever after.

~

I hope you enjoyed *Sea View Cottage*! In the next book, *Sugar Beach Sunsets,* Evelyn's youngest daughter Samantha comes to Cliffside Point to recover, rebuild and find love. Click HERE to read *Sugar Beach Sunsets* now!

If you'd like to receive a FREE standalone novella from my Camden Cove series, please click HERE or visit my website at ellenjoyauthor.com.

ALSO BY ELLEN JOY

Click HERE for more information about other books by Ellen Joy.

Cliffside Point

Beach Home Beginnings

Sea View Cottage

Sugar Beach Sunsets

Home on the Harbor

Christmas at Cliffside

Lakeside Lighthouse

Seagrass Sunrise

Half Moon Harbor

Beach Rose Harbor

Beach Rose Secrets

Prairie Valley Sisters

Coming Home to the Valley

Daydreams in the Valley

Starting Over in the Valley

Second Chances in the Valley

New Hopes in the Valley

Feeling Blessed in the Valley

Camden Cove

The Inn by the Cove

The Farmhouse by the Cove

The Restaurant by the Cove

The Christmas Cottage by the Cove

The Bakery by the Cove

ABOUT THE AUTHOR

Ellen lives in a small town in New England, between the Atlantic Ocean and the White Mountains. She lives with her husband, two sons, and one very spoiled puppy princess.

Ellen writes in the early morning hours before her family wakes up. When she's not writing, you can find her spending time with her family, gardening, or headed to the beach. She loves summer and flip-flops, running on a dirt country road, and a sweet love song.

All of her stories are clean romances where families are close, neighbors are nosy, and the couples are destined for each other.

Made in the USA
Monee, IL
06 August 2024